PRAISE FOR

How She Died, How I Lived

★ "**The writing grabs readers and never lets go.**
Crockett delves deep into the heart of grief and pain through
her narrator, who is witty and vulnerable, making this a
quick but heartrending read. An outstanding debut."
—*SLJ*, starred review

"One of my absolute favorite books of 2018!...
An **unforgettable** and **unputdownable** read."
—*Shelf Awareness*

"Crockett has crafted **dynamic characters** that will stick
with readers long after the book is closed." —*Booklist*

"The narrative voice is highly credible as it canvasses
the **fluctuating range of emotional highs and
lows,** the sine curve of fear and empowerment, and the
fully realized ethical dilemmas that follow a trauma that
hits far too close to home." —*The Bulletin*

"[*How She Died, How I Lived*] authentically
portrays **the real feelings of someone who
survives a tragedy.**" —*VOYA*

how she died, how i lived

Mary Crockett

LITTLE, BROWN AND COMPANY
New York Boston

Copyright © 2018 by Mary Crockett

Back cover photo © Summer Photographer/Shutterstock.com.
Cover candle art © Mr Aesthetics/Shutterstock.com. Cover design by Sasha Illingworth.
Cover copyright © 2018 by Hachette Book Group, Inc.

Little, Brown and Company
Hachette Book Group
1290 Avenue of the Americas, New York, NY 10104
Visit us at LBYR.com

Originally published in hardcover and ebook by Little, Brown and Company in November 2018
First Trade Paperback Edition: November 2019

Little, Brown and Company is a division of Hachette Book Group, Inc. The Little, Brown name and logo are trademarks of Hachette Book Group, Inc.

The publisher is not responsible for websites (or their content) that are not owned by the publisher.

The Library of Congress has cataloged the hardcover edition as follows:
Names: Crockett, Mary, author.
Title: How she died, how I lived / By Mary Crockett.
Description: First edition. | New York ; Boston : Little, Brown and Company, 2018. |
Summary: After narrowly escaping death, a teen struggles to come to terms with her guilt over the classmate who was raped and murdered instead.
Identifiers: LCCN 2017059757| ISBN 9780316523813 (hardcover) | ISBN 9780316523806 (ebook) | ISBN 9780316523790 (library edition ebook)
Subjects: | CYAC: Guilt—Fiction. | Murder—Fiction. | Rape—Fiction. | Dating (Social customs)—Fiction. | High schools—Fiction. | Schools—Fiction.
Classification: LCC PZ7.1.C747 How 2018 | DDC [Fic]—dc23
LC record available at https://lccn.loc.gov/2017059757

ISBNs: 978-0-316-52382-0 (pbk.), 978-0-316-52380-6 (ebook)

Printed in the United States of America

LSC-C

10 9 8 7 6 5 4 3 2 1

for all the lost girls

Wednesday, July 11—
a year and two months ago
Stonehenge Pool

Want to hang this afternoon?

I poked a straw into my sno-cone. It didn't usually come with a straw but the cute old guy who worked at the Hawaiian Chill said he kept them on hand just for me.

What day was it? Tuesday? No, Wednesday. Because Sander wasn't coming back from his eternal camping trip until Friday, and that was still two days away. Two more days of Sander-less summer in the hick town we call home. I stretched out on a lounge chair, pulled the straw out of my Blue Coconut, and sucked the icy sweetness from the end.

The sun was too bright; the pool, too dead. Monica and Andie would usually be here with me, but Monica was at a church retreat all week and Andie had to help her mom clean out their garage.

So today it was just me and the Anonymous Annoying Family. In the shade of a yellow-striped umbrella, below a sky-blue straw hat, Mrs. Annoying drowsed. Her ten-year-old twins were playing some game where they shouted movie quotes and vaulted off the diving board.

The lifeguard on duty—a bony guy with ostrich eyes and a silver lip ring—gazed blindly from his perch.

Annoying Boy #1: "It's so FLUFFY!"

SPLASH!

Annoying Boy #2: "My name is Inigo Montoya. You killed my father. Prepare to die."

SPLASH!

Annoying Boy #1: "To infinity and beyond!"

SPLASH!

I looked back at my phone. Kyle Paxson was a little funny, and not the ha-ha kind. He had my number from Algebra I, back when I was a freshman and he was a senior. But even as a freshman, it didn't take me long to figure out Kyle was a guy best ignored. Harmless enough, but weird.

"Luke, I'm your father!" Boy #2 hollered, but instead of jumping off the board, this time he grabbed a towel from the edge of the pool and whipped it at Boy #1.

"Let it go!" yelped Boy #1, who did a sassy sort of shuffle, kicking his legs to avoid the towel's snap.

"I'm Batman!" Boy #2 growled.

Another chime.

I checked my phone. Kyle again.

> I have some good stuff.

Of course he had stuff.

The idea of getting high was tempting. It was, like I said, summer…and hot…and dead.

I usually didn't partake; it made my mind feel like it was covered with felt and Sander said he didn't like the way I acted. But Sander wasn't around. *Maybe I should do it*, I thought. Like practice for college or whatever comes next.

I had started to type *Ok, where*—when another text came in.

> Heading home early. Need my honey girl.

I took a quick selfie of me in my bathing suit with quirked-up lips—an inside joke—and sent it to Sander.

> Quack

Grabbing my towel, I skipped out to the parking lot and was on my way.

Today
Tomorrow
The rest of my life

The Worst Thing

I guess I have Simon Alexander "Sander" Rushford III to thank. He is, in the final analysis, a two-timing jerk. But he saved my life.

A year ago at Stonehenge Pool, I never finished answering Kyle's text. Instead, I zipped home to shave my armpits and lather my hair with green tea shampoo.

It was Jamie, not me, who answered one of Kyle's texts to a few random girls that afternoon. Jamie who drove her new Ford Escape to Moser Field on the other side of town.

While she was turning onto the park's gravel drive, I was slipping a royal-blue sundress over my head, my towel-dried hair dampening the neckline as it slid past. While she was sitting next to Kyle on the vinyl tablecloth he'd pulled from the trunk of his car, I was bounding downstairs, car keys jiggling in my hand. While she was listening to Kyle complain about how his grandma was always riding his ass, I was on the futon in Sander's basement—Sander's tongue down my throat, his unwashed woodsy smell pressed against me.

While her pink paisley tank top and jean shorts were stripped from her body. While he beat. While he pried open her mouth to put himself in first, then his fist, then a crowbar. While he choked and kicked her. Wrapped her in the tablecloth. Stomped her head.

I was.

I was alive in the dank basement air, Sander's sweat and pine against my skin.

I was kissing, nipping, thinking about the part in an old time-travel movie I saw, where a guy messes with the past and the family photograph he carries in his wallet starts to turn transparent. That's how I felt with Sander's mouth on me. A few more kisses and I'd be completely gone.

I was alive and no one was kicking me. No one squeezed my neck until my throat was raw and breathless and the vomit that surged from my stomach seeped back down my esophagus because it had nowhere else to go. I was alive and running my hands across Sander's shoulders, down his muscled chest. I was alive, breathing hot air on his neck.

Alive and breathing.

And after, while Jamie's mom called first her phone, then her friends, then the police—I lay there under the weight of Sander's outstretched arm, an open pizza box on the floor beside us as he snored pepperoni breath, and I stared at the shifty-eyed cat clock on the wall. Its long black tail swung back and forth, back and forth, a pendulum counting down the empty seconds of my life.

So thanks, Sander Rushford. As it turns out, making me think you loved me while two-timing me with Gemma Cook was not the worst thing you could have done.

Five

I was one of five. The five girls Kyle texted that day. The girls it could have been.

Me. Lindsey Barrow. Taylor Avril. Blair Mattern. Jamie Strand.

The plan was as simple as it was heartless. Draw one of us out to the relative seclusion of Moser Field. Rape one of us. Kill one of us. Take the car. Take the credit cards. Get out of town. It didn't matter who he killed, he told the cops, any one of us would do.

It was, Kyle said, really about the car. He needed one to leave Midland. This place was making him crazy. All the other stuff, like the part where he bashed Jamie's head to a pulp—he said that was just a way to get the car.

He had problems, he told them.

No kidding.

But here's the thing. He also had a car of his own. An old piece-of-crap junker, sure. But it would have driven him, quite literally, out of town.

Maybe it wasn't nice enough. Like he'd made a list.

Girls Who Drive Nice Cars.

He'd noticed my new VW when I saw him by chance at the Hardee's a month or so before the murder. My parents had gotten me a Bug for my seventeenth birthday and it still had that new-car glow. Metallic blue with fancy spoked hubcaps and a sunroof. I loved that car. Named it Pony because it was like getting a pony. That special.

I still love it, in a way. But I can't really, can I? Any love I had for it has been tainted by my hatred for Kyle.

And not that mealymouthed ooh-I-hate-hipster-tattoos or I-hate-the-way-the-morning-show-guy-on-the-radio-laughs-like-he's-spewing-Jell-O or I-hate-the-mind-numbing-Muzak-they-play-in-bathrooms-at-the-mall.

I'm talking full-throttle, rage-on, red-eyed hate.

When they asked him why he'd targeted Jamie Strand, Kyle told them, "She was just unfortunate." Like it had nothing to do with him. Luck of the draw. The way the cookie crumbles.

But if it was a car he truly wanted—my Pony, Lindsey's Toyota, Jamie's shiny new Ford Escape—if it was, as he said, not "personal," then why didn't he just steal one?

Are we supposed to believe he never heard of hot-wiring? Or pocketing someone's keys? He could have tied one of us up. Left us abandoned on the roadside while he drove away. But no, he had to rape. Had to kill.

Some people say he was obsessed with Jamie. Some say that he was obsessed with sex. But nobody, *nobody*, says he was obsessed with cars.

Did he think that would somehow make it all right?

I bashed her head so hard that her skull cracked in three places. But it wasn't personal. I just needed her car.

Kyle texted all of us that day. All the same message. *Want to hang this afternoon?* Followed by something just for us—an offer of pot or money or dinner out or, in Jamie's case, a desperate request for "someone to talk to."

And Jamie was the only one nice enough to give him the time.

She was always nice. *Such a sweet girl*, they said at her funeral. *An angel. Born for sweetness.*

She was born, in fact, with one leg shorter than the other, so she shuffled when she walked. Jamie knew what it was to feel other people's eyes on her—that hum of pity like a stupid song that gets stuck in your head. It might have made some girls bitter. But not Jamie. She laughed before anyone else could laugh at her. She reached out to anyone who didn't fit in. A sweet girl whose sweetness killed her.

No, that's not right.

It wasn't her sweetness. It was Kyle.

You Heard

When it first happened, talk of Kyle and Jamie was everywhere. How he'd been fired from his job at Advance Auto the week before the murder. Stuff about Kyle's nutty grandma. Or Jamie's heartbroken boyfriend. They said Kyle acted weird that July, bragging about how he was going to surprise everyone, do something big. They said Jamie's mother walked the aisles of the Kroger in her bathrobe the day after the funeral.

They said and they said. So much noise. A cloud of gnats that descended on the town.

But weeks passed, seasons. And the talk was swatted away.

So, now, after almost a year of no news, is it wrong there's a dead space in my stomach when Kyle's broad face appears on the front page again? This time with a shaved head, thick black-frame glasses.

Why couldn't they just lock him away and be done with it? But what we get is GRAND JURY TO HEAR KYLE PAXSON CAPITAL MURDER CASE.

Which is stupid because he already said he's guilty.

Even so, it could take months.

Gah.

I lift a clot of mushy green beans from my tray and let the fork drop with a clatter.

I am in the cafeteria of Midland High, five minutes late for my fifth-period psychology class. The hall is mainly empty now, but I still don't want to go out there. I know where it leads. To windowless rooms, uncomfortable desks, droning voices.

All the same, I stand, shoulder my backpack, and walk over to dump my tray.

"You heard?"

I know Lindsey's silvery voice without turning around.

I didn't notice her come in. She eats third-shift lunch, so I only see her in the cafeteria when I'm running late.

"Yeah." I don't have to ask what she's talking about.

Kyle, of course. Now that he's back in the news, the gnats have descended again. Not that Lindsey is a gnat. Her long brown bangs swoop in front of her face and she blows them away. "It's horrible."

She walks with me down the hall. Since she's wearing a navy-blue pencil skirt, like a slinky secretary from a 1940s movie, her stride is shorter than usual, constrained by her hem. I shorten my steps to match hers. The clack of her heels on the hallway tile is so much louder than it needs to be.

"They're doing another vigil. This Sunday," she says. "Mark was putting up flyers."

That would be Mark Lee, official neat freak of Midland High. Of course he's the one organizing the vigil. He's the best friend of Charlie Hunt, the dead girl's brokenhearted boyfriend—and in Mark's role as best friend, he's taken to organizing Charlie, too.

Charlie and Jamie had seemed perfect for each other. Both good-looking, both nice in that sunshiny, pay-it-forward way. He was tall. Smart. She was sweet and friendly. When Jamie's parents got divorced, she moved with her mom into a small brick ranch beside the two-story white colonial where the Hunts lived. Jamie was six at the time; Charlie was four. Literally the boy next door.

People say they grew up in each other's kitchens. They played together, lost teeth together, and in middle school, when it was time for girlfriends and boyfriends, they picked each other. It never mattered that Jamie was two grades ahead of us. They were the sort of people who could cross that line.

Only now, Charlie isn't so sunshine anymore. I see him in both of my classes at the end of the day, sixth-period English and seventh-period gym. He's thinner, shoulders hunched, and he doesn't smile in that far-off way he had. Or talk.

Or do anything, really.

Except run.

When Coach Flanagan sends us out for laps, Charlie takes off like a fox with dogs on his tail. He is fast. And graceful. But his running is painful to watch, at least for me. It's like I see what's really chasing him. And it's not dogs.

"Exhibit A," says Lindsey, pointing to a yellow flyer on the wall outside my psych class. MEMORIAL GATHERING— SUNDAY—7 PM—MIDLAND STADIUM is printed in big block letters at the top, and below is a photo of Jamie: pretty, heart-shaped face; dark, wavy, shoulder-length hair; hopeful eyes. Below that, in a fancy font, SHE LEFT A TRAIL OF BEAUTIFUL MEMORIES EVERYWHERE SHE WENT.

"Hey." Lindsey holds me back before I go into psych. "So all this"—she circles her hand in the direction of the flyer—"it's not sending you back, is it?"

"Back where?"

She scrunches her face, genuinely sad for me. Disappointed, even. "Oh, honey." Then she leans in and gives me a hug.

Lindsey feels warm, like a biscuit. Her hair has a sweet strawberry smell. And despite myself, I give in to the hug.

"What was that for?" I ask when she releases me.

"Nothing." Her face brightens to a grin. "For you! Being you." She pushes her bangs back, and I see that the smile doesn't reach her eyes. "Call me, okay?"

"Yeah," I say.

Just then, a burly guy comes out of psych and barges past us with a bathroom pass. Before the door closes, I half wave to Lindsey and slip into class, walking stiffly to keep my sneakers from squeaking.

Deviant Psychology

"Before we can understand what's considered abnormal, we have to define normal," says Ms. Ramano.

Some might consider Ms. Ramano abnormal. Abnormally short. Abnormally round. She is almost disc-shaped, like the mirrored face-powder cases women carry in their purses. A face-powder case with legs. But she's spunky, and I like her. Plus, she lets me off for being late with nothing more than a stern look. Normal is definitely overrated.

"So once we have a norm defined," she says, "deviant psychology asks how individuals find themselves outside that norm. As with all things, there are various theories."

She scrawls on the whiteboard:

Norm/Psychoanalytic Theory/Cognitive Development Theory

Her words roll into one another—"a diseased mind, inappropriate learning, improper conditioning, the absence of appropriate role models"—and I think about Kyle. Is it his diseased mind that's to blame? I mean, of course it is, right? His mind would have to be diseased for him to do what he did. But is that the whole story?

He grew up like most everybody else in Midland, if not in the same neighborhood as me and Jamie, at least in the same kind. There aren't too many options. There's Longhorn Place with its old fancy brick homes in shady yards on wide, winding streets north of Main. There's Emerald Heights with massive McMansions carved into the narrow hillsides surrounding town. There's the Bottoms by the river, where all the poor people live. Then there's everybody else living side by side in split-levels and ranches and the occasional two-story with porch. The names of the neighborhoods change, but the neighborhoods don't. Kyle lived near Center Park with his grandmother in a smallish frame house with yellow siding, two purple-leafed trees in the front yard, and a garden plot out back. It was the kind of house I imagined might have doilies on the coffee table and dusty African violets lining the windowsill. It could have easily been down the street from me, but wasn't.

But that's just the house. He said he had problems with his grandma. I'm not sure if he even knew his mom. And according to the gnats, his dad shot himself when Kyle was four. So yeah, that's pretty messed up. But does it mean he gets to grow up and beat some girl to death—for her car, of all things? Really?

And then for him to be so nonchalant about it. Like it was just another thing he had to check off his list before he headed out of town "on his quest." That's how he talked about it in the papers, like he was destined for some epic journey. He'd packed her SUV with clothes, deodorant, drugs, a couple bags of potato chips, a box of cereal, a laptop, and $188 in cash. But he was found a day later not thirty miles from home.

It's like he got stuck somewhere in his mind, the way he had in algebra class. Did Jamie die because leaving town was a word problem Kyle couldn't figure out?

Ms. Ramano draws a big red circle on the whiteboard and writes *HUMAN MOTIVATION* inside. "You have to consider what's behind it all, an individual's motivation. What is driving this person—a basic motive like hunger, or a secondary motive, something they aspire to be, for example?"

She turns to us: "What is driving you? Right here, right now, what do you want?"

What do I want? God, what a question. Who knows...

I want to be alive. And to be okay with being alive. To not wake up in the morning and have my first thought be of Jamie; to not lie down at night and have my last thought be of Kyle. I want Jamie to be alive, too. I want to read the paper without the urge to set it on fire in the kitchen sink. I don't want to flinch when I see the shadow of Kyle's soft jaw on every broad, bland face I pass. I want to jog down the street, barefaced, without thinking once about what a crowbar can be used for.

I want my life back. Or someone's life. A new life, maybe.

I want a different past.

I wonder if I would have given him my car if he'd asked me.

In my fantasies sometimes, that's what I do. Sander doesn't text. Jamie's safe at home. It's me at Moser Field. We smoke together. Kyle tells me his life is a shithole. That he has to leave town. I say, "Take my car. You can have it." I hand him the keys. Then I run off into the woods at the edge of the field, and he doesn't follow.

Running

In gym, I watch Charlie Hunt. He is wearing a gray sweat-shirt, hood up, shoulders slumped, face down. I don't think he's been sleeping. His eyes, what I can see of them, have the slightly bruised look of overripe fruit. Beside him, Mark Lee is crisp by comparison, washed and polished. He probably irons his sweatpants. The kind of guy who puts the "butt" in "button-down."

Even so, Charlie—the Charlie from before—used to outshine Mark. He used to outshine pretty much everyone. Before, Charlie had a smile that made people feel like at any moment something amazing might happen. Supernova.

Now his face is the pocked surface of a distant moon.

Anyone who didn't know the two of them might wonder why someone as clean-cut as Mark would hang out with such a...I don't want to say *loser*, but it's probably what someone would think.

For warm-up, Coach takes us up to the practice field and has us run laps. Like usual, Charlie bolts. I don't know what gets into me, but I take off, too, fast, determined to catch up with him. My feet make an obstinate *thwuk-thwuk-thwuk* on the track. I'm a good runner, and though he is, too, I'm gaining. Yeah, he had a head start, but he's running alone, while I am running *against* him.

As we round a bend, I push myself harder. I don't have a plan for what will happen once I catch up, but for whatever reason, I'm determined to run beside him.

At the end of the first lap, he is only a few paces ahead. I put my legs and lungs into it, pounding the track, breathing loud, and then I am by his side. I adjust my pace, matching my steps to his. At first, he doesn't notice me, but after a few seconds of my meeting him step for step, he looks over—not even for a half second, just a glance, but enough to show he's noticed. Then he speeds up.

Now he is running against *me*.

I surge forward. My lungs are burning, but it's a good burn and I drive through it. I no longer want to run beside him. I want to beat him. I want his sleepy eyes to widen at the sight of me as I blow past. I want this, whatever this is, to wake him up.

I imagine we are in a cornfield. The two of us sprinting down the narrow, rutted rows. The wind, the sun at our backs. In my mind, I see myself not just running, but flying, my feet never hitting ground. I slice into the air in front of me, pumping my legs, deepening my breath. Harder. Faster. I run like I was born for this, like I lived for this alone.

A Crumb

The next day in English, Charlie looks at me like I'm some kind of freak. Not blatantly, but enough for me to hear the *blip-blip-blip* of his freak-dar go off.

I squinch one eye at him like I think *he's* the freak.

"All right now." Mr. Campbell's southern drawl booms out over the tops of our heads. His hands, which are surprisingly small for a grown man, rub down each side of his cheek, stroking his cropped beard like it's an exotic and well-loved pet. He is a plaid-shirt-and-crisp-dark-jeans type of teacher, but today he is wearing a thin black tie with the plaid. I'm pretty sure his shaggy chestnut hair teleported onto his head directly from 1982.

"Time for Poem of the Week." He claps his hands once, enthusiastically. "Clarissa, you're up."

Each Wednesday, one of us—a different victim each week—has to stand in front of the class and read a poem. Whatever poem we choose, as long as there's no bad language. We set it up beforehand with Mr. Campbell and he makes copies for the class. As he passes out the papers, Clarissa Coleson shuffles up and slouches in front of his desk. Her bangs, which aren't really bangs but a big hunk of brown hair with a dyed pink streak, blur out her face. She pushes them aside, but when she looks down at her paper, the hair falls again, drawing a pink-and-brown curtain between her and the rest of the world.

"So, this is Emily Dickinson," she mutters. " 'Hope is the thing with feathers...' "

I read the page with Clarissa:

> *...That perches in the soul,*
> *And sings the tune without the words,*
> *And never stops at all,*
>
> *And sweetest in the gale is heard;*
> *And sore must be the storm*
> *That could abash the little bird*
> *That kept so many warm.*
>
> *I've heard it in the chillest land,*
> *And on the strangest sea;*
> *Yet, never, in extremity,*
> *It asked a crumb of me.*

"Good," says Mr. Campbell when she finishes reading, even though Clarissa mumbled half the words. "So, what's your question?"

It's mid-September, only the second one we've done of these, but still we know the drill. The presenter has to ask the class a question about the poem after reading. It's part of the whole Public Shaming event. And worse, it can't be vague, like "What do you think about this poem?" or "What part did you like?" Half the time I don't think even the poets knew what they were talking about, so how are *we* supposed to know some specific question to ask? When we asked Mr. Campbell about the question part, he said, "Point to a single line, or a single word, and ask about that."

And that's what Clarissa does. "It's about the crumb at the end. In the poem, hope is a bird, right, and it sings even in the cold or the storm or whatever. But it doesn't ask for anything, not even a crumb. But I don't get that. I mean, hope isn't like that."

Mr. Campbell raises his eyebrows. "Tell me more."

Clarissa has already returned to her seat. She folds her arms over her chest and stares at her desk like it has the answer. "Hope," she finally says. "It asks for *a lot*. You have to put yourself out there to hope. And then sometimes it all goes bad anyway."

"Excellent question!" says Mr. Campbell, even though I don't think it was technically a question. "So what does hope ask of us? What is required for us to have hope?"

Mr. Campbell looks expectantly around the room, which is suddenly full of crickets. He paces the trail between the wall and his desk.

Paige Sanchez, because she has a huge crush on Mr. Campbell that everyone except Mr. Campbell finds embarrassing, finally pipes up. "Um, it asks us to believe something even if we can't know it for sure?"

"Right! And why should we do that? Why do we hope, even when we can't know something for sure? Even when there's no logical reason?" Mr. Campbell asks.

I always thought teachers were supposed to have an answer in mind before they ask a question, but I'm pretty sure Mr. Campbell is winging it. I mean, how could he know the answer to that question? *Is* there even an answer?

Doe-eyed, Paige stares at Mr. Campbell and chews a fingernail. Russell Soto tosses a crumple of paper across three rows to make a perfect swish in the trash can by the door.

"Why do we hope?" Mr. Campbell asks again.

As it turns out, there *is* an answer to the question and Nick Richert has it. "Because we're stupid."

Laughter spurts from the back of the room. I look back, but Charlie is not one of the guys laughing. Charlie is sitting with his hands on his forehead, like his head hurts.

Hopeless.

The Gathering

There are over a hundred people here, easy. Maybe two. Kids from school, teachers, but also random neighbors, members of the city council, some old folks who are probably from the dentist's office where Jamie worked.

I've come with my parents. They never knew Jamie, but it's their civic duty—payment for having their daughter still alive.

Neither one has a clue how close it came to being me. They know Kyle texted me, of course. I told the police. But I haven't told anyone I almost texted back. That I was a thumb-stroke away from hitting send.

When I see Lindsey here without her mom, I wave her over. It's no surprise Lindsey's here alone. Kind of ironic, though—Lindsey, who is always mothering everyone, is herself pretty much motherless. After her dad left, her mom perfected the Art of Emotional Distance. Mrs. Barrow clocks in on the daily food-and-shelter kind of stuff, but she's not really *there* for Lindsey. It's like she thinks of

Lindsey as a roommate who helps out with the vacuuming and takes care of Veronica, Lindsey's sister who just started her freshman year.

We stand on the manicured turf of Midland Stadium. Our town lives and dies by football, so this is pretty much as sacred as ground gets. Lindsey nudges me and points at the scoreboard.

The screen has a slide show playing on a loop.

Jamie as a toddler with a bow taped to her bald head. Jamie decked out in silver sequins, a spunky six-year-old, twirling a baton in the Fourth of July parade. On the Easter Bunny's lap. Trick-or-treating in a Hogwarts scarf and robe. Here she is maybe fourteen, pushing a boy in a wheelchair. Here in a blue prom dress, a corsage on her wrist; behind her, a smiling Charlie with his arms around her shoulders. In her graduation cap and robe. In the dentist's office where she worked, kissing the cheek of a silver-haired lady in a neon-green beret.

Roland Foggerty, our balding mayor, climbs onto the stage that's been set up at one end of the football field. The picture on the screen changes to a live feed of the mayor as he walks to the podium. Blue blazer, red tie.

"Today, we close the book on a troubling chapter for our city. The man responsible for the brutal death of one of our beloved daughters has admitted his guilt. He is awaiting the sentencing trial, which will determine whether he faces life in prison or the death penalty. Time will tell his fate. But this gathering is not about him. This gathering is about Jamie Tatum Strand." The mayor pulls a cloth handkerchief out of his coat pocket and wipes his sweaty forehead.

"Anyone who met Jamie was deeply touched by her magnificent spirit," he continues. "She had a smile for everyone. She never let her physical challenges get in her way. She always stood up for what was right, even with one leg shorter than the other."

Lindsey rolls her eyes. "I think I just barfed a little in my mouth," she whispers—but it's one of those loud stage whispers that anyone around us would have to be deaf not to hear. The back of my head tingles, and I'm pretty sure the people standing behind us must be giving us a nasty look.

I glance back, but I don't see angry old people. What I see, behind a clump of middle school kids, is Monica and Andie. If I had to guess, I'd say they are now purposely *not* looking my way. My best friends.

Ex–best friends.

But no, that isn't quite right either. It's not like they're my mortal enemies. They're not my ex-anything. They're just not in my life anymore. We...drifted, I guess.

I keep looking back and eventually Monica can't avoid seeing me anymore. She gives me a nod, then trains her eyes on the stage, like the mayor's glistening forehead is the Eighth Natural Wonder of the World. Andie never even looks.

I don't blame them, I swear. Lindsey says I pushed them

away, and she's right. Maybe they just weren't screwed up enough for me. After the murder, when they talked about Jamie, I felt like they were really talking about me. Like you could insert my name, my life, in the blank. And if they talked about anything else—the normal high school sighs and whines—it just seemed cold.

At the end, it was all petty stuff. Monica liked someone who liked someone else, and I suppose I couldn't muster the appropriate enthusiasm for all the drama that ensued. Meanwhile, Andie swore a girl in her World History class was mimicking her style. The same floral top from last week, the same cropped jean jacket from the week before. Like the fate of the world rested on the fact that no one else wore her signature flats.

I blew. Said a bunch of mean stuff you can't take back. So yeah, maybe "drifted" is an understatement.

They pretended like they forgave me, like it was still okay between us. But after that, they didn't really make an effort. And me—well, everything had come to seem so useless.

For a while, I got stuck with Jamie, I guess. Wrapped in that tablecloth on the side of the road. How could I expect them to stay there with me?

I'm not sure even now I know my way out.

Beautiful Girl

The varsity cheerleaders walk through the field with cardboard boxes, doling out candles. By the time they make their way to us, Jamie's mother has publicly wept, her father and stepmother have publicly wept, and her brother has stared vacantly into the crowd, a bloody flake of tissue paper stuck near his ear where he nicked himself shaving.

I spy Mark and Charlie down front, close enough to be caught in the floodlights aimed at the stage. Otherwise, there are only two field lights on, and they're far enough away from where I'm standing that I can almost feel the dusk settle on my shoulders. We light our candles, but it's windy and we have to shield the flames with our hands to keep them from blowing out.

Someone reads a sad poem. Someone sings a sad song. Jamie's brother thanks everyone for remembering his sister.

"She had the funniest smile," he says, "and when she laughed, you just wanted to laugh, too. That's how she was. I wish she were here, laughing with us right now."

Can she laugh, I wonder, wherever she is...In the ground? Skipping across clouds? Strolling down streets of gold?

The obituary said she was "welcomed to heaven by her grandfather and grandmother."

So let's say Jamie *is* up there, getting her heavenly reward for being kind to some a-hole who would (and did) bash her brains in. Let's say she's watching us. Would Heaven Jamie *laugh* at all the off-key singing? At the tissue on her brother's cheek?

For a while after Jamie was killed, the world didn't laugh. But the world got over it.

To everything there is a season. Turn, turn, turn.

And so we turned, too. Even the four of us who knew it could have been our faces on the memorial service poster. We all turned, though some of us took longer than others.

Taylor Avril was probably the worst. For months, she walked around like a backup singer for a metal band, hair tangled, eyes ringed with week-old eyeliner. She stopped eating, stopped sleeping. When she stopped showering, Lindsey showed up at her house and refused to leave until she used soap.

That's Lindsey's way. She wants to fix everyone—even those like Taylor, who would rather rot.

But now Taylor's in her first year at Premiere Cosmetology in Roanoke. So I suppose Lindsey got her way.

She's at the vigil, too. The crowd makes an arc around

the stage, and I see Taylor on the other side, holding her candle inches away from her lips. The light casts tiny half-moons in her eyes. Her hair is a soft purple now—cut short, but with a few long beaded strands. I guess she's been her own beauty school test case one too many times.

An Asian guy with saggy jeans and eyebrow piercings is hanging on her shoulders like a coat. He's wearing a black T-shirt with a big red fish on it.

The stage people start in on another song, this time posting lyrics on the scoreboard.

You were our light, you were the one to make us smile, but you were only here, baby, for too short a while.

We're supposed to sing, too, but my voice sucks so I just watch the crowd. A line of people sways in unison, like the Whos from Whoville. Or old drunks at a Zac Brown Band concert.

The wind has quieted down now, and the candles stretching across the field make a hopeful little galaxy. I glance up to see if the stars can match them, but all I see past the lights is an inky blue vastness. The stands are empty, a cup that holds nothing but dark sky.

Empty, except for . . . A woman sits halfway up one set of stands, entirely alone. She's wearing a camel-colored coat and a black old-lady hat. Small, round-shouldered—not remarkable at all. Only, why is she there alone? Not singing. Holding an unlit candle in a gloved hand.

Maybe I'm paranoid, but it's almost like she's looking

right at me. I lower my candle and turn to stare at the stage. When I take a quick glance back, the old lady's head is angled toward the stage as well.

I nudge Lindsey and nod toward the woman. "Who's that? In the stands?"

Lindsey glances over, shrugs, and launches into the chorus. After forever, the music rises and the voices around me wobble into an awkward silence. The screen goes dark for a second, then the slideshow of photos starts back up. Everyone stands there for a second, not sure what to do. The mayor takes the mic and waves us off. "Good night, everyone. Be safe!"

As the crowd breaks, Lindsey and I head over and talk with Taylor and her friend.

Taylor doesn't introduce us to the guy, but Lindsey compliments his shirt. He tells us it was made with an actual dead fish that he rubbed paint on like a rubber stamp.

We talk about nothing that matters—beauty school, our school, the way the mayor stood too close to the mic and sang way out of tune. Everything but Jamie. Anything but Kyle.

I scan the stands, but there's no old lady now. Even so, my neck prickles like I'm being watched.

"You guys should come by," Taylor says. "I have a place set up in the basement. I could do your hair."

"What do you want to do to it?" I say it like it's a joke, but I'm serious. I don't want purple hair.

"I'll figure it out. The hair will speak to me," she says.

"We totally should," says Lindsey.

"Yeah, maybe," I say, but I'm thinking, *Not a chance.*

It's like a little reunion—the three of us, dead Jamie on the screen.

Blair Mattern, the other girl Kyle texted that day, isn't here, but she was quoted in the newspaper last week. She is the oldest of us—the same age as Kyle—and she moved to Los Angeles late last year.

According to the article, the day of the murder, Kyle invited Blair to dinner at The Pink Envelope, which is the fanciest restaurant in town. When she refused, he told her he was going to be famous, that she'd see his picture on the front page of the newspaper. He even hinted that he might kill someone.

Blair said she'd written it off as his general weirdness. "I don't want to think about it. I should have done something," she told the newspaper guy. "Jamie was a beautiful girl. She shouldn't have had to lose her life."

Lose her life. It seemed an odd way to put it. Where did she lose her life, in Kyle's crowbar?

It's like everything is our fault. *I should have done something.... She lost her life.*

But Kyle *killed* her. *He* did it. It's not Blair's fault. It's not Jamie's.

And I know, no matter how much it feels that way when I'm alone late at night, it's not my fault either. It's not mine.

A Minor Point

The unfortunate difference between knowing something and believing it to be true.

Rosencrantz and Guildenstern

The Monday after the vigil, Charlie Hunt raises his hand in sixth-period English and volunteers to die.

Friday we're reading *Hamlet*, and Mr. Campbell has this idea that we need to act some scenes out to really "wrap our minds around it" (his words, not mine). To be fair, *Hamlet*'s a bloodbath, so pretty much everyone has to be willing to die. Most of the girls are holding out for the part of Ophelia, since she's young and pretty and her death is romantic, as far as deaths go. Plus, her lover-boy Hamlet is almost surely going to be Nick Richert, who has that whole hot-jock-who's-too-smart-to-be-a-jock thing going.

"I'm taking orders. Who wants Rosencrantz and Guildenstern?" Mr. Campbell asks. "They don't have too many lines, and they both die offstage."

Charlie, who has been quiet to the point of nonexistence, puts out his arm, elbow bent, like he's turning right on a bike.

A half-second later, I raise my hand. I'd rather have a

boy role than be either the whacked-out Ophelia or the whacked-out queen. Plus, I like the idea of not so many lines. The momentum of Charlie's hand causes some sort of sonic ripple in the air, because as soon as my hand goes up, Felix McKenzie's hand follows suit. And then James Forrester's. It's like we're doing the wave at a ball game.

"Hmm," says Mr. Campbell, "I saw your hand first, Charlie. Who was next?" He is asking Charlie, not the rest of us.

Charlie shrugs, silent. Mr. Campbell waits, then goes on like he'd never asked.

"Sorry, James and Felix," Mr. Campbell says. He points at Charlie, "Rosencrantz," and then at me, "Guildenstern."

After doling out the rest of the roles, Mr. Campbell tells us what scene he wants each group to prepare for. Charlie and I are supposed to work on the part where Rosencrantz and Guildenstern are first reunited with their old friend Hamlet.

At first, they're joking around like frat boys. But then Hamlet asks them whether or not the king sent for them. They try to dodge the question. But Hamlet won't drop it. It's a test. Hamlet wants to know who he can trust.

I could have saved him some trouble.

No one. Trust no one. No testing required.

Charlie drags his desk over to mine and sits across from me. I tell him I can read for both Guildenstern and Hamlet while we practice since Nick, who has indeed been cast in the starring role, is busy with another group.

Charlie says nothing, so I start as Hamlet in a low voice: "'Oh God, I could be bounded in a nutshell and count myself a king of infinite space, were it not that I have bad dreams.'"

Then I raise my voice to do Guildenstern. "'Which dreams indeed are ambition, for the very substance of the ambitious is merely the shadow of a dream.'"

I lower my voice to be Hamlet again. "'A dream itself is but a shadow.'"

Charlie sighs and runs his hands through his hair. "'Truly, and I hold ambition of so airy and light a quality that it is but a shadow's shadow,'" he drones, looking himself like a shadow's shadow.

"Hey, can I ask you something?" It's not in the script, and he looks at me like he's worried I have rabies.

"I wanted it to be different," I say. I'm pretty sure we both know what I'm talking about, but I say her name anyway. "Jamie." Someone has drawn the profile of a cartoon face with a red permanent marker on my desk, and I press into its outline with my thumb. "But that's...that kind of wanting isn't worth much. It doesn't change anything. You know, since I haven't learned how to warp time or whatever. Still, what happened...I don't know how I'm supposed to be okay with—" All the good words are apparently busy in everyone else's mouths. The ones I'm left with seem bald, awkward, wrong. I blurt them out. "I just get so angry. It makes me sick." *Too loud*. I quiet my voice, but that's wrong, too. It comes out like I'm whispering a dirty joke. "It's like I can't get over it. I mean, how are we just supposed to be okay with what happened?"

He looks at me a long second, his eyes full of some sad thing. Animal sad. Like those fish that have lived for so long in underground pools they've evolved to be born blind.

"I'm sorry." I can't believe I'm saying this, to Charlie Hunt of all people. Or at least the broken husk of Charlie Hunt. "I shouldn't have brought it up."

"I just—" he says. "I gotta go." He closes his book, grabs his backpack by the strap, and takes off down the aisle.

The room ripples in his wake. A blur.

"Charlie all right?" Mr. Campbell asks me a minute after the door swings shut.

"He was feeling sick," I cover. "He needed to see the nurse."

Stuck

Charlie isn't in gym next period. And he isn't in English or gym the next day. But Mark Lee gives me stink eye while we're doing our laps Tuesday, so I'm guessing something was said. I keep running, though, and now I'm running against Mark. A stand-in for Charlie. But Mark is too slow, easy to beat.

The track spools out before me like a tired song. Above, clouds puddle in the sky.

I shouldn't have asked Charlie anything. I should have read Hamlet's next line and finished the scene and kept my mouth shut. It's not like Charlie has the answers. Clearly.

But still, I want them. And not just for me. I want answers for Lindsey and Taylor Avril. For Jamie's mom, her dad, her brother. Blair Mattern. For the silver-haired lady at the dentist's office where Jamie worked. For Charlie himself. How are any of us supposed to get over something like this?

And of course every day I wake up, don't I? I wash my face and put on clothes.

But it's not normal yet. It's not *la-di-da*, how it was before. Back when I believed I got to choose what to do with my life. When I believed I got to choose to keep living.

As my legs pump out the final lap, I think about that kid story. *Can't go over it, can't go under it... Oh no, gotta go through it.*

But there's no way through that I see.

I try getting excited about my future. As if me wanting all the traditional teenager things makes it *okay* for me to want all the traditional teenager things. I try to focus on plans for graduation and college and meeting new people and living on my own and someday being an archaeologist or criminal profiler or whatever that woman who lived with the gorillas was. I try to appreciate the fact that I'm running outside under a cool blue sky.

I thank the ground for keeping me and I breathe.

Poem of the Week

English Wednesday, Charlie is back.

He doesn't look at me, but I'm not sure if that's his general he-never-looks-at-anyone thing or a specific he's-not-looking-at-me-because-I-was-an-insensitive-jerk thing.

We are not doing *Hamlet* today because we have rough draft reviews for our college application essays. We're supposed to research a real university's question so we can use it when we submit to places this fall, but I haven't gotten that far, so I'm just going with the generic "Describe a person you admire" and recycling an old Mother's Day paper.

Mr. Campbell has told us to bring a book so we can read quietly on our own while he meets with one person at a time.

"But before we dig into our essay reviews—" Mr. Campbell rubs his hands excitedly. "Poetry waits for no man! That's right, kids. Poem of the Week time. Who's up?" Mr. Campbell consults his list. I am surprised when he calls Charlie's name. "Front and center, Mr. Hunt."

Charlie pulls his notebook from his backpack and walks to the front of the class.

Instead of handing out copies, he bends open the notebook and says out loud, "How to Get Over It." And now he is looking straight at me. And there is nowhere for me to go but here and nothing for me to do but listen.

> *I've learned about the space*
> *between a proton and a neutron.*
> *And I can calculate the shape*
> *of normal distribution.*
> *But I'm not going to figure out,*
> *not now, not ever,*
> *how to get over it.*
>
> *Not because it's impossible,*
> *improbable, unknowable—*
> *not because I can't,*
> *but because I could.*
>
> *I could, I might, forget.*
>
> *The way she'd close her eyes*
> *and go inside the music.*
>
> *The cross-eyed smirk she'd give*
> *when I said something stupid.*

The curly red wig
she wore in the rain
that Halloween, singing loud as thunder
"The sun'll come out tomorrow..."
And tomorrow, it did.

I won't get over it.

I hold the burning loss of her
so tight
it sears a hole in my skin—
a place where I can go
to begin
to remember.

Where she can still be near
and I can go on, for her sake,
from this side of the divide.

Where I can talk to silence
and hear the silence talk back.

He looks for a second electric, like the old Charlie. Supernova Charlie.

"Damn."

It's a whispered damn, the damn of admiration. And I'm not the one who whispers it. Mr. Campbell does. I don't think he realizes he spoke out loud. He forgets to ask Charlie for his question about the poem.

When Charlie passes me on the way to his seat, the hair on the back of my arms stands up. I sense my own skin, for maybe the first time ever, shimmering.

Matched

In gym next period, I don't run against Charlie.

I run with him, beside him. And when we're done, panting, our hands on our knees, I say between breaths, "Campbell was right. That poem. Damn, Charlie. Where'd that come from?"

He straightens, shrugs, and walks to the side of the field, where Coach Flanagan waits with tennis equipment. The coach sends us in groups of four to the courts. Charlie and I are paired with the next ones in, Mark Lee and another guy, Jared Hilley.

Jared, or JJ as he tried to get everyone to call him when we hit ninth grade, crushed on me last year. He was always showing up in weird places, smelling of some tropical cologne. But of course I was all about Sander then. And when Sander and I broke up before he left for Virginia Tech, I was all about forgetting—a fact that Jared used to his advantage.

What did I want to forget?

Only everything.

Sander. Sander's hand up Gemma Cook's shirt.

Andie and Monica off in a distant solar system, orbiting their own little planets.

The way my dad clearly didn't know what to do with his worry or his hands so he tried to pet my hair when I was at the breakfast table.

The way I flinched at his touch.

Jamie. And how much I hated myself for wanting to forget Jamie.

Kyle Paxson.

Seeing Kyle outside of Hardee's. How normal and boring it was.

The nightmare where his fist hammers my jaw and teeth spill from my mouth like loose beans.

That I could feel so much like a blackbird. Oil-slick feathers. Hollow bones. Blunt, useless beak.

Knowing that Kyle Paxson is not the *only* Kyle Paxson.

So, yeah, getting wasted is awesome for forgetting, and I spent more than my share of weekend nights wasting away in someone's basement or garage.

That lasted a month or two of weekends, and then Fridays and Saturdays melded into Sundays, and Thursdays, Wednesdays, and my grades tanked and my mom freaked and Lindsey staged an intervention. Lindsey hadn't been that close of a friend before, but after Kyle, the way she kept standing between me and the brick wall I was trying to crash myself against—*that* made us close. Like she got what I was feeling, what I was trying not to feel. And even though she was feeling something different, she was there. Not judging, just there.

Jared was around during the wasted weeks, too; I was lucid enough to remember that I made out with him at least once. It was the sort of zero-to-sixty all-tongue assault that seems hotter when you see it in the movies than when you're actually one of the participating tongues. Lindsey eventually pried us apart and drove me home—but not before I fell on top of the snack table on the way out the door.

I don't remember too much from that night, but I recall my head flopped forward against her car's dashboard when she was trying to strap me up. Maybe the whack of impact woke me for a second, cleared my mind. "Do you hate yourself enough yet?" she asked me, but not in a mean way, and then gently settled me back into the cradle of the passenger seat. I felt, for the first time in months, safe. Maybe even loved. Nothing brings two girls together like a violent murder, right?

As it turns out, Lindsey's intervention was well timed, in that 1) I woke up with salsa in my ears, 2) Jared is almost certainly a man-whore, and 3) drinking my way to oblivion never actually got me there.

I'm not at all into Jared now. Or probably even then. Plus, over the summer, he grew a scraggly goatee sort of thing. And got a skull-and-crossbones tongue stud. Seriously, yuck.

Now that I have to share a tennis court with him, I'm hoping he's forgotten the whole tongue and salsa thing.

"'Sup?" Jared says, nudging my elbow as we walk to the courts.

"'Sup?" I echo.

He hangs back then, a half-step behind me, and I know he is looking at my butt. Smooth.

"Doubles," Mark says, way too eager. "Me and Charlie against you guys?"

I suck at tennis, and I'm pretty sure Jared sucks, too. Meanwhile Mark is on the school team. Not sure about Charlie.

I shrug. Jared gives a cocky nod. We take our places on the court. Jared has the ball and gets in serving position; I go up front. Charlie stands catty-corner from me, across the net, while Mark plays backcourt.

When Jared serves the ball, it goes high, and the "Jared sucks at tennis" theory is confirmed. Mark could have run down to the corner store, grabbed a bag of beef jerky, and made it back in time to slam the ball low and fast across our net. I dash for the return but swing at empty air. The ball whizzes past me and hits Jared in what must be, judging from his howl, boy parts.

"Holy MOTHER!" He holds himself, dancing around in a sort of painful hoochie-coochie move.

"Ooooh." Mark cringes.

"What's up, JJ?" Coach Flanagan barks from two courts over. He jogs over to assess the damage, pats Jared on the shoulder, and tells him to "walk it off."

"Give him a few minutes," Flanagan tells us, then jogs

back to the group he'd been supervising, which consists of Amanda Wells and two girls named Allison—all from the girls' soccer team.

Mark bounces the ball. Twitchy. Eager to get back in the game.

Charlie stretches. I stretch.

He bends. I bend.

I realize I'm mirroring him, and I start to feel awkward about it, so when he bounces on the balls of his feet, I intentionally do the opposite. Only as I squat down, I realize that looks awkward, too. So then I stop doing anything and try just to stand there. Normal. One hand by my side, one on my hip.

He gives me a little smile, like he knows what's going on in my head. Which of course he can't. Right?

There's something different about him today. Maybe it was that poem. Reading it, writing it? Something. He seems livelier, more *here*. And I feel inexplicably glad about it.

"So, you good?" Mark calls to Jared, who is limping along the back line of the court, still semi-hunched. "Man up! Let's get this party started."

Jared straightens. Grimaces. "Whose serve is it?" he asks, his voice tight with pain.

"Mine," Mark calls.

I send Jared a "sorry" glance. I wish I could tell him there's no need for him to act all tough. It doesn't matter to me, and he's not impressing anyone else either. But that's not the kind of thing you say out loud. At least not to a guy.

45

Instead, I ask Mark, "What's the rush?"

"Is there a problem?"

"What's. The. Rush?"

"JJ's good," Mark says, though Jared clearly is not. It kind of makes me want to kick Mark in the gonads and see how *good* he is about it.

Jared hobbles over to his position on court.

"Give him a few minutes," Charlie says to Mark. "Come on, dude."

Mark gives Charlie a surprised quirk of the eyebrows. And I can see why. For the past year, Charlie has been stumbling around like a zombie, and Mark has been there for every stumble, propping him up, spoon-feeding him brains. And now here Charlie is telling Mark what to do.

"Yeah, okay," Mark says. He walks over to the fence, his back to us, tossing the ball in the air and catching it as he goes.

I grin at Charlie. Not the wide-eyed Charlie from before, exactly, but not the sleepwalker from last week either. Someone in between. He almost grins back.

What Love Is

The good thing about having gym last period is the showers. I actually have five minutes to take one.

When I get to the parking lot, my ponytail is still wetting my neck, and I smell like lavender.

Lindsey leans against the hood of my VW, chewing gum. Mrs. Barrow's transmission went out in her Chrysler, so for the last two days she's been driving Lindsey's Toyota to get her back and forth to her job downtown. Which means I've been giving Lindsey a ride to and from school.

"Hey, beautiful," I say. "What's up?"

Lindsey's legs seem extra long today, maybe because her skirt seems extra short. Definitely more than an index card above the knee, which is school regulation. But adults always cut her slack. It's that whole wise-beyond-her-years thing she has going for her. Since she was fifteen, she's carried two part-time jobs—night cashier at the Big Lots and teachers' helper at the Baptist after-school program. Lindsey stretches her gum from her mouth like pulled taffy, rolls it into a wad between her fingers, then plops it back in and keeps chewing.

She tugs my wet hair. "Aren't you cold?"

"No, Mother." I shrug Lindsey's hand off my neck and eye her skirt. "Aren't you?"

She does a twirl. "It's the price of looking fabulous."

"You're in a mood."

"Robert asked me out!"

"Linds!" I give the perfunctory squeal. "It's about time!"

"He was real smooth about it. He asked me if I'd be at the game this Friday, and then said maybe he'd catch me after."

That doesn't sound like much of a date to me. It sounds, in fact, like an offer to be his third-string plan for a hookup. A distinct possibility from what I know of Robert Leuger. Not that I know much. He was sweet and clueless enough in middle school, the kind of kid you'd share your peanut butter sandwich with because he lost his lunch, but he had some sort of freaky growth spurt the summer of our ninth-grade year, and started lifting weights or something, because now he struts the halls of Midland High, a football deity, ripped and blond and breaking hearts.

Lindsey has been drooling over him since he winked at her after the first pep rally of the year, and now she's taking what was probably a random comment from him like it's some kind of contract. She's super excited, though, so I put on my poker face and duck into the car.

"What?" she asks me when I pull out of the parking lot.

"What what?" I say.

"It's all over your face."

"My skin?" I tease, turning onto the main road. "Yeah, I generally leave it there."

But I know what she's saying—that she can tell I'm not convinced about the whole Robert thing. So much for my poker career.

"Really," she says. "What?"

"It's just," I say, "you have to be careful with guys like—"

"It's Robert," she says. "*Robert*. He's not one of those—"

"I know, Robert's great. But he might be looking for a hookup and you—"

"I'm what?"

"Well, you're the best person I know at telling everyone else what to do—"

"Wha—?"

"No, not like that," I cut in quickly. "*Good* advice. You give everyone really *good* advice. But you don't have your head on straight when it comes to that guy. It's like you can't hear your own sense. What is it you always say? 'Think it through.' Well, that's what *you* need. You need some distance.'"

She crosses her arms. The radio fills the silence between us. An 80s power ballad. *I walk down that road...alone, girl...alone. And there at the end, I find what you left. Who's to blame?*

"Because that's what love is all about, being distant and logical." Her sarcasm thrums like an out-of-tune guitar.

"Is that what love is?" I ask, serious, but then I start to sing full throttle with the song, *"Is that my heart? Is that my heart on the road in the rain?"*

She shoves my knee, but gently enough that it doesn't screw with my driving. "Jerk."

"Sorry." I let out a little laugh. "I just don't want you to get hurt."

"That makes two of us," she says, and I can tell she's already forgiven me.

Lost Twins

"Maroon or silver?" Lindsey holds up a dark red T-shirt in one hand and a silver tank top in the other.

"The shiny one?" I guess.

"This is not a test," Lindsey says. She tosses the maroon tee on the floor of her closet and slips the tank top over her head.

"Yeah." I take another look at her. "Definitely that. It brings out the sparkle in your eyes."

She bats her lashes at me. "Toss me my mascara," she says.

I take the tube from the table beside her bed and throw it. It hits her in the forehead and bounces to the floor. "Ow." She bends down to pick up the mascara, rubbing her head. "Remind me never to play softball with you."

I stick out my tongue and lean back on her pillows.

"So what are you going to wear?" she asks me.

I look down at the jeans and pale-green T-shirt I already have on. "Jeans," I say. "T-shirt."

She checks the clock on her phone. "There's time for us

to swing by your house if you want to change. Or you could borrow something—"

"Come on." I turn over on my side and watch her poke a dangly sea-glass earring through her left lobe. "It's a football game, not a fashion show."

"Says who?"

"Says me. And it's too cold for that skirt. Or is it a belt?" Lindsey wiggles her rump.

"I think you might be sending Robert the wrong idea."

"Maybe it's the right idea." She gives me a wicked grin.

"Okay. Just don't get your heart all wrapped around him. Promise me," I say. "For your own good."

"All right. I promise."

But I can tell she's lying.

"Anyway," she goes on, "what's with you? You didn't go all Mama Bear when I was seeing Eddie."

"You didn't *care* about Eddie. Eddie was just a— whatever. Someone to make out with."

"Ouch. Poor Eddie."

"Ouch, but true."

"Maybe that's what *you* need. Someone to make out with," she teases. "It would get you off my back."

As I drive to the stadium, Lindsey rolls her window down. The air is oddly warm for late September, and things smell wrong. More earthy rot than crisp leaves.

Instead of sitting in the stands, we find a spot on the grassy hillside near a goalpost. From here, we can see the little bucket of our lives. On the left side in maroon and silver, the people from our school, all the ones we scribble and eat and yawn and gossip and pee with every day. Then, on the right, a mirrored universe in blue and gold. A mirrored universe that has arrived here tonight for the express purpose of beating our butts in some stupid manly game that requires helmets and swearing and sweat.

I wonder if our doppelgangers are out there, too, just across the field. I spy big, blond Maria Madison in her short maroon skirt with her silver pom-poms and wonder if the big blond girl in the short blue skirt with the gold pom-poms on the opposite side is her secret identical other.

If so, where's my lost twin?

She and I must have parted ways over a year ago. As far as I know, she never stood over the casket of a mangled dead girl, certain it could have been her inside. So wherever Twin Me is and whatever she's doing, she's not quite *me* anymore.

And ironically enough, neither am I.

"Hey, you in there?" Lindsey asks, waving her palm in front of my face. "Whatcha thinking?"

"Nothing." I shake my head. "Everything."

"Philosopher," she says, then squeals. "Ooh! There's Robert!"

The band has started to play and our team rushes on the field, breaking through a big paper banner that reads SPARTANS! in hand-painted letters.

From this distance and in his uniform, Robert is unrecognizable. We know, though, that he is number twenty-nine. "Lucky twenty-nine," he says, whatever that means.

Luck isn't with him tonight, though. I don't know much about football, but even I can tell that what happens on that field isn't good. Dropped balls are skittering across the turf like runaway jumping beans. Boys are piling up on other boys. There's the *whack* of helmet on helmet and the *ooof* of shoulder to gut.

By the fourth quarter, the scoreboard reads 7–32 in favor of Chilton when the sky crackles and a few drops of rain plop down. With a sizzle, the sky flares. The lights in the stadium surge.

A ref blows his whistle, calling the players off the field. People stand. Some put on ponchos and sit back down. Others make a run for the covered underbelly of the stadium. Lindsey looks up and a fat raindrop splashes her eye. She wipes it, smearing her mascara down her cheek.

"Come on." She pulls us both up, and together, as the rain starts to pour, we run toward an opening in the cement flank of the home stands.

We lean against the archway, out of the rain, but soaked, shivering. Lindsey's top is like something from a wet T-shirt contest. I look down. Mine is not much better. Even though we're away from the crowd, I fold my arms over my chest, covering my nipples the best I can.

The rain starts to come in slants and we step back, deeper into the stands.

"Let's get some coffee," Lindsey says.

"Hot chocolate," I say.

She grins. "Hot chocolate!"

Fifteen minutes later, we sip our drinks, which are closer to warm brown water than melted chocolate, but whatever. "Sorry," I say.

"For what? You didn't know the line was going to be so long." She takes a sip. "And you didn't brew this god-awful stuff."

"Not that," I say. "I mean for the game. I know how excited you were to see Robert play."

"Oh!" She laughs. "Nah, I'm good." She wags her eyebrows. "The sooner the game officially ends, the sooner we start with the post-game activities."

"Ah," I say. "Well, this isn't letting up. They've got to call it, right? So what's next?"

"Robert said he'd text me when he's free," she says. "You can go on. His truck is here. I saw it in the parking lot."

"I thought the players had to ride the bus."

"Not seniors."

I consider leaving. I'm already soaked, so running the rest of the way to my car isn't going to make much difference. But I tell her I'll wait.

"I don't want to get wet," I joke.

After a few more minutes, a voice on the loudspeaker calls the game and the crowd thins. People make their way through the parking lot in zigzags, avoiding puddles, getting drenched.

Ten minutes pass, then twenty. Thirty. Lindsey checks her phone for the millionth time, but the only message she gets is from her sister, Veronica, telling her to pick up toilet paper on the way home. The rain putters to a stop.

The stadium is pretty much empty now. It's just us, the old Lions Club guys who run the concessions stands, and the stadium staff.

"You gals all right?" a gray-haired lady wheeling a mop bucket asks.

"We're good," I say. "We're waiting for someone."

"The gates are closed, sweetheart. Nobody can get in."

"One of the players," I say. "He's probably showering or something."

"I don't know," she says. "The buses have already left."

I look at Lindsey. Her bangs hang in limp coils over her forehead, and the smeared mascara has dried to her cheek.

"Let's wait outside," she says.

"Sure," I say, and we head out.

The parking lot is mostly bare, dark and wet.

"Where'd Robert park?" I ask.

Lindsey points to an empty quadrant of the lot. No truck. No nothing. Light from the lampposts makes yellow streaks on the dark pavement.

I put my arm around her shoulders. "We must have missed him," I say.

Under my arm, Lindsey's shoulders start to vibrate, like she's trying unsuccessfully to hold something in.

"Hey, hey," I say and turn to hug her. Her tears follow the same silent path down her cheek that the rain had, this time washing the mascara away.

Red

The first time I saw Charlie Hunt, we were ten. He was wearing a red baseball cap and running across the school yard after Mrs. Domingo's sandy-furred mutt.

"Catch 'im for me, honey, can you catch my Harvey?" Mrs. Domingo called in a voice that was both high and gravelly. She stood in her bathrobe at the end of her front walk and swatted at the air. Her house, a white bungalow with slate-blue shutters, sat across the street from the elementary school, and her mangy little dog was always breaking out. "Harvey! Here, Harvey!" she called. I later learned the kids had renamed the dog Humpty because of his doggish compulsion to hump random people's legs.

Charlie was wiry then. He hadn't yet hit his growth spurt, and his legs were gangly as he sprinted across the field. I was new to fourth grade. It was October when we moved here, so everyone knew everyone except me. Our teacher, Mr. Brewster, a sad man who wore fuzzy sweaters, had given me one of those fat, log-like Tootsie Rolls when we broke for recess. He'd done it out of pity, but to me it still tasted sweet. I had shoved the entire candy into my too-small mouth, and the brown juice running down my chin turned icy in the air.

When Charlie reached the dog, he scooped him up with one hand without stopping, cradling him like a football to his chest. He ran toward me, then past me to the curb, where Mrs. Domingo met him to collect the wriggling wad of her mutt. "Oh, you're a good boy. A good boy," she said, and I wasn't sure if she was talking to Charlie or the dog.

Eight years later, whenever I taste a Tootsie Roll, I still imagine that ball of fur running amok while little-kid Charlie breezes past. I suppose that vision of him, his hat askew, a red blur, is pressed somewhere against the curve of my mind. Quilted now with other memories, paper-thin, that have built up, layer by layer to this, tonight, right now:

Grown-up Charlie Hunt as he perches against the counter in Matt Graybill's kitchen—long legs, red Solo cup in hand, a dazed, drunk look on his face.

I haven't been to a party for months, but it is Saturday night and Lindsey has spent the afternoon alternately moping and raging about Robert. She has guessed and second-guessed (and four-hundredth-guessed) everything she did or didn't do the night before. And because I'm her friend, I listened.

But I'm not certain I can hear the words *asshole* or *don't care* or *my fault* any more without seeking out the nearest cliff for a nice cozy jump.

And so, we made a plan. I told my mom I was going

to spend the night at Lindsey's, and Lindsey told her mom she'd be spending the night with me. And together, hand in hand, metaphorically at least, we set out for the great wide world—or the living room dance floor at Matt Graybill's house, whichever came first.

"What can I get you ladies?" Matt's little brother, Dylan, is manning the drinks.

"Aren't you a little young to be playing bartender?" Lindsey asks. We slip off our coats. She is dangerous tonight, wearing a lacy chemise over a V-neck tank and white short-shorts over pale pink leggings. Her entire outfit is confused, like her underwear is trying to escape.

Dylan looks at her as if she's covered with whipped cream.

He reaches past the assorted half-full bottles of gin and vodka on the counter, fills two red cups from a keg, and hands them to us. I set mine down and rifle around in a cooler for a can of soda instead. "Driving," I say, which is true. But it's also true that I haven't partied since the whole facedown in salsa thing. Plus, it's Lindsey who needs mood alteration, not me.

I pop my can and raise it to Lindsey. "Cheers!"

She bangs it with her cup, sloshing foam on my wrist. I toss my coat on the back of an empty chair.

Without moving his head, Charlie lifts his eyes to the two of us.

"Cheeeers," he says, drawing out the "eeer" in a slur, not bothering to raise his cup. "I haven't seen you at one of these things for a while." With his free hand, he points at me.

"I haven't been," I say.

"Get comfortable," he says. "It never ends." Which I suppose makes a drunk sort of logic.

"Right," I say, and Lindsey pulls me out of the bright kitchen, through a large, dimly lit living room full of noise, dance music, and sweat. Arms and hips pulse with the bass line as we dodge our way through the crowd. When we reach the edge of the room, Lindsey takes a gulp of her beer and sets it on a coffee table. She starts to dance across from me, tilting her shoulders like a desperate boat. I put down my soda and dance with her, hoping I don't look as awkward as I feel.

We inch our way deeper into the room; Lindsey raises her arms over her head and shuts her eyes as she sways. After a minute, I feel something brush against my back and turn to find Jared Hilley gyrating in the general area of my butt. I think for the second time this evening of Mrs. Domingo's dog.

"Hey, girl," says Jared. Very Ryan Gosling. The beer is frothy on his breath.

"Hey," I say, still dancing. I ease away, creating a cushion of space between my body and Jared's. The song transitions into an elaborate guitar riff and Jared's hands start to twitch in a face-melting air guitar. "You still play?" I ask him.

He nods, enthusiastic. And I wonder if I've encouraged him in some way I didn't intend to.

I step away and do a little spin. But when I turn, I notice Lindsey isn't dancing. She is standing. Staring.

At Robert.

He wasn't supposed to be here—he was supposed to be at Tony Somebody's bonfire out in the woods near Eagle Creek because Tony Somebody is on the football team and rule number one of the football team is "Players Party with Players"—but here's Robert, regardless, broad shoulders blocking Matt Graybill's kitchen doorway. The light behind him makes the tips of his blond hair seem to glow.

"You want to go?" I touch Lindsey's shoulder. "Come on."

She shakes her head. "I'm here to dance," she says, and she starts up her engine again. But she might as well be listening to chainsaws for all she hits the beat.

I do a sort of shuffle-dance, keeping my eyes on her face. Meanwhile, my radar, invisible, is sending out pings, bouncing off walls. Without looking, I sense the space occupied by Jared, the space occupied by Robert, and beyond, the space occupied by drunken Charlie.

There is movement behind me—not Jared's dancing, but a more general crowd-making-way movement. Lindsey's eyes widen, which means Robert is walking toward her. I make way, too.

Robert slips in beside Lindsey and puts his lips next to her ear. Whatever he says, it's working. She rolls her eyes like she's pretending not to give in, but with another word from him, a slow smile tugs at her lips and she flushes a rosy pink.

Oookay, I think. *So much for the last eight hours of my life.*

It kills me how stupid she is about that guy. But whatever. It's her heart, not mine.

Jared moves closer, like he's about to say something, but I pull away. "Thirsty," I say, and step back, making a bee-line for the coffee table where we left our drinks.

I so don't want to be here—the extra in a bad teen movie. *Lonely girl at party.*

Robert holds Lindsey's hand and leads her out of the living room, back through the kitchen. She catches my eye on the way out and gives me a happy little wave. I wave back, not smiling, but trying not to frown either.

I glance down at my soda and, beside it, Lindsey's red Solo cup. It's half full. I pick it up instead and take a sip. The beer tastes lukewarm, bitter and ashy, like someone put a cigarette out in it.

"Wanna dance?" Jared has caught up with me. He thumbs his goatee in a way I'm sure he thinks is sexy.

I let out a frustrated breath.

He leans against the wall behind us. "What's wrong?" he asks.

"Ugh," I say, and that pretty much sums it up.

My phone vibrates. A message from Lindsey.

!!! Heading out wiht Robert. Don't wait forme. Lol. Talk tomorow. Bugs!

Lindsey is a bad speller, but what she lacks in spelling skills, she makes up for by being sloppy. For some reason, she turned off the auto-correct on her phone a week ago and never turned it back on, so now half her texts read like she's an extraterrestrial who learned English by scrolling through the comments section on YouTube.

K

If she were paying attention, she would know that means I'm irked. But what does it really matter if I wasted an entire day marinating in Lindsey's big vat of misery, listening to her wail about Robert? What does it matter if I lugged us both out to this party where neither one of us particularly wanted to be in some misguided attempt to cheer her up? What does it matter if we're supposed to be having a girls' night…because WHO NEEDS THAT JERK ANYWAY? and GIRL POWER! and CHICKS BEFORE PRICKS… BESTIES BEFORE TESTES! What does *any* of that matter if Robert, who up till twenty minutes ago was, and I quote, "the asshole to end all assholes," waltzes in and bats his eyelashes in her direction?

Yes, they are nice eyelashes. But really, Lindsey, really?

I take a gulp of her beer. Then shuddering, chug what's left.

"Look, Jared, I'm not great company right now," I say.

Empty cup in hand, I make my way back to the kitchen where the keg awaits.

Pig Latin

Twenty minutes later, I'm downing my second refill when Dylan Graybill jabs my shoulder. "I thought you were driving," he says.

"New plan!" I give him a sloppy grin as I finish the cup and toss it in the general direction of the sink. "Where's the bathroom?"

"Down the hall." He points past the living room.

I slither my way through the crowd, moving with the music. *I'm a snake*, I think. *A sneaky snake. Who needs to pee.* The thought of it makes me laugh, because, you know, beer.

I slide through the dance pit and halfway down the hallway, but before I can reach the Vessel of Sweet Relief, someone swats my bottom. I pivot on my heel, and now the swatty hands grip my hips and a bristly chin presses against my neck.

"What the—?" I try to pull away.

"You're so hot."

"Ugh. Get your—"

But then a surge of burly mass is driving me backward, crushing me against the wall.

Panic bolts through my body and I push back hard, but he—*who is he?*—is made of grizzly bear hormones and gut.

"Get off!" I yell, thinking back to my self-defense teacher, Miss Nancy, in her baggy sweats. *Say it girls: "Knee to groin!"*

Steeling myself, I ram a blunt knee into his privates. The guy, a blur of brown, stumbles back, and I exhale.

"What's your problem?" the guy barks, holding his privates.

"*You're* my problem!"

"Come on, babe. You know you—"

"Who ARE you?" And then it hits me. Todd Firebaugh. The dude who blows on a maroon plastic horn at every pep rally. One of those long horns that make a crap-ton of noise.

"You okay?" It's Jared, but his voice sounds oddly high, like the cartoon version of his voice. "This guy giving you trouble?"

My eyes dart from one to the other. "This guy" is about two of Jared in bulk alone.

A hand still cradling his groin, Todd turns on Jared. "LEAVE."

Jared straightens, his shoulders expanding. "Bite me."

Todd takes the first swing, but Jared dodges to one side and jabs Todd in the ribs.

Snorting, Todd gives an ugly grin. He shoves Jared against the wall, "Okay, let's do this."

"Back off!" I jump between them, holding out my hands like a traffic cop.

"Step aside, babe."

"I'm not your babe!"

He looks at me like I'm spouting pig Latin. And yeah, I might be slurring a little, but I'm certain I'm speaking actual words.

"You're just some tease, aren't you?" Todd gets up in my face, exhaling his sour breath. "You think you get to walk around, shaking your ass, licking your lips—"

"Are you insane? Yes! Yes, I get to *walk*! And I get to take my ass and my lips with me when I do!" My heart is beating out of my chest, but I look right at him when I say it.

"Unbelievable! You're such a slut!" He clamps his hands around my shoulders.

Is this really happening? My mind throbs with the bass of the music and I can't find my breath anywhere. What will get him off me? Finger wrench? Ear slam?

Head-butt!

I hear Miss Nancy's voice in my head, "Chin down. Aim the top of your head at their face. Move in hard, like you're letting out a big sneeze."

I grab Todd by the ears, tuck my chin, clench my teeth, and pound the crown of my head hard into his nose. There's a loud *thwak!*, and Todd's hands break from my shoulders.

Staggering, he wobbles to one side, and I spring away.

It's then I see who's behind him. Charlie, fists clenched. "Leave. Her. Alone."

My first thought is to get as far away as fast as possible, but Todd and Charlie are between me and the way out. So I'm there for it all: Todd shaking it off, wiping blood from his nose with his forearm, laying into Charlie with both fists; Charlie pushing him back, striking with a fierceness I didn't know a drunk could muster. It all goes in a quick blur. Someone gets someone in a headlock—bodies tilting in a mass—grunts and thumps, some kicking.

Jared and I stand there like forgotten marionettes, dangling by a single frayed thread.

Charlie steps back, then throws himself into a punch, making a dense *thunk* against Todd's chin. Blood sprays, and my stomach sinks beneath the floor.

It ends with Charlie pinning Todd against the wall, delivering one punch after the other. Todd looks like a demented bobblehead.

"What the f—" I look to Jared, my head blaring with pain. "We've got to stop...we've got to stop...."

I don't know if I'm making sense, but Jared nods, grabs Charlie by the shoulders.

"Lay off," he says. "You don't want—"

Charlie turns, fist raised, face raw, eyes wild. No trace of the Charlie I know.

"Stop it," I say. He lowers his fist, his back turned to Todd, who after a second regains himself and, from behind, slugs the broad side of Charlie's jaw.

Charlie's head jerks. He falters to the floor.

"Holy mother! Is he okay?" Jared angles himself in front of Charlie, putting himself directly in the path of Todd.

"Back away!" I yell, though it's not clear who I'm yelling at. I kneel down to check on Charlie. He looks at me through bleary eyes.

By now, everybody from the living room has crowded into the mouth of the hallway. A few boys chant, "Fight! Fight! Fight!"

Matt Graybill squeezes through the crowd, takes in the blood-splattered wall, a picture of a barn in snow hanging sideways on its nail; Todd Firebaugh, breathing heavy, rubbing the fist of one hand in the palm of the other; Charlie and me on the floor; Jared in between.

"What the hell!" Matt puts one hand on his hip and points the other at the general mayhem.

"It's not...it's not..." Todd starts.

But I can't say exactly what Todd Firebaugh thinks this is *not*, because he never finishes.

"You." Matt points at Todd, then the three of us. "All of you. Out!"

Light of Morning

Light. Sharp. Pinpricks to my eyes.

I clamp shut, tunneling down, back to the den of sleep. But the light is still there. A thick smear of it crosses my eyelids. A thrum of white.

My neck feels crooked, like it's one of those angled wrenches that come with a make-your-own-furniture set.

Everything is bent metal.

Everything is clotted gravy.

Everything is dull roar.

I force my eyes open. My first question: Am I going to puke? My second: Where am I?

It doesn't make sense.

I'm half-sitting, half-slouched over the arm of a sofa. Someone's arm rests heavy across my lap. Brown hair, boy body. I'm in a garage—no, it's one of those big, stand-alone sheds, fitted out like a man cave. In front of me, a flat-screen TV; beyond that, a band setup, complete with drum set, keyboard, speakers, mic stand. I turn my head. On one side, a mini-fridge, and on the other, a recliner with Jared Hilley, mouth open, snoring.

I check my clothes. Jeans and top—intact. All my buttons buttoned. I wiggle my toes. Shoes off, but socks still on.

There's a snort, then a cough. Jared wakes and looks over at me. "Hey. How you doing?"

I pat my hair, which is matted and stiff, and then wipe something wet—drool?—from my cheek. Is this a question that really needs to be answered?

He stands and stretches, rumpled, in the same jeans and Van Halen T-shirt he was wearing last night.

Beside me, the boy-body shifts. Charlie Hunt in profile, black-eyed and bruised—but sleep has turned him younger, less guarded, more like the little boy who chased stray dogs all those years ago.

"Is he all right?" I ask.

"I wouldn't want to be him this morning. Or Todd." Jared holds a hand out to me. "You, either, for that matter. You up to standing?"

I nod, push Charlie's arm aside, and Jared hoists me gently to my feet.

"There we go, Sleeping Beauty."

How did I get here?

That's when it comes back.

The fight. Charlie, Jared, and me, out on the street, in no shape to go home, in no shape to drive. Jared saying he knew a place—a couple blocks away, a guy in his band who wouldn't mind. Us walking the streets like a wolf pack, bony shoulders hunched against the dark. There's a weird black-hole quality to the whole thing. I remember arriving here, settling onto the sofa, exhausted, Jared getting me a Dr Pepper from the mini-fridge, but the rest is lost in space.

"Nothing happened last night, right?" I ask.

He looks at me like I'm a two-headed unicorn. "What's your definition of nothing?"

"You know." I gesture in the general direction of my body. "You guys didn't—while I was out?"

Jared blinks, like I threw dirt in his eye. "Are you serious? We're not—do you really think—?"

"Sorry," I say, but he has already recovered. He puts on his good-ole-boy mask.

"It's okay." He wets his lips, and I see a flicker of the skull-and-bones tongue stud. "You know I'm at your service whenever you want," he says. "You just name the time. But you're gonna be *there* when we get together. I don't want you to miss a second of all this." By which he means his general manliness, I guess.

"Um…" I'm not sure how else to respond.

There's movement on the couch. Charlie sits up, running a hand over the mess of his hair. A clump near his temple is jutting out at a right angle in a way that looks sort of absurd and sort of cool.

"Is there any food?" His voice is sandpaper.

"Let's see," Jared says, walking over to a cupboard beside a small utility sink.

Charlie rumbles to his feet. He rubs his neck and groans. "You get the license plate for the truck that hit me?"

"That bad?" Jared asks.

Charlie shrugs.

Gah, what I wouldn't give for a toothbrush. Or a bathroom.

We grabbed our coats on the way out of the party, so in the pocket I have car keys, cell phone, my ID, and a few bucks in cash. But that's it. No hairbrush even.

"Jackpot!" Jared tosses a box of cheese crackers at Charlie.

There's a rustling sound as Charlie burrows into the box. He comes up with a big handful of crackers and starts shoving them in.

In the glare of morning, he looks like a strung-out raccoon.

I must not look much better. I'm pretty sure my hair smells vaguely of beer.

"Oooh, even better!" Jared pulls a box with leftover pizza from the mini-fridge. He sets it out on a big metal footlocker that serves as a coffee table. "The breakfast of champions!" he declares as he and Charlie plop down on the sofa and dig in.

Jared holds out the box to me. "There's a piece here with your name on it," he offers, mid-chew.

"Not unless you want some puke to go with that," I say.

"Yeah, pass." He pulls back the pizza box and sets it on his lap.

"I guess I should thank you guys," I say.

They look up at me, confused.

"You know," I say, "for stepping in. For not letting Todd—"

"That guy's an ass," Jared says.

"Well, anyway," I say, "I appreciate you doing that for me."

"I would have done it for anyone." Charlie has a grim look, and I'm not sure if he's mad at me or Todd. Or life. "I can't stand guys like that. They think they can do whatever they want."

Or Kyle, now that I think of it. Maybe that's who Charlie is mad at.

Charlie is taller than Kyle. Stronger than him, I'd bet. He could probably take Kyle in a fight. It must kill him that he wasn't there to stop what happened to Jamie.

"So that's how you spend your weekends—fighting crime?" And really, I am curious. Is this a regular thing?

"No." He shakes his head. "I spend my weekends... There's nothing special about how I spend my weekends."

Jared picks up the last two pieces of pizza and folds them over to make a kind of pizza sandwich. "We should head on," he says. "I know Motor is good with us being here, but his old lady is a piece of work. And she might come sniffing around. You up to driving?" he asks me.

I nod.

"Think I could catch a ride with you?" Jared asks.

"Sure." I jingle the keys in my pocket.

"You're not looking too solid," Charlie says.

"Just need some air," I say.

We creak open the door, creep through the yard and down the street. Sunday is mostly quiet. A middle-aged couple on bikes passes by. A woman walks her dog.

When we reach his car, Charlie digs in his pockets, rifles around, comes up empty. "Hell. I left my keys at the party."

We look a few houses down, toward the Graybills'. There's a minivan in the driveway. "No way am I going in there." He lets out a puff of breath. "I'll text Matt, ask him to bring them to school on Monday."

"I'll give you a ride," I say. "My car's just at the other end of the street."

As the three of us walk out together, making our way down the tree-lined block of the upscale neighborhood, Jared hums. It takes a second before I place the tune.

"Over the Rainbow."

And yeah, I do feel a bit like Dorothy, as if I just fell from the sky.

Jared could be the Scarecrow when he lost half his stuffing.

Charlie might make a rugged, slightly dented Tin Man.

And the road, bathed in the bland light of midmorning, curves away, toward a glowing, green world.

What Was

The Tin Woodman, as it turns out, is too long-legged for my little Pony, and his knees stick up in a flamingo-esque angle in the passenger seat.

"Here," I say, twisting down to reach the lever below the seat, my face way too close to his knees. I pull the handle up, feeling the blush rise in my face. "Scooch back."

"Ahhhh," he exhales as his legs straighten a bit. "Thanks."

"You got enough room back there?" I ask Jared, as I scoot my seat up.

"It'll do," he says, though I'm sure he's just being nice.

The cell phone in my jacket pocket vibrates and I check my messages. Three from Lindsey—two earlier and one just now.

Sorry abot taking off. Oy! Robet!

Get home ok? Call em.

Where are you?????

Hey! In car. Talk soon. I want details!

"Are your parents worried?" Charlie asks as I pocket my phone.

I shake my head. "They think I was at Lindsey's," I say.

A blotch of blood is crusted on his chin, and his bruises are starting to ripen into plums. His face looks like fruit salad. Menacing fruit salad.

I realize I'm openly staring at him, and I shift my eyes away from his face. Starting the car, I tell myself I absolutely should *not* be staring at Charlie. I maybe had a crush on him once upon a time, but that was so long ago I hardly think of that little girl as being *me*. We were total kids—the new girl and the boy in the red baseball cap. I didn't even have breasts.

I drop off Jared first. He gives directions from the back seat that land me in an alleyway behind a small apartment complex. Maybe twelve units, each with its own little cement patio on the back.

I hop out and lean the driver's seat forward as he detangles himself from the back seat. "Later, gators!" he says, taking off.

Charlie's next. I know where he lives, but I let him direct me there anyway. A few blocks down is his house, white with black shutters, and right beside it, Jamie's.

I wonder how he stands that. Every day, just to get to his car, he has to walk by an entire world full of her.

Full of what *was* her.

It's a miracle he's kept it together. Sometimes I can't, and I wasn't even that close to Jamie. I mean, what I knew about her, I liked. You'd have to be an a-hole not to like her. She was, as I've mentioned, exceedingly sweet.

It's so unfair. Here I am, my own mean self, while she's in the ground.

Here Kyle is. Here Charlie is. Here's Lindsey. Taylor. Blair. Here's Kyle's grandma. And Todd Firebaugh. And Jamie's mom and dad and brother with the bloody tissue paper near his ear. Here's the judge and the cops and the jury. Here's the silver-haired lady in the neon-green beret, with Jamie's kiss still on her cheek.

Here we all are walking around and sometimes smiling and getting drunk and dancing and fighting and kissing stupid boys and dyeing our hair purple. Some of us might go to college or get married or grow old or die peacefully in our sleep.

It's wrong.

But how can living be wrong?

For a while I thought everyone else had some secret knowledge. Like they'd all taken the class. A Survival Guide for Survivors.

On the dashboard, my solar-powered daisy in its plastic flowerpot dances and waves.

"This is you, right?" I ask, keeping my eyes on the road.

"Yeah."

When I pull over, he opens his car door but doesn't get out. I want to say something else. Too many somethings. *Thanks for fighting Todd.* And *fighting is stupid.* And *that bruise under your eye looks like a small South American country.* And *I've thought about your poem.* And *I remember you with that goofy dog when we were kids.* And *do you think about Jamie all the time, like every minute of every day? Do you think about Kyle?*

But what comes out is, "Do you run?"

He glances at me from the corners of his eyes. "Is that a trick question?"

"No." I laugh, nervous. "I just meant, I run sometimes. You know, on that greenway down by the river."

"Yeah," he says, scratching behind his ear. He shrugs. "Maybe I'll see you down there sometime?"

"Maybe."

He hops out of the car and crosses the lawn. When he nears the door, I start to wave, but Charlie goes in without glancing back. I take one more look at the glossy black door, then pull away.

No Place Like Home

I sneak upstairs for a quick shower, then trail wet foot-prints to my room. I'm dizzy from the steam, and the top of my head still aches from where I crashed it into Todd's face. Wrapped in a towel, I topple like a downed redwood onto my bed. My eyes tug closed. *Just for a minute*, I tell myself, but the swell of fatigue is overwhelming. I want to text Lindsey—find out what happened with that jerk Robert Leuger, but my phone is in my coat pocket, a million miles away. It would require standing and walking. Or at least dramatic stretching. I consider sending an FU text to Todd Firebaugh, but I don't have his number.

The last thoughts I have before I slump into sleep are about the scent of brown sugar and the dampness of my hair.

"You've come for me?" A voice, soft as air, seeps from a doorway. A girl's voice, but not a young girl. She could be my age. It could be my voice.

I don't answer. And then I am on a beach, strolling toward the water. The surf rises and settles, a yellowish brown, clogged with the long hair of the drowned.

At the edge, water laps my feet, and there's the voice again. "You've come?"

I don't want to look. I want to keep moving forward, but there is no forward, only ocean. So I turn around, as if it's my duty. I crack my knuckles to prepare myself for what I am going to see, and yes, I'm not surprised to find her there.

Jamie.

Maybe five feet away, floating above ground like in a painting of Jesus.

She isn't the way I thought she'd be, the way Kyle left her, crumpled and bloodied. Instead, she is...perfect. The shiny-new-penny version of herself.

She wears a long blue dress, her hair curled and gleaming. Even her eyebrows have a tidy look—as if they've each been brushed one hundred strokes. Her cheeks are rounder and redder than they were when she was alive, and she doesn't limp when she moves. Midair, she glides.

I try to smile at her. I try to say, "I'm sorry." But I'm stuck.

Instead, she speaks. "There's so much air here. I'd forgotten." She looks up, awed. "So much sky."

"We have other things. Bridges and benches. Squirrels. Oh, we have cupcakes." She lets out a happy sigh. "They're prettier than yours. Like every wish you had as a girl—*everything you ever dreamed*—squeezed into a single perfectly iced cupcake."

She glides closer, and the brightness in her cheeks dims. "When I bit into it, though"—she makes a grimace—"it tasted stale—like sawdust." Then her face lightens again with a serene, philosophical smile. "Some things just aren't meant to be."

"I'm sorry," I say—finally getting my words out. But now it's wrong, too. Because it seems like I'm apologizing about her bad cupcake. "I'm sorry," I say again, hoping she understands me.

Hoping she can forgive me for having all this sky.

Opera

The kitchen table is scattered with mixing bowls, flour dust, random wooden spoons, a spilled box of raisins, the shredding of carrots, upturned bottles of spice, and smears of goo. My mother is nowhere to be found, but a platter mounded with gorgeous brown muffins sits on the counter by the sink.

Patting my stomach, which feels emptier than usual, I snag a muffin and retreat to the den.

The house feels empty, too. No sign of parents. The clock on the mantel reads a quarter after five. I've been asleep up in my room all day, and I feel achy from being in bed too long.

I should catch up on homework. Or go run. Or call Lindsey.

But what I do is I sprawl out on the couch and channel-surf my way to a Bugs Bunny marathon.

I am watching Elmer Fudd, decked out with a magic Viking helmet, sing a love song to the cross-dressing Bugs Bunny, when my mother comes in.

"There's my girl," she says, perching on the end of the

couch. She squeezes my calf. "You and Lindsey must have been up all night. You were sacked out."

"I guess I'm hitting a growth spurt," I say, though we both know I'm pretty much done growing. "Where were you guys?"

"We brought Chinese. General Tso's." She smiles, knowing it's my favorite. I watch her as she tugs a hair tie from her wrist and pulls her long brown hair back into a ponytail. A slice of late-afternoon light shines through the window and lands on her profile in the space between her eye and ear. She is beautiful, with full lips and rich brown eyes that look mysterious even to me. My dad said I could be her twin when she was my age, but I don't see it. I've always felt dull next to all her color.

"Oh, hey," she says, her smile fading. She shifts her body so she's facing me full-on. But then she doesn't say anything more—just searches my face like she's trying to find the *X* on a treasure map.

After a second, I ask, "Hey what?"

She blinks, then looks back at the screen, where a bunch of women wrapped in white towels talk about their armpits. "Nothing. Did you have a good time last night? What did you guys do?"

"Listened to music. Talked." Both true, though not exactly the truth. I consider telling her about Todd Firebaugh and Charlie and Jared, but what would be the point? She'd never let me out of the house again.

"Lindsey's a good nut," Mom says. "I'm glad you have her for a friend."

My mom gnaws at her lower lip, a sure sign she's hold-ing something back.

"What were you going to say?" I ask. "Tell me."

"Oh, it's just—" She's staring now at the TV, but her face has gone blank, like she wouldn't notice if the women dropped their towels and started pole-dancing. "Your father got a call on Friday. From the Commonwealth's Attorney's office. They want to talk with you. About Kyle Paxson."

"What?" I sit up. "But why?"

"You know, that text he sent you."

"But he's guilty. He said so. He sat up there in front of everyone and said he did that to Jamie."

"I know, jelly bean, but they still have to build their case."

"What do you mean? I thought it was over."

"It's not. They have to decide…" My mom picks up the remote and fiddles with the battery compartment, snapping it out and back in place, out and back in place. "They have to decide his punishment. Whether or not he gets the death penalty."

Oh, right. *That.* When they caught Kyle, the police knew it was him right away. It wasn't some big mystery, like you see on TV. He told them he did it, and I thought he'd be locked away, end of story. But that's too simple for the American justice system.

"They're going to have the sentencing hearing in a few months. They want to talk to you and Lindsey and the others."

"But we've already talked to them."

"You talked to the police," she says, tucking a hunk of hair behind my ear. "These are the *lawyers*. They want to talk with you, and then maybe you'll have to testify in court."

"No way." I lie back down on the couch, feeling a thin layer of unreality seep between me and everything else.

My mom squeezes my calf again, but this time she keeps her hand there.

"Is he going to be there?" I ask. "Kyle?"

She rubs my shin. "I think so."

I pull my leg away, curling up on my side. She reaches out, pats my foot, and says, "If you want to talk, your dad and I are here."

She perches there a minute in silence. Then she leaves, and I hear the clank of plates as she sets the table for General Tso's.

Happy

Monday morning, I haul myself out of bed.

I'm not sure if Lindsey will be getting a ride with Robert so I text her.

Need a ride to school?

Yes!

When I pull into the parking lot for her apartment building, I text her that I'm here and wait. The apartment building is that small, old-fashioned brick type that has a single entrance with a hall and stairway leading to eight little units—four up, four down. The street is old, quiet, and, except the apartments, stocked with small, practical houses that look like they haven't been touched since the 1950s. The only thing that might qualify as cutesy is the pink flamingo somebody stuck near a mailbox a decade ago.

After a few minutes Lindsey bounds out her door, wearing a cropped jean jacket over a tight neon-orange T-shirt dress that reads MORE ISSUES THAN VOGUE in sparkly black letters. Long black socks and orange high-heeled boots complete what I can only think must be her bid for Hot Witch of the Year.

I wonder if she knows yet about us needing to testify, but I doubt it because she's all bubbly when she climbs in the car. "Hello, darling," she drawls, leaning in quick as a jackrabbit to give me a playful peck on the cheek.

"Hey!" I say. "You look...um...That dress is...bright?"

She sticks out her chest. "Makes my breasts look awesome, *n'est-ce pas?*"

"Um, yeah," I say. "Plus, it's so...modest. You know, *modest*...like when people *don't* go around talking about how awesome their breasts are?"

"Tried it. Hated it." She laughs.

I give a weak smile and stare at the steering wheel.

"Hey, you okay?" she asks.

So I tell her about what happened after she left the party—about Todd and the fight.

"That ass-wipe," she growls. "That absolute prick."

I nod and start driving.

"So, what happened with you Saturday?" I ask once we hit Main Street, trying to make my voice light. "You and Robert...Did you guys—?"

"Oh my God, he is so—I swear, I'm *marrying* him. He doesn't know it yet, but he and I are totally going to—"

"You can't be serious."

"What?" she asks, clueless.

"Gah, Lindsey, are you hearing yourself? That's..." The idea of Lindsey settling down forever in some picket-fenced love shack and baking pies pretty much strips any semblance of tact from my tongue. "That's some bat crap."

"Don't you think Robert—"

"*Marriage?* We haven't even gone to college, Linds. You're just talking, right?"

"I'm not sure I'm even doing college." She glances down and picks at a thread sticking up from the band of her sock.

"What? Okay, that's the *crap of* bat crap. Like a big pile of crap took a crap. That."

"*You're* the one who wants to go to college. You're smart. You got that whole fight-crime-and-tame-the-gorillas plan. But that's not me. I never wanted anything but to find a good guy, get a little house, maybe have a baby somewhere down the road. I've never wanted anyone but Robert."

"Ugh. Seriously? But what about—*life*? Don't you want to go out dancing with some guy you've never met? Or do...whatever it is married people *don't* do?" I veer to avoid a stray jogger. "Think about it, Linds. We haven't seen the Eiffel Friggin' Tower. We've never gotten thrown out of a bar. We can't even get *in* a bar. We haven't jumped out of a plane or hiked the Appalachian Trail. We've never gone skinny-dipping."

"Calm down. It's not like he's asked me." She flips down the visor. "He *will*. But he hasn't. Yet."

"And that's going to be enough? Don't you want something more? A good job doing...something?" I wave my right hand aimlessly.

"I like my job."

"Big Lots?"

"Well, no, not that one. But the church. And Miss Mirabelle says I should apply to teach at the camps next summer."

"And that's...I don't know, Linds," I say. "That's great. I just don't want to see you stuck."

"I love Robert. I *love* him."

"Does he love you?"

"Yes."

"He told you?"

"No. Not in words."

"You can't believe the *words* when some guy *says* them. I mean, look at Sander. If Robert hasn't even *said* it..."

"You just can't—" She is staring out the passenger window, and her voice comes to me muffled and flat. "Why can't you be happy for me?"

I glance over at her as I pull into the senior parking lot. She looks like a balloon that's had all its air drained out.

"No, you're right. I'm sorry," I say. "I *want* to be happy for you. I mean, it's your life, right? Whatever happens, I'm happy for you."

When she doesn't answer, I poke her leg and paste a smile on my face. "See, this is me. Happy." I point at my face.

"I see." And when she looks at me, her eyes are as tired as my smile.

There Are the Players

So I'm officially a rotten friend.

Rotten person in general.

I'm not anyone's rotten girlfriend, though I'm sure I'd be especially rotten at that today, too.

I'm on autopilot as I drift through the halls.

When I'm leaving psych, Ms. Ramano holds me up, waving me over to her desk as everyone else is shuffling out the door.

"I heard some things about this weekend," she says, once the room clears. "Some kids were talking in my first-period class. There was a fight?"

It seems like a question, but I don't answer.

Ms. Ramano sighs. She is wearing a black dress today, like a short and lumpy grim reaper. "Do you know anything about that?"

"Not much," I say.

"But something?" she says.

"Not really," I say.

"Look." She doesn't touch me, but her gaze is so intense, it feels as if she has tipped my head down to peer into the bland moon of her face. "Look, if someone did something to you, it's okay to talk about it."

"Nothing really happened," I say. "I'm fine."

She searches my face for some crumb of a lie.

"For real," I say.

And even if I were inclined to talk to Ms. Ramano about that a-hole Todd Firebaugh and his filthy, grope-y hands, what is there really to tell? That he *might* have *tried* to force me—you know, *maybe*, if Charlie and Jared hadn't stepped in? That he made me feel scared and dirty and small?

Because I'm pretty sure the world doesn't much care what *might* have happened. It's not interested in how small I *feel*. To the world, I'm just another drunk girl at a party.

Fuck the world.

"Well, if you need help, you know you can talk to me," Ms. Ramano says.

"I've got to get to English," I say, hiking my backpack higher on my shoulder. "But thanks." I stop on my way out the door. "It's good to know, you know…whatever," I say, not sure what words I'm looking for.

In English, the words don't come any easier. We are back to *Hamlet*, doing our scenes for the entire class.

Nick Richert, in a tight black T-shirt, makes a disturbingly hot Hamlet. The entire female population of the class is practically drooling. Not to mention Doug Howe, who is gay, and Russell Soto, who might be.

When it's time for me and Charlie to get up there next to Nick, I have trouble focusing on anything but his muscles.

Mr. Campbell lets us hold our books for reference, but he doesn't want us just reading.

"*Act!*" he proclaims. "*Own* your character! Be *dramatic!*"

"O, there has been much throwing about of brains," I read, having no clue what I'm saying.

Nick as Hamlet gets all up in my stuff. I stare, mesmerized, at the way his collarbone emerges from the neckline of his shirt.

"Do the boys carry it away?" he asks, his voice like hot maple syrup. He places his hand on my shoulder and lets it drift slowly down the curve of my arm.

"What?" I murmur.

Charlie, a shop-worn Rosencrantz, pries us apart, declaring something equally perplexing: "Ay, that they do, my lord; Hercules and his load, too."

I sway slightly, trying to hold it together until my last line of the scene.

Nick steps back, offering his next speech for the benefit of the girls in the front row. Something about his uncle... blood...philosophy.

When I miss my next line, both Nick and Charlie look at me expectantly for a beat. I stare back, clueless. Then Charlie steps in, announcing stiffly, "There are the players."

I can feel the heat of him beside me, the comfort of him.

The bruise on his cheek has faded from yesterday's purple to a vague moss green.

I nod, as if it all makes sense, and mouth a tiny "thanks"—relieved that I'm in this with Charlie.

Hamlet and his freakishly alluring collarbone mean nothing to me.

Ducks

I look for Lindsey, but she isn't waiting for me after school, and when I call, she doesn't answer. I know she's pissed at me, but even so, it isn't like her to avoid me—or her phone—and I'm worried.

It's Monday, not one of her days with the after-school kids, so I drive by her apartment on my way home to make sure she got there. I don't see her car, and when I knock, no one answers.

> Where are you?

She doesn't answer.

> Want coffee?

But that doesn't work either.

She probably just lost her phone. It's happened before. I slip back in my car and drive.

When I get to the turn onto Main, I find myself steering left, toward the river, instead of right, toward my house.

Just because Lindsey isn't answering, it doesn't mean she *isn't*. I know that, of course, but while I drive, I find myself inspecting every car I pass, trying to remember little details, as if they might be important later. *Yes, Officer, it was a powder-blue LeBaron with a dent in the front fender and a license that began "QRT."*

Would it have helped? How would I have described Kyle, anyway? *White male. Twenty-one. Glasses. Baby face. Not fat, exactly, but soft. Harmless.* A weird guy in a world full of weird guys. I never bothered to look twice.

But as I inspect the tenth car I pass, I can't help feeling that something's been stripped from me. What normal high school senior thinks this way, like a PTSD grandpa prepping for end times? I should be worrying about college applications, not whether the guy with the beard has Lindsey stuffed in his trunk.

When I get to the river, I park where I usually do, in the little gravel patch near the eternal cluster of ducks.

I pull the crank and, leaning my seat back, focus on the ducks. Their random waddling, pecking, fluffing. I watch curled yellow leaves drift down from a tree on the bank. And I think about that dirt-wad Todd Firebaugh.

I guess I should just be happy he didn't get me alone in some room.

And I am.

But I'm also sick of being thankful that some horrible thing miraculously *didn't* happen to me.

I'm sick of thinking, *Oh, goody, that guy who wanted to rape me got the crap beat out of him.* Or, *Yay! the dude who wanted to kill me is up for the death penalty.*

Are either of those things even remotely good? Yeah, they're better than the alternative, but still, they suck.

I check that my doors are locked and then close my eyes for a second.

When I open them, it's dusk and my neck is stiff. There is a noise—a knocking. I look up, confused, and see a hand and a dark blue sweatshirt sleeve in the dim light outside my window.

I follow the arm up to find the sharp angles of Charlie's face as he squints down.

"You okay?" His voice is muffled through the pane.

I nod and pop the lock, then realize I can't open the door without it ramming into him.

"Yeah, you?" I say through the glass.

He cups one hand to his ear like he can't hear me.

I open the car door, slowly enough that he has time to scoot out of its way. Behind him, ducks scatter, a couple edging down to the water.

The movements of the world seem strange, an awkward animal ballet.

"Hi," I say as I climb from the warmish womb of the car out into the brisk river air. "You getting ready for a run?"

"Just finishing one up," he answers. "I parked down in

the other lot, but passed you on my way out. And since you were still here on my way back, I wanted to make sure you were okay. You looked pretty washed out today."

"I was." I smirk. "Always nice to hear it, though."

He laughs. "Sorry." A stray duck waddles over to peck at the ground around his shoe. "How are you? You know, since Saturday?"

"Okay. Yeah, better." I comb my fingers through my hair, which feels ratty and frizzed. "So, thanks again—for stepping in, I mean, with Todd."

"Yeah, that guy." He says it like it's all that can be said.

And for a minute, it is all that we say.

Charlie finally breaks the silence. "Those ducks look hungry," he says. Then, "That sounded so random. I've got some crackers in my car. Want to walk over with me?"

"Trying to lure me away to my doom?" I tease, and then when I realize what I said, I put my hand to my mouth, like I could shove the words back in. "I mean, no, I mean…" I scratch the back of one leg with the toe of my other shoe, feeling my face go hot and speckled. When I glance up at Charlie, he's not looking at me. But not I'm-so-pissed-I-can't-make-eye-contact, more just giving me space.

"Sorry," I say. "Let's go get those crackers."

I'm glad for the quiet as we walk. At Charlie's car, we toss crackers, listening to nothing more than the *guk-guk-guk* of ducks peppering the air.

Then, while my brain is preoccupied with keeping my left foot *out* of my mouth, I open up and shove the right foot in.

97

"That bruise on your cheek is hypnotic....Uh, I didn't mean that how it sounds."

Up close, his bruise is almost beautiful. At the center, a deep purple boat drifts in a lake of green.

"Are you getting me back for what I said earlier about you looking washed out?"

I laugh. "Can I touch it?" I ask, knowing that asking is weird, and that wanting to is even weirder. And kind of not caring, either way.

He tilts his head to one side, considering. "Will you be gentle?" His tone is joking, almost like he's flirting, but I'm serious when I nod *yes*.

As if I'm petting a small odd creature, a baby hedgehog or something, I reach up to brush his cheek with the pad of my index finger.

"Does that hurt?" I ask.

"I hardly feel it," he answers. For a second his face relaxes, then something shuts down in his eyes. He pulls back just enough to break contact, and I drop my hand.

"That's what I get for drinking," he says.

The ducks have formed a semicircle around us. They shuffle closer with eager beaks.

I take a cracker from Charlie's box and toss it into the mosh pit. A duck lunges, chomps. The others flutter enviously.

"So, it's like that?" I gesture toward his bruised cheek, but I don't touch it. "Drinking, I mean. It makes you want to fight?"

"Mostly it makes me forget why I *don't* fight." He passes me the cracker box and dusts the crumbs off his hands. "I didn't used to be that way. But now, it's like there's this...I don't know, like this acid in my stomach, just *there*. It boils up—and I *want* to fight. I want to fight, drunk or not."

"Because of what? Kyle?" I spit his name out without thinking, like it's a hunk of gristle.

Charlie flinches.

"Because of him," he says. "And now this trial..." His words drift away, and he digs into the gravel with his heel, making a jagged line.

"What?"

"Nothing," he says.

"My mom said Lindsey and Taylor and I will probably have to be at some hearing. In the same room with him. For the sentencing or something." My voice goes up at the end. It's my way of asking Charlie if he has to go, too.

He keeps his eyes on the river. "Mrs. Strand told my mom she and Daniel, Jamie's brother, have to make an impact statement. I wish I could, but it's only family. Which is...It's not like I wasn't impacted."

He crunches a handful of crackers and showers the ducks with crumbles. "I'm going to be there, though. I want to see that bastard's face when they make him pay for what he did. I want him"—and I'm not sure if he's even talking *to me* now. Just getting it out—"I want him to know we remember *her*, that every day, we think about *her*. But he's forgotten. Less than forgotten."

99

It's a lie. We haven't forgotten—but the lie doesn't matter. The idea of it, the wish of it—that's what matters. Kyle said that we'd see him on the front page, but why should we give him what he wants? And not just Kyle. Why should any a-hole who stalks or kills or shoots up a crowd get his name in the paper?

Maybe we should stop naming them. Stop showing their picture.

We could replace "Cowardly Asshole" for their name and show a wilted carrot for their face.

Breaking news: Cowardly Asshole shot ten people and then himself at a mall in Atlanta earlier today.

"I want to forget him, too," I say. "After it happened, I drank too much, so I wouldn't have to think about him. And for a while, it worked." I toss a cracker. "I was...blissfully stupid."

A fat white duck nudges aside a small brown one and claims the cracker.

"This is where I need to change the subject," I say, keeping my eyes for a moment on the elaborate duck dramas playing out at my feet.

Charlie tries for a smile, but it doesn't take; he shakes out a few crackers and throws them at the fringe of the duck cluster. One cracker skitters to a stop right in front of a small speckled gray duck who pecks at it tentatively. Another duck, big and white and bully-ish, edges him aside. The first duck, the little one, circles aimlessly.

Charlie aims another cracker at the small duck's feet—a

gift. This time the little guy snatches it up and waddles off to enjoy it in the relative quiet of the bank. It's silly, but it warms my heart that Charlie was watching out for him.

"That was kind of you," I say.

"What?" It's not the ask of someone who wants to hear his kindness spoken of aloud. It's the ask of someone so used to doing kind things that he doesn't realize he's done one.

Messages

Between Monday at 9:15 PM and Tuesday at 11:22 AM, I have sent the following text messages to Lindsey:

> Sorry.

> Really.

> I get it. I rained on your parade. I'm a parade-raining jerk.

> If you forgive me, I'll sing the piña colada song at your wedding.

> Your wedding with Robert.

> If you DON'T forgive me, I'll sing the piña colada song at your wedding. With Robert.

> I will give you a huge mugging. Yum!

> No, not mugging.

> I am typing mugging. Not mugging.

> MUGGING! MUGGING! The things my mom bakes! MUGGING!

Unlike, Lindsey, I have NOT turned off auto-correct.

> I hate my phone.

It is not in her nature to hold a grudge, and I know she loves my mom's muffins, but she still doesn't answer.

Did I piss her off *that* much?

On the second day of her silence strike, I wait around after lunch as the third shift files in like ants following invisible trails to food.

My thumb absently smooshes the roll on my tray until it's paper-flat. Five minutes. Ten. I am beyond late for psych, but still no Lindsey.

I try not to let it bother me.

It doesn't mean anything happened, I tell myself.

But when I go to dump my tray, instead of Lindsey, there's Todd Firebaugh, two tables away. His face is like a freaky still life, the marbly red of uncooked steak.

I want Todd to be frowning into his tray of corn and lasagna; I want him to bang his own head with his fists. But of course, he's not doing any of that. He's chewing with his mouth open as he talks to some hunched-over green jacket in the seat across from him. And he's grinning his big goonish grin.

The sight of him there, corn rattling around his mouth like yellow teeth, makes my chest tighten with anger.

Without thinking, without any sort of conscious plan, I hold my milk when I dump my tray. It's like I'm being led by a force outside myself when I take a swig and keep it in my cheeks. I walk the ten feet to Todd's table, letting the warmth of my mouth infuse the milk with what I hope is venom.

Leaning over the back of the guy in the green jacket, I stare at Todd until he looks up at me, square in the eye, and I spit my mouthful of milk in his face.

He splutters, enraged, wiping his eyes with his sleeve.

I drop the carton, then walk away.

When he calls "Bitch!" down the long empty hallway, I don't stop. I don't even look back.

Strawberry

I pass Lindsey after school outside the Jiffy Lube. The sight of her, healthy and whole, fills me with relief. Mostly relief. I'm also a little pissed I have to feel relieved in the first place. And a little pissed she hasn't answered my texts.

She's wearing another bit of outrageousness. A short dress as purple as it is tight. Against the flank of Robert's cherry-red truck, she looks determinedly cheerful, like a young girl's makeup kit.

I consider pulling over, but it's too weird between us right now.

I think about Monica and Andie. How many silences sprang up in the spaces we used to share. There was that blowup, but there was also all the stuff that led to the blowup, when I stopped talking, stopped answering their texts or calls. Before I knew it, I was on the other side of a wooden bridge and I had set it on fire behind me.

I turn, circling around to the Jiffy Lube again, but Robert's truck is already gone, and Lindsey with it.

I pull over and text her one more time.

Forgive me.

When I get home, I can tell from the driveway my mom's not back yet. She does freelance writing and usually works from her home office, but she's meeting with a client this afternoon.

I hate coming home to an empty house, so I go in the front way. It's more open than the kitchen entry. There's an easy sight line from the street.

As I fumble with the key, a red something on the welcome mat shimmers in the afternoon light. I pick it up—a candy wrapper, the old-fashioned kind that looks like a fake strawberry, red on bottom, green twist on top.

It must have fallen out of someone's pocket.

Which is weird because no one ever comes to this door.

I hold the wrapper in my open palm—the tint of a memory rising from it in little ripplets. I know I've tasted that hard strawberry shell, the liquid in the center. But when? This is not a type of candy my parents ever buy, or my grandparents. And it's not the kind of thing you get for Halloween.

Then I remember. It was Kyle. In that algebra class. He'd have a whole pocketful of them sometimes, and he gave me some once.

I chuck the wrapper to the ground like it's diseased; it skids off the front porch and lands under a bush.

Okay, okay, breathe in, breathe out.

I look over my shoulder, scouring the street for signs of life.

This is stupid. I'm being stupid, right? Kyle is locked up in some jail cell somewhere.

There are a thousand ways that wrapper might have randomly ended up here. Maybe a Jehovah's Witness dropped it...or a Boy Scout selling popcorn. Or, I don't know, a roving clown.

Still, I can't help feeling a needle of fear puncture my spine as I enter the foyer.

"Hello?" I call. No one answers. But then again, murderers lurking in closets generally don't announce themselves.

I deadbolt the door behind me, hating how paranoid I've become, then walk through the house, checking each room. When I'm done, I text my mom.

> I'm home.

> Just getting ready to leave. I'll be there soon.

In those minutes of waiting, the house feels like a tomb—so quiet that the lack of sound becomes its own noise. It reminds me of those final lines from Charlie's poem:

> *Where I can talk to silence*
> *And hear the silence talk back.*

What must it be like for him—speaking into the void, listening for Jamie's voice in every empty room? With a death as brutal as Jamie's, what would anyone even say?

There is no *I miss you, but I know you needed to go.*

No *you're better off this way.*

I even wonder about *welcome to heaven,* no matter what the obituary suggests.

Because who wants to go to a heaven that plays harp music and acts like it never happened when somebody just bashed your skull in?

Heaven should be pissed.

I flop on the couch, toss my backpack on the coffee table. Opening my government notes, I listen for a minute more to the empty house, thinking of that strawberry wrapper. Just a random candy wrapper, about as harmless as you can get. It probably blew there on the wind. It's stupid that I let it unnerve me.

Then I stuff in my earbuds and drown the silence out.

Outside

Behind me, the late Wednesday afternoon sun is a warm hand on my back. I am eating a tart green apple as I perch on the cement wall of one of the ginormous circular planters outside the main entrance to the school. It is so huge that they've not only filled it with a bunch of scraggly flowers but a good-sized tree in the middle as well. A dozen people could fit around the perimeter, but this afternoon it's only me and a few stray freshmen.

Mr. Simpson let me finish my trig test after school. And now, I am watching the deserted parking lot like it's a time-lapse movie that hasn't started yet.

Someone comes up behind me and covers my eyes. Dry, calloused fingers. The smell of sweat and cologne. Coconut. A faint underlayer of motor oil.

"Hello?" I try not to panic. *This is normal*, I tell myself. *No one is abducting me. This is what people do.*

"Hey there, hot stuff." The cologne should have given

him away. His choice of words definitely does. The voice is Jared's.

I reach one hand up and pry the fingers off my eyes.

"Hot stuff?" I say. "Really? What decade is this?"

He shrugs. "You can't deny what you are, baby."

I stifle a laugh.

"Least I made you smile," he says.

"I'm laughing *at* you, not with you," I tease. "What are you doing here, anyway?"

"Mr. Wirt," he says. "Apparently making a homemade stink bomb in the chem lab is frowned upon. So now I have detention for the rest of the week. What about you?"

"Math test," I say, then wiggle my apple core, "and snack." I toss the core in some weeds along the side of the school building, then rummage around in my backpack. "I think I have some peanut butter crackers in here if you're hungry." My fingers land on the plastic wrapper and I pull the package from my bag. "They're kind of smooshed." Dubious, I hold it out for Jared to inspect. "Really smooshed...."

"Thanks." He takes it. "I don't mind smoosh. And I'm *always* hungry." He winks suggestively.

"Sometimes I think you were raised by porn stars," I say.

Now it's Jared's turn to laugh.

"I'll have to introduce you to my parents sometime." He flicks out his tongue-stud.

"Gross." I guilty-laugh.

Popping open the end of the wrapper, Jared shakes the cracker crumbs into his mouth like he's drinking.

"So," he says, chewing, "my band is going to be playing Saturday at Bobby's Barn."

"What band?"

He swallows. "We call ourselves The Operators. Me and Randy, Tyrell, a couple guys who work down at the warehouse, Joey and Motor. You know Motor—the guy whose garage we slept in."

"Seriously? What kind of songs do you play?"

"Gecko Blue, Dragon Interrupted, some original stuff." He crumples the wrapper and stuffs it in his jeans pocket.

"I'm sensing a strong lizard theme."

"You should come Saturday."

"Maybe," I say, but I can't quite see myself hanging out alone at Bobby's Barn on a Saturday night, and all signs suggest that Lindsey has given up on me.

Plus, I don't want to lead Jared on.

"Where you headed after this?" he asks.

"Home."

"Mind giving me a ride?"

"I guess not." I shoulder my backpack. It'll be good to have company, even Jared's. "Ready?"

"I'm always ready for you, hot stuff," he says.

I shove his shoulder. "Someone needs to teach you how to talk."

Huckleberries

Lindsey finally texts me back Wednesday night.

> Hey. Not ignorinh you. Lost phone charger. Plus busy. Work and school and Robert. You ate still my huckleberry. We good?

I smile. The huckleberry thing was from an old Western we watched over the summer. Some guy kept telling everyone "I'm your huckleberry," which seemed extremely funny to us at two in the morning, and for the next week we could hardly say hello without announcing that we were each other's huckleberries in our most southern accents.

Instead of texting back, I call her before she has time to put her phone away.

"Busy how?" I ask.

"Hey to you, too," she says. I hear a guy's deep voice in the background, talking to something that beeps.

"Busy with Robert?" I ask.

She giggles. I take that as a yes. "You're one to talk," she teases. "I saw you drive by with JJ today."

"What? Where were you?"

"Front field bleachers, waiting for Robert to get done with practice. Imagine my surprise when you two just hopped into your little Pony and cruised on by. So what's the deal?"

"No deal. He needed a ride."

"Uh-huh. I bet. So did you give him a *ride*?"

"Ugh!" I say. "I'm gonna clean your mouth out with soap!" We joke about it, but it's actually something Lindsey's grandma did to her when she was little.

More giggling. More guy's deep voice.

"You're busy," I say, "but call me later?"

"Sure," she says. "I'll call you. Oh, and Robert has to go out of town with his folks Saturday. His cousin Andrew's got a thing. Maybe we could have a girls' night out."

"Yeah, sure," I say. "But do you really think you should go around telling everyone about his cousin's 'thing'? I mean, that's kind of personal, isn't it?"

She laughs this time, not giggles. "It's *your* mouth that needs cleaning, young lady!"

I grin so loudly she can probably hear it through the phone. "So Saturday," I say. "Girls' night, right?"

Relays

In gym Friday, Jared comes up beside me and pops me on the leg with a big purple elastic workout band. It's been raining that miserable October rain and we're inside, doing stretches.

"Ack!" I squawk, popping him back with my green band.

"Girls! Settle down!" Coach Flanagan yells at us, even though one of the "girls" is clearly a guy.

"You know," I whisper to Jared once Flanagan has turned away, "you don't get to go around popping random people."

"Whoever said you're random?" he whispers back.

"Puh-lease." I roll my eyes.

Jared looks like he's about to say something, but the coach roars, "Relays!"

Flanagan waves us all over to one side of the basketball court, where we clump up like overcooked noodles.

Beside me, Shavelle Rylan tosses her braid and mouths a mock "Yay!"

Mr. Flanagan grabs a handful of batons from a cart.

"Here! Roland! Joe! Other Joe! Randy!" he barks, striding across the free-throw line as he points to where the newly appointed baton-people are supposed to stand. "Now, the rest of you, line up behind them. Six in a line! Move, people, moooove!"

I squeeze in behind Randy, Shavelle, Jared, Mark, and Charlie.

As we wait for the coach to blow his whistle, Jared leans over and yells past Charlie and Mark at me, "You coming Saturday?"

I give him a blank look.

"The *band*, at Bobby's Barn. It's going to be badass."

"Ummm," I say. "I'm not sure—"

TWEET! Coach blows his whistle, and Randy, Other Joe, Joe, and Roland take off across the length of the basketball court, filling the gym with the clatter of feet pounding the hardwood.

After a moment's distraction, Jared turns back to me and picks up where he left off, shouting, "It's going to be epic. We're going to burn—"

Randy blasts across the line, passing Shavelle the baton. She stomps off in an awkward canter.

"Tell her, Randy," Jared says, nodding toward me. "Tell her we're going to burn that place up."

"We're...gonna...burn it...up," Randy pants, getting in line behind me.

Jared turns to Charlie and Mark. "You guys'll be there Saturday, right?"

Mark shrugs. Charlie nods, pulls at the neck of his T-shirt. "Yeah," he says. "I was thinking I'd go."

"See," Jared shouts. "Everyone's gonna be there."

"Okay." I hold my hands up in surrender. "Okay, I'll come."

Jared grins. "Good. There's a song I want you to hear," he shouts just as Shavelle crashes into him from behind. From there it's like dominoes: Jared pushes into Mark, who stumbles back into Charlie, who does an awkward side step to avoid falling into me, which he ultimately doesn't avoid (but thanks for trying anyway). And at the end, there's Charlie pressed up against me, one hand on my rib cage, the other gripping my arm—which he yanks toward him to keep me from falling to the floor—and which ends up pressing me even harder into his chest.

I look up into his face, with the scab on his chin, and his lips that curve like a dove's wing, and his mesmerizing bruise, and his deep, almost rust-colored eyes, and—*no, no, this is so not good.*

That's when I admit what I maybe should have known all along. I've been telling myself that Charlie might be able to help me figure out how to deal with Jamie's murder, and that's...not entirely a lie. But not the whole truth either. It is what it is, but it's also an excuse for some other true thing.

Because I don't only want answers. I want to kiss him. Not a comforting kiss either, not a kiss that intends to save anyone. I want to watch the veins in his hand as it glides down my arm, to feel his fingers twine with mine. I want his other hand to glide that half inch higher on my chest. I want him. God help me.

In a half second, everyone straightens. Jared grabs the baton from Shavelle and starts running across the gym. But Charlie and I remain tilted together for a half second more. I'm not about to break away. And his face, mapped with some unspoken emotion, makes me wonder if he wants me like that, too.

Limits

Lindsey comes over early Saturday and we paint our fingernails and watch the latest two episodes of *Baby Mamas* in the den. The first episode features a country singer who has kids with three different women, each tough and spike-heeled—the kind of women who would bite one another's ears off in a cage match. The second shows a hippie cult leader who has eight different "soul mates" and fourteen children, all living on the same commune and eating organic vegan meals at a huge picnic table.

"Can you imagine trading off like that?" Lindsey says. "'You have him on Friday, I get him on Saturday.'"

"Who knows," I say. "Maybe on Saturdays they all get him at the same time."

"Gross! I'd never share Robert," she says, pushing her bangs off her forehead with the flat of her hand, careful not to touch her hair with her still-wet silver sparkle nails. "I mean, please. Have some limits."

"You guys are getting serious?" I ask, careful to keep my tone even. *No judgment here*, my voice says, *just asking*.

She doesn't answer, though, and I'm worried she's thinking about last time we talked about Robert, when I shoved my whole marriage-bashing rant down her throat.

"It's okay," I finally break the silence. "I'm not going to say anything."

She gives me the look that means, *Well, but…*

"I'm not going to *think* anything either," I say. "I'm just going to listen. I want to know how you're doing, Linds. I swear."

So she tells me about Robert, how gorgeous he is (which I already knew), how sweet (which I can't entirely believe), how sexy (which I can). She says she's sure he's serious about her, that there are "some things you just have to trust to love."

I keep my mouth shut this time and give her a big hug when she's finally done going on about the wonders of Robert Leuger, future husband of the century.

Then we talk about everything else. Lindsey, who spent the week in a phone-less, Robert-induced haze, is clueless about most things non-Robert. At least most things in my orbit. I start by catching her up on Todd Firebaugh and the milk.

"You spit in Todd Firebaugh's face!" She snorts. "Now there's something I would have liked to see."

"It was stupid," I say. "I mean, it's not like it changed anything, except for making him pissed at me. But it felt really good."

"I bet," she says.

"It makes me so mad that just because I've got this"—I point to my butt—"some guy thinks he gets to grab it. It's messed up. It's like…" *It's like Kyle*, I think. We haven't talked yet about Kyle's trial, or hearing, or whatever they call it, and I'm not sure how to bring it up, or if I even want to.

I take a chip out of the bag on the coffee table in front of us and chomp it, stalling. Too late, I realize that chip dust is magnetically attracted to almost-dry nail polish. Two fingers and the thumb of my right hand are now coated with salty little nubs. I lick the thumbnail; it tastes vaguely chemical, but the nubs don't go anywhere.

"Ugh." I hold out my hand for Lindsey to inspect.

"You should do both hands like that," she says. "Think of it as glitter."

I take another few chips, filling my mouth to keep it from asking the inevitable.

"So," says Lindsey, while I'm still chewing, "what about JJ? Is something going on with you guys?"

The question takes me by surprise and I cough. "Ack!" Bits of chewed chips spray out of my mouth, splattering everywhere.

"Geez, spitfire!" Linds holds up her hands and ducks for cover. "Back off. I'm not Todd."

"Sorry," I say, swallowing. "But God no! Jared and I are friends…or not even friends. He's just around sometimes."

"But we're going to see *his* band tonight."

"Yeah, but," I say, picking a wad of chip out of her hair, "Jared isn't the only one who's going to be there."

"Hmmm," she says. "Who else are we looking for?"

I think about saying "no one" or "anyone in cowboy boots" or whatever, but I'm so glad to have Lindsey back, I just tell her the truth: "Charlie."

"Charlie?" she asks, like she can't think who I mean. And then it dawns. "Charlie *Hunt*? CHARLIE!?"

I bite my bottom lip and squinch up my face, like that will somehow hide me.

"Okay," she says, "this is starting to make sense. I always wondered if somewhere deep down you had a thing for Charlie. But dude, that's tough. I mean, Jamie…" She drifts to silence, like her name says it all.

"I know," I say. "I know. What am I thinking? I'm not going to act on it. I just, I just like being around him, that's all. I'm not stupid."

"You're kidding, right," Lindsey says, more a statement than a question.

"Charlie is off-limits. I know it," I say.

"Not off-limits, but it could be rough," she says. "Especially with the whole sentencing thing coming up."

And there goes the inevitable.

"They called you?" I ask.

She nods. "I've been kind of freaked," she says. "I never thought I'd have to see his face again."

"Yeah," I say, thinking of Kyle's bland round face—the owl with the wolf hidden inside. "I know what you mean."

The Operators

Bobby's Barn is dark and cavernous and stinks of fried food and vomit—not to mention an industrial-strength musk intended to cover up the stink of fried food and vomit.

The front entry hall is carpeted, but most of the floor is a flat yellowish linoleum tile, like in park bathrooms or the kitchen of the homeless shelter where my parents volunteer. The first thing I see when I go in is a long bar. A half-dozen slump-shouldered guys with beers are scattered among the dozen stools. A wiry guy in a corduroy shirt and two middle-aged women in V-necks and tight jeans are pouring drinks. The wiry guy bobs his head to the blare of old rock music as he pours.

Beside the bar, a windowless, wood-paneled room stretches out like a yawn. There are maybe ten blocky tables, a dance floor, and a side room with an electronic dart board and a huge flip-flop on the wall. In the corner where the band is setting up, a handful of guys shuffle around, plugging cords into big black boxes and saying things like "test one two, test test" on the mic. It's not really a stage because it's on the same level as the rest of the room, but still it's pretty cool.

Lindsey and I claim one of the back tables. In my magenta peasant top and Lindsey's hot-pink glamour-slashed T-shirt, we stick out like a pair of flamingos at the duck pond.

A waitress comes over and asks us what we want. Only different words. She says it like this: "What can I do you for?"

She must be nearly fifty, with chalky lipstick and a silver skunk streak running down the edge of her thick black hair.

What I really want is water, but it sounds so babyish. I look at Lindsey and she looks at me. "Um, do you have food?" I ask.

"I'll get you menus," the waitress says, and ambles off toward the bar.

While we wait, two burly men in trucker hats come in and scan the room. The first one wears a dirty frayed jean vest with a patch over the chest that looks like a snake engulfed in flames. The second man, heavier and if possible dirtier, wears a camo T-shirt and has a thick silver chain between his belt loop and the wallet in his back pocket.

Vest starts toward the bar, but Camo holds him back, nodding toward us. The men nudge each other; the gruffness of their voices carries over the dull strains of "Born in the U.S.A." I can't make out what they say, but it must be about us because the men laugh in that way men do, and instead of keeping on toward the bar, they prowl down the length of the room, their faces lit with predatory grins.

I intentionally look away, first at Lindsey, then at the band. Suddenly, the most interesting thing in the world is the sight of Randy Keaton hiking up his pants as he carries a coil of wires. Jared, who is at the mic, tunes and re-tunes his guitar. When he sees us, he grins and waves.

I return a small wave, but I'm not sure he even sees it because at the same moment a guy in a baggy orange T-shirt comes up and starts asking Jared something. Jared takes off his guitar and the pair walk together to a complicated-looking sound board on the far side of the room.

Without looking, I can feel the press of Camo and Vest as they near us and sit at the table beside ours. There's the clatter of chairs and the overwhelming stink of gasoline. Like one of them bathed in the stuff.

"School must've let out early," Camo barks, then gives a whistle that almost sounds like a sigh.

I am suddenly glad both Lindsey and I decided on jeans tonight instead of skirts.

When the waitress returns with our menus, I hold up the white laminated sheet in front of me like a shield.

She stops at the men's table on her way back to the bar. They hoot and flirt with her and demand something called the Draft Horse.

Lindsey, who has been watching the pair as brazenly as they've been watching us, snorts and rolls her eyes. "So."

She taps the menu, turning to me. "What do you think's edible here? Mozzarella sticks? Curly fries? Nachos?" She flicks her hair carelessly. "It's hard to screw up nachos."

"I don't know. Pool nachos, ballpark nachos," I say. "Nachos at the fair."

"Point taken," she says, plunking down the menu like she's punctuating her sentence. "They have fried pickles."

"Ugh." I make a face. "No thanks."

"You girls never had fried pickles?" Camo cuts in. Loud, like the conversation belongs to him.

"Never had fried pickles?" Vest echoes. "You ain't lived till you try you some."

"We can't have that," Camo booms. "Let's get these gals some pickles." He bangs his table like Henry VIII calling for the head of one of his lesser wives. "Darlene!"

Lindsey fakes a smile. "Thanks, but we can take care of ordering for ourselves." She angles her chair away from their open mouths, their table, their universe.

"No need to get all uppity," Vest says, a dog with a flat tail.

"Come on, now, we won't bite." Camo scoots his chair closer to our table. "Least not much." He guffaws like he's his own stand-up comedy routine.

Lindsey turns back to face him, this time with acid in her expression. "Maybe you have trouble understanding the Universal Language of No, so let me translate: WE"— Lindsey pauses, pointing her index finger back and forth between the two of us—"want YOU"—she jabs a finger at Camo and Vest—"to LEAVE. US. ALONE."

And when she turns her back on him this time, it's a closed door.

"Well, ain't that some Grade-A bullshit," Camo snarks to the empty air. "You try to be nice, and this is what you get."

"Some people too uppity for their own good," Vest mutters.

"Bitch . . . on the rag," Camo growls.

It's a fine line, I realize. You want them to go away, but not to get so pissed they wait for you in the parking lot with their shotgun or pocketknives or a random screwdriver.

I keep my face blank, like I don't notice the exchange. Like I'm just watching the band do its band-setup thing. No disrespect. No rubbing salt in the wound. I'm invisible.

It's the same thing possums do, I think, when they get caught in a car's headlights: pretend they're not there.

Which may explain why there are so many dead possums in the road.

After a minute more of grumbling, Camo and Vest get up and move to the bar.

I make sure they're as far away as they're likely to get before I lean over and whisper in Lindsey's face, "You're my hero." Her eyes are still tense, but she grins.

The waitress, Darlene, comes back with two frothy beers in huge glass mugs. "Huh," she says, when she spies the men across the room. She clunks the beers down on the empty table and turns to us.

"What'll you girls have?"

"A basket of fries, a Dr Pepper, and...What do you want to drink?" Lindsey asks me.

"Water," I say.

"Got it." The waitress picks up the abandoned beers and heads off to the bar just as Jared comes up on the other side of the table. He sits in an empty chair.

"What's the word, Thunderbird?" he says, looking at me.

When I don't answer right away, Lindsey asks, "You ready for your gig, JJ?"

"Ready as I'm gonna get." He cracks his knuckles and leans back in his chair.

"Aren't you guys supposed to have started?" I say. "Where is everybody?"

There's none of the people who seem to show up at every First Friday concert or civic center headliner. No short guy wearing Viking horns. No whirling dervish in a hippie skirt. No dad playing air guitar.

And yeah, no Charlie either.

"We don't start till nine," Jared says. "It'll fill up soon."

One of the older guys in his band comes up behind Jared and flicks his head. "What you doing, jawing with these girls? Come give me a hand with the speakers."

"Duty calls." Jared winks before he walks away.

Feathers

By the time Charlie shows up, Bobby's Barn is thumping with sweaty bodies and electrified sound. The dance floor is packed with the bar's regulars, plus a bunch of friends of Jared, Randy, and Tyrell.

I'm surprised how good the band is. Randy plays bass, Jared guitar, one of the old guys is on drums, the other sings and plays guitar, Tyrell is on keyboard and (for a few songs) saxophone. They're way too loud, but decent. Better than decent.

Lindsey and I are on the floor with a group from school. Mostly girls dancing in a clump. The burly bar guys are leaving us alone now. Safety in numbers.

The waitresses have marked a big Sharpie X on the hand of anyone who can't show her an ID, so we're all hyped up on caffeine instead of stumbling drunk.

I see Mark first on the fringe of the dance floor. His fine black hair splays out as he bops up on the balls of his feet and then down, then up again, which I think is Mark dancing. I look around for Charlie and find him in a shadowy spot near the wall, his face turned away from me. There is a pretty dark-haired girl in front of him, and he's moving his head the way he does when he talks. Judging from the numbers of nods, he's having a longish conversation with her. Either they are shouting over the band or reading each other's lips.

She is not a girl I've seen before, but she's much too young to be one of the bar regulars. Probably somebody's friend from another school. A school where they know nothing about Charlie. And if they've heard of Kyle or Jamie at all, it's some urban myth version with Jamie visiting a psychic a week before the murder or ending up buried alive.

The anonymous girl suddenly laughs, then grabs his hand and tugs him out into the middle of the dancing. The music is grinding, pounding, more angry than romantic. Charlie stands there, stiff, for a few seconds, then slowly—like an egg cracking—begins to dance. You can see the music moving up his body. His feet, knees, hips, shoulders—finally his head is banging, fist pumping....a regular poster boy for teenage rebellion.

He seems so...un-Charlie. So free.

With that other girl, who doesn't know his sadness.

I need to take a minute alone.

"Hey," I yell to Lindsey over the music, "I've got to go pee."

She cups her ears.

"Pee," I yell again, then leave.

129

Beyond the far edge of the bar, a short hallway leads to the bathrooms. Two women are already ahead of me in line.

Beside me, a small hawkish woman with a feathered cardboard crown is eyeing the men's room, which stands empty, door open.

"It's not that bad," she says to the woman in a red mini-skirt at the front of the line. "I've been in there before. The ladies' is just as bad."

"Should I?" the woman in the red mini asks, squirming and flapping her hands in that *I've gotta go so bad* way. "Will y'all stand guard?"

"Sure, go ahead—" the feather-crowned woman starts to say, but they are interrupted by another woman, one who hasn't been waiting in line at all. The new woman brushes past the three of us and enters the men's room. She flips her glossy black hair and gives us a wet smile. "I'm just gonna go in here," she says as she closes the door.

"What in holy hell was *that*?" Crown-woman asks. "Did you see her? She just waltzed on past like Cleopatra parting the Red Sea!"

"Well, maybe she didn't—" the woman in the red mini starts to say.

"You're damn right she didn't!" Crown-woman is clearly drunk. She puffs out her cheeks like she's holding her breath.

The women's restroom door finally opens and a large lady with round glasses lumbers out. The miniskirt woman who has been holding herself squeezes past her into the bathroom and slams the door.

At the same moment, Cleopatra scoots out of the men's bathroom and back toward the bar. Crown-woman glares laser beams in her back.

"Line breaker!" Crown-woman yells, though the woman is long gone. "You best not mess with me! I'm wearing feathers!"

She turns my way, I suppose since I'm the only one left in line. "Did you see, she got on these leggings like they was pants!"

I nod, though in fact I didn't notice the woman's leggings at all.

"They're not pants, lady; they're leggings!" she fake-yells after Cleopatra.

I try to figure out what kind of expression I can put on my face without pissing Crown-woman off. The best I can do is something that feels like confused.

"Here." She points to the men's bathroom. "You go ahead, honey. I'm not so rude as to break line."

"But you're ahead of me," I say. Ignoring me, she takes my shoulder and presses me toward the men's room.

"It's just like the ladies'," she says again, then grins and waves like she's just sent me on my first cruise.

I shut the door. The room is small and dirty. A bare bulb on a cord hangs from the ceiling. The yellowish light makes everything look like a photograph from the 1970s. I cough and cover my nose, certain I have smelled that particular combination of rot and wetness somewhere before.

It is not quite so loud here—the bass line, a muffled throb; the drums, a distant thump. Leaning back against the door, I close my eyes. The room may be disgusting, but at least there is no one looking at me, and there is nothing I have to see.

The muscles in my face relax, my waxy attempt at a smile melting away.

I don't want to go back to the dance floor, with the leering men and the pretty anonymous girl and Charlie dancing like something's unraveled inside him.

I wonder where Twin Me is now. Is she in a bathroom somewhere, thinking about a boy?

Is she in Paris? In the back of a truck? On a rooftop somewhere, counting stars? At Tattoo King in Roanoke, picking out a flute-playing raccoon in a tutu for her shoulder?

The handle rattles at my back. Apparently I've had this grungy oasis all to myself for long enough.

I straighten, prepare my face, and open the door—to find Charlie.

Of all people in this crappy little bar in this crappy little town in this crappy little world. Charlie.

There is still a line for the ladies' room, though Crown-woman is nowhere to be seen.

"Hi," I say.

"Hi," says Charlie. He nods at the door I just came through. "This is the guys', right?"

"Yeah, sorry, there was a line for the other," I say, feeling the redness rise in my face.

I scooch out of his way, but he touches my arm.

"Hold up. You have something. There." His hand hovers at my temple.

I comb my fingers through my hair.

Charlie's smile is a question I can't interpret.

A blue feather—it must have come from the woman's cardboard crown—drifts off my shoulder and onto the floor.

For You

When I get back, the band is between songs. The old guy who plays guitar is propped up on a stool, jawing in the microphone. He tells a convoluted story about how he used to be a heavy drinker, and then one night he was working in his shed, drunk, and he cut off the tip of his pinky with a saw.

"It was the best thing that ever happened to me," he says, holding up the offending finger and waving it patriotically. "I lost some bone, but I found Jesus. And Jesus, praise Him, gave me this guitar."

He sounds kind of drunk—slurred and light on logic—but since the whole story is about how he quit drinking, I'm hoping he just talks that way.

Lindsey is still on the dance floor. Instead of joining her, I sit at our table. I'm thirsty, but my water is empty, so I eat a few fries, which only makes me thirstier. I could use a soda, but our waitress is nowhere around, and I'm not sure how to order something at the bar. Do you squeeze between people on the barstools or is there some particular place you're supposed to stand? Do you pay when you order? How much are you supposed to tip?

It's possible I'm overthinking this.

The whole night I've felt like I was on some foreign planet where words mean other words.

I see Charlie when he returns from the back hallway. Not that I'm looking for him. The girl he'd been talking to is now talking with a guy in a Thor T-shirt. But Charlie isn't walking in their direction; he seems, in fact, to be heading toward me.

I try not to watch him, to act like I haven't seen him at all, so if I'm wrong, if he strolls right on by, takes a turn, sweeps that other girl in his arms and there—smack-dab in front of the Norse God of Thunder—sticks his tongue down her throat, at least I won't be looking.

I don't need to see Charlie, though, to sense him. It's like my brain is wearing night-vision goggles.

He doesn't veer. I feel the table shift slightly as he sits down beside me.

"Hi again," he says. "Can I sit here?"

"Sure," I say, turning to him, feeling jittery. "Sure. Of course."

"So what do you think of the band?"

"They're...burning the place up," I say.

Charlie laughs. "Yeah."

I stare at his lips. Then realize I'm staring at his lips, which are full and dusky red and infinitely kissable. I feel myself swallow but I have nothing to swallow and for a second I think I'm going to choke on the dryness in my throat.

"You okay?" Charlie asks.

I nod, still staring at his hypnotizing mouth.

"Yeah," I say. I am suddenly unable to move my eyes. Is this what guys feel like when they keep looking at girls' breasts? Like they know it's wrong, but they're not in charge?

I need someone to smack me. Where is Lindsey?

Under the table, I grind the heel of one foot down on the toes of the other. The pain helps bring me back. With a snap of my head, I look out at the crowd and spot the back of Lindsey's pink ripped shirt in a crowd of girls.

So far, so good, I tell myself. *Now when you look back, focus on something other than Charlie's lips.*

I don't trust myself with his face, so I go in low, staring at my hands on the table instead.

"Hey." Charlie's fingertips nudge the edge of the table, skirting the frame of my vision. When I don't look up, he props up his pointer and middle fingers like they're little legs and walks his hand over to mine. One of his finger-feet pokes the back of my hand. "You sure you're okay?"

"Sorry." I say. "I'm good."

"Do you…?" he starts, but drifts off. Lowering his head, so it's closer to my frame of vision, he reaches up and gently tilts my chin, and now I'm back looking at his lips.

"It's okay," he says, and I'm thinking, *Okay how? Okay that I want to drown myself in you?*

"I could use some fresh air." He grins, slowly, like he's reading my mind. "You want to go outside?"

And I don't know if I should be embarrassed or happy. I

can guess what an invitation to the parking lot of Bobby's Barn has meant for countless girls in the past. I wonder if it means the same thing for me.

Before I answer, I want to know: Am I reading him right or am I just hearing what I want to hear?

And is that *truly* what I want anyway? An invitation to make out with Charlie in the parking lot of a roadhouse in the brisk October night?

"So what do you think?" He nods in the direction of the exit. "Want to head out?" His voice skims over possible meanings, but doesn't settle anywhere.

I open my mouth to ask something, though I'm not sure what, and—*eeeeeeeeee!*—the stage microphone makes a high-pitched squeal. Everyone in the room simultaneously cringes and turns to look at the stage. Jared is there, in a spotlight, with a single red rose in his hand. He steps back from the microphone, like the light is blinding him. "Whoa!" he says, and people in the crowd good-naturedly laugh.

"So, um." He adjusts something on his guitar and steps back in the spotlight, up close to the mic. "I wrote this song for a very special person," he says. He cups the hand with the rose at his forehead like the brim of a baseball hat and squints out at the crowd. "I can't see her, but she's right back there." He points in the general direction of our table. A wall of faces turn in my direction.

I look behind me for some other girl.

"This." He lays the rose down on a stool beside the mic. "This is for you."

And then he begins to play.

People say we don't belong together
But maybe we just don't belong
In a black-and-white world
Every guy, every girl
Singing some sugarcoated song.
Bright eyes grow darker
Searching the horizon
For the things only you can see
But I know we can get there
Yeah, I know we'll get there
If you'll only reach for me.
Reach out for me.

Reach.
When this town has locked you out
When the gray clouds scream with doubt
When you lose what you're all about.

Reach.
When you don't know where you've been.
And your nightmare's closing in.
Think you'll never love again.
Reach for me.

Oh reach, oh reach,
reach for me…

The Starting Gate

The song is good, beautiful even, but I don't stay to hear the end of it.

With every note, every word, I feel another lifetime of redness pool in my face.

And here's where you know for sure I'm not a nice person: After the first verse, while a boy I kissed is still standing in front of a room full of drunks, singing words that shimmer with stardust—while he's singing them *to me*—I bolt.

Without even looking in his face, I grab Charlie's hand, tug him up, and lead him out the door. My need to be released is almost a physical thing, and it makes me fidgety. Like a horse at the starting gate, I can't get out fast enough.

In the parking lot, I can still hear Jared's music, but not the words. It's all muffled sound, a distant radio.

A few random people are leaning against a parking post, smoking, talking low and sloppy in that half-drunk way. Fixing my eyes down, I keep Charlie's hand in mine as

I lead him past the group, around the side of the building. When we get to the dumpster, I stop, suddenly thick with the realization that I don't have a plan.

I look up, and sure enough, Charlie is studying me like I just sprouted a second head.

"So, you and JJ...?" he asks.

I don't know how to answer him. In fact, I'm not sure I even have it in me to speak at this particular moment. So I don't. Instead, slowly, I reach up and feather my fingers across Charlie's bruised cheek.

He leans back against the cement of the building, and I'm glad it's not too cold out. Brisk, but not bad for early October.

Without letting myself think, I stand on my toes and paint my lips ever so gently onto his.

He stops me with the same question, soft as an exhalation: "So, you're not? You and JJ?"

"No," I say. "We're definitely not."

Charlie's smile brings out a dimple I'd forgotten he had. "In that case," he says, and he pulls me to him.

His kiss isn't as gentle as mine. It's eager, messy, demanding, complicated.

Irresistible.

For a few minutes, I'm lost in the touch of him. The absolute *thereness* of him. I'm soaring above all the crap in my life. There's no *everything that happened* or *who Charlie was* or *who I've become* or *poor Jared singing his beautiful song to an empty chair.*

And then I make the mistake of letting myself think.

When I stop kissing him back, everything feels tilted and raw. Like someone else was using my body without me knowing.

Charlie's eyes are still half-closed as I pull back. His face is the way I imagine his face looks when nobody is watching. Vulnerable. Hiding nothing. It makes my heart pinch.

I try to convince myself I would have made out with anyone right then just to get away from Jared and all that earnest guitar playing.

It's not about Charlie, I tell my brain.

But it's always been about Charlie for me. At least sort of. Only, I know it can *never* be about Charlie because how can Charlie be with anyone after Jamie?

Anyone, and me in particular?

Then there they are, the words I never wanted to think: *How could Charlie* not *blame me for living when the girl he loved died?*

"Sorry. Sorry," I say.

"Sorry?"

"I shouldn't have. We shouldn't have."

"What? Why?" Charlie looks lost.

"Look, I can't do this." And I'm in bolt-mode again. I step back, pull my cell from my back pocket, and start texting Lindsey, *Got to go. Now. Meet me out…*

But before I finish, before I press send, Charlie's hand claims mine. "Hey, whoa. What's going on?"

"We shouldn't be doing this."

"Why not?" He looks impossibly earnest. Like he really doesn't know.

"Because," I say. I pull my hand from his, put my phone back in my pocket. "It's not right."

"What's not right?" He bends down to my level so I have to meet his eyes.

My face answers for me.

"Okay," he says. He slides his hand down my shoulder and holds my hand again in his. "Okay. Why do you think *this*"—he squeezes my palm—"you and me, is a problem?"

"Jamie wouldn't want—"

"You don't know that. You can't *know* what she'd want. And she can't tell us."

I remember the dream where Jamie came to me as an angelic floaty thing. I didn't think to ask what she wanted, and what she did say was all nonsense—though it probably wasn't Jamie in the first place, just my subconscious.

"Look, don't you think I've been over all this?" Charlie asks. "I've been up one side of it and down the other. Like it was playing on a loop in my brain. But here's the truth, and I just have to accept it: The truth is that Jamie's...She's gone. And as much as that—as much as that *hurts*, it's not going to change."

Charlie lets go of my hand and runs his fingers through his hair. He leans back against the wall again, bending one knee and propping the sole of his shoe against the cement.

"I've been writing more, you know, since I did that thing in Mr. Campbell's class," he says. "It's like it's just pouring out of me. And getting some of that stuff down...I can think things through for once. I can let myself—I don't know, like I don't have to hold it in my head the whole time. I don't have to hold on so tight to...to..."

I look at Charlie's hands, not his face. His left fist is flexing and letting go. Flexing and letting go.

"I'm not going to forget her. I'll never—never. It's just—I can't—do we have to talk about this?"

I shake my head. "So where do we go from here?"

"How should I know?" Charlie says. I look up and the gleam from a parking lot light is reflected back in his eyes. He shrugs. "But is it going to hurt to find out?"

I lean into him then, resting my head just below his collarbone. Thinking, *Yeah, this could hurt. This could hurt a lot.*

But out loud, I whisper, "I guess not."

A Song Like That

"I looked for you everywhere."

Lindsey's reflection is staring me down through the full-length mirror that hangs over my closet door. She puckers her lips as she unscrews her gloss, but her eyes are on my face, reflected behind her. She's spending the night for real at my house this time, and it's just us, so I'm not sure why her lips need to be any pinker than usual. Still, she layers on the gloss like armor.

"JJ's up there singing his heart out. And you've—disappeared." She turns to where I'm sitting cross-legged on the bed. "And when I *do* find you, it's like your brain has been taken over by aliens. So, what's the story?"

After Charlie and I were done talking, I didn't want to wade back through the swamp of humanity in Bobby's Barn to find Lindsey, so he walked me to my car. From there, I texted Lindsey to come out. And yeah, I was pretty spacey on the drive home. I'm not sure she got two coherent words in a row from me.

"No story," I say, feeling my smile give me away.

"Yeah, and that goofy look on your face is...because what?" She perches beside me on the bed. "Come on, this is *me* you're talking to."

I grin and chew the skin around my fingernail, a habit I'm trying to quit.

"Or *not* talking to, as the case may be." Lindsey taps her foot.

"I'm talking," I say. "I'm talking, I'm—" I spread out my arms, which could mean anything from *give me a hug* to *wow, the universe is huge.* "It's just—" I flop back on the bed and start making these little burbly giggle sounds that are entirely beyond my control.

"Are you—are you *drunk*?" Lindsey asks.

I giggle more, shaking my head and holding my sides.

"Ooookay." Lindsey lies down on her side so her face is only inches away from mine. She sniffs, as if trying to catch a hint of the green, mulchy scent of pot. "Did you smoke something?"

"No," I spurt out, laughing harder, even though I'm not sure what I'm laughing at in the first place.

"So while you were missing," she says, "I happened to notice that I didn't see Charlie anywhere either. Hmmm." She rubs her chin in a Sherlockian gesture. "Your little giggle fit wouldn't happen to have something to do with that, would it?"

"Kind of," I say.

"Aha!" Lindsey squeals. "I thought so!" She pushes

herself up on her knees and half bounces on the bed. "Tell me! Tell me! Tell me!" she shouts.

"Shhhh," I say. "You'll wake my parents."

"Tell me everything," Lindsey whispers, poking me in the ribs.

"I guess, you know, we sort of got together."

"Ahhh—!" Lindsey yells again, and then when she hears herself, she soundlessly mimes *Ahhhhh!*

"I know." I say. "I can't believe it."

She curls up on the bed beside me. "So is Charlie a good kisser?"

"It's not even really about the physical stuff. I just like being with him."

"For the record, that's what someone says when the physical stuff sucks."

"No, no," I say. "He's a good kisser."

Lindsey squints, like she's trying to peer through a fog of lies.

"He's a *great* kisser," I say. "Really. Great. I mean it. Really. Like, wow!"

"You know, when you're defensive like that," she says, her voice tease-y, "it almost seems like you have something to hide."

"Screw you," I say.

She laughs. "Go on," she says. "Great kisser, and…?"

"Great kisser, and I guess we're just going to see where it goes."

"Oh, geez, I bet this is going to kill JJ."

"Don't say that!"

"It's the truth, isn't it?"

"No," I say.

"Yeah, well, it is."

"Jared will live," I say. "He—he doesn't even really know me. He's just...full of hormones or something."

"That song, it was really—"

"Yeah, I heard it," I say. "Some of it."

"And he was looking for you after. The whole time he was playing, he kept scanning the crowd."

"Look, Jared's nice. I'm sure he'll find some girl who just wants to listen to him strum his guitar all day long," I say.

Lindsey snickers. "His guitar?" she says suggestively.

"Yuck!" I say. "Where's my soap?"

"Oh, come on," Lindsey says. "*You* said it."

"But *you* thought it. And anyway, what I meant was that he's going to find someone right for him. Someone worth a song like that."

"*You're* worth a song like that."

"No," I say. "No, I'm really not."

"Of course you are," she says. "*I'd* write a song for you like that, if I wrote songs."

"You're such a goofball," I say.

"Ohhh...your eyes, they remind me of marbles. Beautiful, beautiful marbles..." she sings.

I laugh. "Are you sure *you* didn't smoke something? Maybe I should sniff your hair."

"Hey, so, what about—" She sits up.

"What about what?" I ask.

"Never mind," she says. She stretches, exaggerated. "You ready to turn in?"

"Sure." I toss a pillow down to the bottom of my bed. It's a twin, so Lindsey and I always sleep head to foot.

I change into sweats and toss a pair to Lindsey, then turn out the light. But as I lie there in the half dark, making room for Lindsey's knees, I replay that stretch in my mind, and I can guess what she was thinking:

Jamie.

What about Jamie?

"Hey," I say in the dim room. "Do you think it's too weird?"

"What?" Lindsey's voice is muffled by her pillow.

"You know, me and Charlie."

"Because...?" Lindsey stalls.

"Because of what happened," I say. "I mean, Charlie's kind of in a no-man's-land, right? And I have my own, I guess you'd say, *issues.* Do you think there's any chance it could work?"

Lindsey doesn't answer right away.

"He's not really over it," I go on, "and it's not like I even *want* him to be. I mean, you don't just get over something like that."

"Are you over it?" Lindsey asks.

"I guess," I lie. "Are you?"

"I guess." After a minute, she adds, "Sometimes I really hate Kyle."

"Yeah," I say, and this time I'm telling the truth. "Me too."

"Do you think he's going to get it?"

"Get what?" I ask.

"You know, the 'ultimate punishment.'"

Death.

I picture Kyle in an orange prison suit lying back on a metal table. Beside him, a doctor with a long coat and a fat needle waits. I imagine on the same metal table Jamie's mutilated body, her face crusted with blood.

"He deserves it," I say.

And then it's my bloody body on that table. Lindsey's. Taylor's. Blair Mattern's. If he could have, Kyle would have killed any of us. Maybe *all* of us.

"He definitely deserves it." I know I am right. And that rightness thrums in my chest like a pulse.

There is no punishment Kyle Paxson doesn't deserve.

How to Fight Dirty

Lindsey and I hide in my room most of the morning, listening to music, complaining about the paper we have to write for Mr. Harrel's government class (the same class—though I have it third period and Lindsey has it seventh), and analyzing each other's dreams.

I dreamed of swimming across a lake, which Lindsey says represents emotional questioning, while the marching band played fight songs on the opposite bank, which she says represents my need to overcome. She doesn't specify *what* I need to overcome, and I don't ask.

Her dreams are not so easy: Her mother, her sister, and Robert drift away in a hot-air balloon, while she's stuck in the city below where there's some sort of epidemic that makes people lose their skin.

"Um," I say, "maybe you're afraid of something?"

"Like what?"

"You know, like losing your skin?"

"Well, that's literal." She gives me a look. "You're really not good at this, are you?"

I shake my head and suggest we go find breakfast.

My mother is at the kitchen table with the crossword puzzle and a cup of coffee. "The prodigal girls return," she says.

She is always saying things that don't make sense. I've learned to ignore it.

"Hungry," I say.

"There are muffins." She states the obvious, gesturing toward a platter on the counter. "Or you could fix yourself a bowl of cereal. There's yogurt, oatmeal—"

"This is good," I interrupt, aware my mother will go on listing everything edible in a ten-mile radius of the kitchen if I let her. I take two muffins and pass one to Lindsey.

"Thanks!" I call over my shoulder as we skirt out of the kitchen to the den.

There, Lindsey turns on the TV and clicks through the channels until she lands on some celebrity gossip show. My phone chimes in the pocket of my sweats. It's from Charlie. I'd added his number last night and then texted him so he'd have mine. As I open the message, my insides go rigid, like they're on heightened alert.

Thinking of you, beautiful. Time for a run today?

I grin and pass the phone to Lindsey, who gets an evil smirk on her face and starts typing.

"What are you doing?" I yell. "Stop it!" I try to grab the phone, but Lindsey swoops aside, still typing.

"Don't!"

She stands up on the couch and, holding the phone above her head, snaps a photo of me as I try to wrestle the phone from her hands, then gives me a devilish look and clicks what I can only guess is *send*.

"What, do you want this?" she asks, the picture of innocence, and holds out the phone to me.

"You suck," I say, taking the phone from her outstretched hand.

"That's what you get for not having sisters," she says. "If you had a sister, you'd know how to fight dirty."

When I check it, there's a message to Lindsey. Not Charlie. And an unflattering picture of me—well, mostly my hand—grabbing for the phone.

> I'm messing with your head. This is what it looks like. Love you! Ha!

"Oh, you double suck!" I laugh, relieved.

"You know I'd never do that," she says. "You just looked so pleased with yourself." She plops down on the sofa and takes a sip of her coffee. "So, are you going?"

"Going where?"

"Running. With Charlie?"

I like the sound of that. *Running with Charlie.*

"Yeah," I say. "Yeah, I think I am."

Running

The path by the river is smattered with leaves. I try to keep my mind on the darkness of them as we pass. The wetness of them. The way they glob up in the gutter between the greenway and the road.

I am thinking of leaves because I don't want to think.

The smack of our soles against the pavement makes a comfortable rhythm.

Leaves are safe. Leaves, leaves, leaves.

The way I feel for Charlie isn't safe.

I love how fast he is, how he smiles when I come up beside him. Even the casual smile of one runner to another feels…*glowy*. Like there should be angels singing choir-like in the trees.

We don't talk. I guess he doesn't feel the need. I'd probably babble out of nerves alone, but I don't want to embarrass myself by panting in this cold air.

When we reach the end of this stretch of the greenway, he's hardly winded as he asks, "You want to hike up the hill?"

I nod and we slow to a walk. The path ends in a big circle near a parking lot. As we head across the lot, he matches his pace to mine, walking beside me, and I wonder if we should be holding hands. He doesn't take my hand, though, and I don't take his.

Together, we make our way through the woods, up and up. There's still green in the underbrush, some ivy-ish and ferny-looking stuff, but mostly just brown earth and yellowed, fallen leaves.

The path ends, opening to a vast, grassy meadow, which goes on for almost a mile before it lowers to the road. Beyond, another mountain rises, immense and speckled with the orange of October.

On the hill where we've arrived, there are maybe a dozen big wooden jumps where people train their horses. Some look like stairsteps, others like little houses for gnomes.

I've been here before, but I'd forgotten the view. After the long climb through the trees, it's almost too open, too gorgeous.

I love being here with Charlie—the world in front of us.

Two years ago, I might have said *forever* was in front of us. But I know there's no such thing. Because of Jamie. Because of Kyle.

It's like that country song "Live Like You Were Dying."

And mostly, I do.

Or maybe I just live like some random boy might at any moment slaughter me.

It's not the way they describe it in the song.

"What would you do," I ask Charlie, "if you knew you were going to die tomorrow?"

"Hmmm." He looks up at the sky, down at the grass. "Where did that question come from?"

"Country music." I laugh because the truth sounds so ridiculous. He doesn't answer at first, so I climb onto the end of a nearby horse jump and walk along its ridge, holding my arms out on either side for balance. When I get to the other side, I squat and angle my legs around so I'm sitting. "So...? What would you do?"

"I'm not sure." Charlie comes over to lean against the jump, right next to me. "Maybe I'd spend the day with my family, just hanging out. Maybe I'd try to write something, you know, to leave behind. Some sad little yawp to prove Charlie Hunt was here." He pushes off the log and looks out at the view. His back is to me when he says, "Maybe I'd go see Kyle. Maybe I'd...I'd..." He turns toward me, shrugs.

"You'd spend your last day with Kyle?"

"I mean, it'd be the end anyway, right? And it'd feel pretty good to beat the crap out of him."

"Oh," I say. I hadn't thought of that. The bruises on Charlie's face are faded yellow and brown in the afternoon light, like the leaves.

"I don't know, really," he says. "Most likely, I'd be right here, doing just what I'm doing. Here, with you." Taking my hand, he pulls me from the log. He steps closer so the length of our bodies touch, like we're slow dancing without the music. "This isn't such a bad last day," he says. Then Charlie is kissing me, and I'm kissing him back.

It's a good kiss. More deliberate than in the bar parking lot. Not so full of questions. And for a minute, I give myself over to the softness of his lips, his earthy boy smell. I'm in a beautiful void, and I never want to leave.

Then he pushes my hair back from my cheek, tucks it behind my ear. "What about you?" he says. "How would you spend your last day on earth?"

"Who knows," I say, "maybe this *is* my last day." It's the truth, too, but I don't laugh at it.

"You shouldn't say that," he says, and when he looks into my eyes, I'm not sure it's me he sees.

"I *don't* know. No one does. . . . Jamie didn't know."

"Just stop." He steps away, and the warm space where his body had been shielding mine goes cold. "You can't live like that."

"But I *do*," I say. "Most the time, it's like I'm . . . like I'm not *living* at all. I'm just some girl who, for whatever reason, isn't dead *yet*. A girl he didn't kill."

"I hate him. God, I hate him."

I know that hate. I feel it. But seeing it on Charlie's face—his beautiful features twisted and hollow—makes me sad more than anything else.

I touch Charlie's cheek. "You sure you don't hate me, too . . . ?" This time I don't say her name, but there can only be one way to fill in that blank. *For living when Jamie died?*

"Why would you even ask that?"

He pulls me close, so there's no need for me to answer, only feel the comfort of his arms around me, trembling the smallest bit from all he's holding in. I press my ear against his chest, listening for his heartbeat. When I find it—quick and strong—I smile at the wonder of it, its steady persistence. *Tha-thum, tha-thum, tha-thum.* The best sound I've ever heard.

Strange Blooms

Monday morning, I'm walking to my car when I see in my periphery a blur of colors beside our front door.

Flowers—a willowy bouquet of yellows, purples, and whites in an openmouthed glass jar. I walk closer. They look to be mostly wild flowers, the kind you find at the neglected edges of things, around the train tracks or behind the convenience store. Airy and open and gorgeous, except for a single clump of blooms that doesn't seem to belong: five tight-fisted carnations colored a pale blue. Artificial-looking, like they've been dyed.

In the jar, there's a clear plastic trident-thing sticking up, and tucked in its prongs, a small tan envelope.

I snatch the envelope up and do a tiny happy dance, singing under my breath, *Charlie sent me flowers, Charlie sent me flowers!*

I fumble open the envelope and slip out the note.

There, in tight cursive letters:

It's not your fault

Four words.

No charming cliché. No overblown emotion. No signature even.

I'm not sure what I was expecting, but not this.

It's not your fault? I feel like a popped balloon. *What isn't my fault? What does that even mean?*

I think back to yesterday, on that hilltop. How we were talking about Jamie.

I guess it could make sense in that context.

It could actually be kind of sweet, right?

I mean, the flowers are pretty, and he took the time to get up early and pick them or buy them at Kroger's or wherever.

Because here's the thing. I have only received flowers one other time in my entire life, and that was when my dad took me to the father-daughter dance for my Brownies troop, so I'm not about to let this—my *first* time ever to get flowers from a boy, not to mention a boy I really *really* like—be ruined by a somewhat cryptic, vaguely creepy note. I mean, he probably wasn't even awake when he wrote it. Or maybe he was quoting a song lyric or something and I just don't get it?

I quick Google "it's not your fault," but all I get is a million hits for *Good Will Hunting*.

I stuff the note in my jacket pocket and pick up the

flowers, holding them at arm's length, admiring their color against the blue-frosting sky.

They truly are beautiful. Bright and shimmery.

I don't have time to take them inside, so I set them in the shade beside a shrub where they won't get too much after-noon sun.

Happy—and determined to be happy—I jog to my car.

Alas, Poor Yorick

When I get to English class, I can't keep my eyes off Charlie. Mr. Campbell has made us move our desks into a sort of crooked horseshoe. "It's a circle of trust," he says. "I want you to see each other when you share your free-writes." I try to keep my face forward, but my eyes keep veering to my left, where Charlie is sitting.

It's not just that he's good-looking, though he *is* good-looking. It's that he's... *Charlie Hunt*. Which to me is synonymous with some sort of cosmic magnet that I've been trying to avoid for the last half of my life. But now, I guess I get to look at him all I want.

And not only look, but I can—well, for one, I can now admit (if only to myself) that even when I was at my craziest over Sander, I would have dropped him like a hot brick if Charlie had shown the least interest in me.

But Charlie was always with Jamie. And now he's, well, not with me, exactly. But sort of. I mean, he got me flowers. And she's...

It's messed up. *A sprinkle of guilt baked into every delicious bite!*

Mr. Campbell booms, "Alas, poor Yorick! I knew him, Horatio!" We're at that place in Hamlet where the prince finds the skull of his buddy Yorick, the court jester, and starts spewing crazy-talk to him.

"You know the Long Theater Building on Main Street? Where the social service offices are?" Mr. Campbell asks. "Well, a long time ago, it was used for plays. The guy it's named after, Jedidiah Long, left that building to the town in his will. He also left money to organize an acting troupe for the theater. But"—Mr. Campbell raises his arm and wags his finger dramatically—"Mr. Long had one stipulation. After his death, he wanted his skull to be taken from his corpse and used as the skull of Yorick in a production of *Hamlet*."

"Ewwww," says Paige Sanchez. "So, was it? I mean, did they actually *do* that?"

Mr. Campbell sighs with satisfaction, giving Paige the *that's just the question I wanted to hear* look. "I have no idea, and no real way of finding out," he says. "There's no written record, and anyone who might have once known is long dead. Which leads us to one of the main themes of *Hamlet*: the uncertainty of life, and the mystery of death. We can never know... well, pretty much *anything*, can we? Can we know by looking at someone the state of their soul? Can we guess what consequences our actions will have? The entire play is about our inability to really know what the heck is going on."

Mr. Campbell plucks a large, skull-shaped candle off his desk.

"And then we come to Yorick." He gives the skull-candle a lazy toss. " 'Where be your gibes now? Your gambols? Your songs?' Hamlet is essentially asking Yorick, the court jester from his youth, where his life has gone. 'Here hung those lips that I have kissed....' So where Yorick's lips were is now just skull. It's like Hamlet's trying to figure out exactly where that line is between being alive and playful and fun, and being dead, rotted down to the bone, in a worm-eaten grave."

I can feel the tension spike through Charlie's body from two feet away.

Geez, I think toward Mr. Campbell, *do we really have to do this?*

Because if skulls and graves make *me* think of Jamie, what must Charlie be thinking?

Inside I scream, *HOW CAN YOU BE SO OBLIVIOUS?!*

I don't care that I'm not being fair. I get that it's *Hamlet*, which is pretty much a big parade of death. I get that the only outward indication of Charlie's agitated state is the index finger of his right hand tapping the edge of his desk, lightly, but at a sugar-high pace. Even so.

"So for your free-write, I want you to meditate on death. What can we know about it? What does it mean? Get out a clean sheet of paper. I want you to write for five minutes. Don't worry about grammar. Just keep your pencils moving. Start..." Mr. Campbell checks the wall clock, and then, when he realizes it reads 10:11, where it's been stuck all year, pulls out his cell phone and sets the timer. "Now!"

I feel like I'm going to be sick.

How can I possibly write about death?

Instead, I stare at the floor, focused only on the curved line of feet across from me. It's like one of those words that can be read backward or forward, only made out of shoes; from left to right: boots, flip-flops, tennis shoes, heels, tennis shoes, flip-flops, boots.

Next to me, Charlie is bent over his desk, writing furiously, like there's not enough paper in the world and he has to use it all.

I pick up my pen, doodle something to avoid making actual words. *Write whatever you're thinking*, Mr. Campbell said, but the words I'm thinking are best not committed to paper.

Fartwad. Asshat. Prick.

I scribble a few random words, put my pen to my lip like I'm in the "thinking" pose, and stare some more at other people's feet.

Finally, the five minutes are up, and Mr. Campbell makes us go around and "share" our free-writes. And share we do.

Someone has a dead grandmother, dead fish, dead cat. One boy whose name I don't know feels way too guilty about accidentally stepping on a stinkbug. Clarissa Coleson reads a pro-vegan poem that rhymes "Barack Obama" with "sock-sore llama," and Nick Richert's paragraph is nothing but a list of questions that only a zombie could answer.

When Mr. Campbell gets to me, I rub my eye with my knuckle, fold over my paper of scribbles, and tell him it's kind of personal. "Could you maybe skip me this time?" I ask in my most pitiful voice. I'm not much of an actress, but Mr. Campbell's not much of a judge of character either.

He nods. "Just this once."

Finally, it's Charlie's turn. This is what he reads:

> *You asked us to write about death. I want to write about love.*
>
> *They're not the same, but they link us together in the same way. Death and love. They both wrap us up in their cords, and they don't let go.*
>
> *And when they mix—when death takes the one you love so far away you can never touch her again, you can never hear her voice, you never see her smile—when death leaves you alone in a room with a wooden box, and inside that wooden box is another box, and inside that box is another, and it just keeps going on and on until you finally get to the smallest box, and that box you can never open—that doesn't mean the love is dead, too.*
>
> *It's still there—you're just alone with it.*

Alone in a room with a box.
Until maybe you aren't alone anymore.
Until maybe there's someone beside you.

He stops there, but I can tell by the way he turns his paper there's stuff he's not reading. More on the back of that sheet, more on the next page.

Oh, wow, I want to read the rest.

He looks hot. Not gorgeous hot—though that, too—but I mean physically *warm*. Almost blushing.

Mr. Campbell makes it a rule not to comment on our free-writes, but just to "let them breathe," as he puts it. Even so, he gives Charlie a curious look, kind of like a dog who's just heard a high-pitched sound, before moving on to Felix McKenzie and his dead guinea pig.

So, I can't help thinking, *is Charlie talking about me as the one beside him?* I am, for what it's worth, literally beside him at this very moment. Does that count for anything?

I try to catch Charlie's eye, but he's staring at his own hands.

Which means...what?

Crap and son of crap. An instruction manual should come with every boy.

I write, "Thanks for the flowers..." on a corner of my page, rip it off, and slip it on his desk. He glances at it and gives me an odd look.

"Okay! Places! Who's up next? Hamlet! Horatio!

Queen! King! Doctor! Dead Ophelia!" Mr. Campbell calls out the list of people for the next scene.

Rosencrantz and Guildenstern are already done for, so Charlie and I stay in our seats as "audience."

He passes me a note with a penciled question mark.

I'm not sure what that means, but in return, I pass him an exclamation point and three asterisks.

Then the scene starts up and any more note passing would be too obvious, so I discreetly check my phone under the table, as if the answer to all things boy will miraculously appear on my screen. What I discover, instead, is a text from my mom.

> Hi. Just got a call from the Commonwealth's Attorney's office. They want to talk with you this Thursday after school. You're free that day, right? Nothing to worry about. I'll be with you. Dad, too. Love, Mom

Ugh. Thanks, Universe. Way to come through.

Friendly

Charlie waits for me after class, taking longer than I suspect is genuinely necessary to gather his stuff and scoot his desk back where it goes.

When we get to the door, he walks beside me, close enough that the backs of our hands brush against each other.

I can't help but grin. It's *almost* like holding hands.

"So, that was pretty deep in there," I say. "Do I get to read it?"

"What?"

"All that furtive writing," I say, and when he still pretends to be clueless, "page two."

"Hmm." He taps his chin with his forefinger. "I don't think page two is in the contract."

"Hmm." I tap my chin right back at him, teasing. "I don't think we *have* a contract."

"Well, maybe we should," he says, but he doesn't go on to say what that contract might include. As it turns out, I'm glad he doesn't because when we round the corner to the locker rooms, I hear Jared's voice mix with the other gym sounds. And I think about what Lindsey said: *This is going to kill JJ.*

While I don't "like" Jared, I do like him. He is, sad goatee and tongue stud aside, a decent human being, and I don't want to hurt him. I pretend that I need to dig something out of my backpack as we pass the open gym doors, which puts a respectable distance between Charlie's hand and mine.

When we get to the girls' locker room door, which can't be seen from the gym, Charlie draws me close, kisses me softly on the cheek. Even though it's just a little kiss, it seems so intimate, exceptionally sweet. Like a gentleman's stolen embrace from one of those nineteenth-century costume movies my mom likes to watch.

"So was that a hint?" he says, as he pushes open the door for me.

"What?"

" 'Thanks for the flowers,' " he quotes.

"No hint," I say, confused, "just, you know, thanks." I give him a quick smile and step into the locker room just before the door swings shut.

"The rumors are true!" a voice trills before I'm even fully in the room. "You and Charlie Hunt."

It's Allison Hampstead. She, Amanda Wells, and Other Allison, as everyone calls her, are all on the girls' soccer team. Of the three, Hampstead is definitely the alpha. She stands by the sink with her hip out, a teenage goddess in pale pink bra and matching panties.

Amanda and Other Allison stop what they're doing and look at me. I feel like I just walked in on someone else's surprise party. A vaguely threatening surprise party.

"Hey," I mumble, approximating what I hope is a friendly wave, and walk to my locker, where I try to become immediately invisible. As I start to undress—all too aware that my sky-blue undies with kittens do *not* match my neon-orange sports bra—Other Allison says, her voice snuffly, like she has a cold, "So, Charlie. He's so mysterious. I didn't think he'd ever get over…*you know.*"

I am thinking simultaneously: *Is he over her?* and *Why won't she say Jamie's name?* and *Why couldn't I have worn my black bra today?* and *I hope I don't catch what she has.*

"It must be weird," she says.

"*So* weird," Amanda kicks in. "Was it a hookup or—?"

"Do you ever think, you know, she's still *here*? Like a ghost?" breathes Other Allison.

"Uh," I say.

"Come on, Ally," snaps Amanda. "That's just stupid."

"She could be, you don't know," wheezes Other Allison. "Did you see that show—?"

"Anyway." Allison Hampstead shoulders Other Allison out, pushing herself and her perfect bra fully inside my personal air bubble. "It's wild about you and Charlie. I mean, it's so…unexpected." Her pastel lips, which coincidentally match both bra and panties, make a perfectly tied bow.

"It'll be interesting to see if it can last. Who's taking bets? Girls?" Amanda holds out her hands like she's carrying two invisible trays.

"Um, excuse me." I try not to elbow anyone as I tug my gym shirt over my head. I reach for my shorts and step into them, then square my shoulders, thinking, *I'm not naked anymore, bring it on.* "What exactly do you guys want?"

"Huh," puffs Allison H. "We're just being friendly!"

"It's just that Amanda has this thing for—"

"Shut up, Ally!"

"Okaaaay," I say, putting it together: Amanda must have a crush on Charlie. Of course. All the estrogen swamping the locker room air suddenly makes a little more sense.

"Well, then, to answer your questions," I say, picking up my shoes. "No, I don't think Jamie has come back to haunt us. No, it's not a hookup. And even though you didn't ask: No, it's really not any of your business."

I scoot past them, heading to the gym, hopeful my inner bitch has put an end to the capital-D Drama.

When I hit the gym, though, it soon becomes clear that Drama isn't done with me yet.

Confused

I walk in, thinking I'm going to go find a quiet corner. I'm going to slip on my shoes, lie low, and spend the next forty-five minutes doing whatever peppy thing Coach Flanagan has planned for us with the two nets set up at opposite ends of the gym.

Charlie is talking with Mark Lee. It's not like I'm trying to listen, but the tension in their voices makes them louder than usual, and I can't help but hear their words.

"I thought—" Mark shakes his head. "Whatever."

"Come on," says Charlie. "It's like *every* Monday."

"My point exactly. We do it *every* Monday."

"So this once—"

"Whatever. No biggie." Mark turns, rolls his eyes. He catches sight of me on the bleachers and shoots me a hostile look.

The rest of the girls trickle out of the locker room, including the now-clothed Allisons and Amanda.

That's when Jared slides in beside me. He puts his hand

on my knee. "Heeeey." He drawls the "hey" out like it's lyrics to one of his songs.

"Hey," I say. I stare at his hand.

"So I lost you," he says.

From the flirty way he says it, I'm guessing the dude gossip network isn't quite as efficient as the girls' soccer team.

I'm not sure what to say, so I don't say anything.

"Saturday night," he goes on. "Did you—did you happen to hear—?"

"VOLLEYBALL!" Coach Flanagan roars. He blows his whistle and stretches, his muscles rippling—the signal that class has officially started and we're all supposed to pay attention to him and his hyped-up biceps. "Who can tell me the basic rules of the game? You! Randy!"

"Uh, you hit the ball over the net."

"And...?"

"And the guys on the other side hit it back."

"And...?"

"And, yeah," says Randy. "You try to win."

"Close enough!" bellows Flanagan. He rattles off some rules and then clumps us into teams of eight. "It's going to be crowded. Volleyball usually calls for teams of six, but I got to squeeze you all in there, so stay aware!"

By proximity, I end up on a team with everyone who's been making my life so confusing for the last ten minutes.

"Move, people. Move!" Flanagan barks.

I pop up, glad to have a reason to catapult Jared's hand off my knee.

In a group, we amble over to our side of the net, lining up like the cast for a reality show. Angst, hormones, and too much eyeliner.

In the back row are Mark, Charlie, me, and Jared. In front, the Allisons and Randy, with Amanda directly in front of Charlie. She bends down to stretch, displaying her prominent and, to be fair, rather perky backside.

Ah. Well. I flex my hands, give a mental shrug. Jealousy has never been my thing. In some ways, my life might make more sense if Amanda gets her way.

Yes, Charlie is lovely. He has a special, I guess you'd say, *glow*. That may be the word people use for pregnant women, but really, it fits him. Even in a gray T-shirt under the fluorescent lights of the gym, he glows. The problem is, to me, he's *too* beautiful. It gets me all tangled up inside.

I don't like worrying about what he's thinking. I don't like worrying about what other people think he's thinking. And especially, I don't like *wanting* him so much.

Because wanting is dangerous. It can all be taken away.

So go ahead, Amanda's Butt. Do your damnedest.

Coach blows his whistle. The ball starts flying.

"Aaaak!" Randy yells.

Joe Pinsky's spiked ball shoots past Randy and rockets toward a spot on the floor between me and Jared. With an inelegant "Umph," I propel myself toward the ball. What I don't see is that Jared is diving in from the other side, going low. My knee connects with his forehead, giving a resounding *thwack!*

He falls back, and I fall with him—momentum sending the whole of my body skidding across his. We land in a heap. I'm suddenly aware that my right boob has ended up in his eye socket and my armpit is straddling his ear. My right thigh, meanwhile, is wedged between his legs, where—*oh, oh, tell me that's not what I think it is.*

I untangle myself, trying to pry my body from his without causing any more damage.

"Are you okay?" I kneel beside him.

Jared looks stunned. I'm not sure he even sees me. I move my hand in front of his face. "Jared?"

I look over my shoulder, where Charlie, Mark, and the rest are huddled.

"Maybe we should get the school nurse?" I say.

But when I turn back to Jared, he locks his eyes on my face. "You're sooooo beautiful," he slurs, his voice earnest and low.

"Uh, is your head okay?"

"Do you have any idea how much I love you?" he says. Not loud exactly, but loud enough that anyone on our half of the gym could have heard it.

I look up; now Coach Flanagan and a bunch of others have circled around.

"I think he hurt his head," I tell the coach. "I knocked into him. With my knee. He's—he's confused."

The coach squats down, peering in Jared's face. "You okay, champ?"

"Her eyes sparkle. Isn't it pretty? Like they're made of glitter," Jared says.

Shavelle Rylan leans over me. The tip of her braid, wrapped in a fat rubber band, thuds against my ear. "That boy's got it bad."

"He's just," I say, repeating it for myself as much as for her, "he's just confused."

My Undoing

Mark and Randy walk Jared to the nurse, who calls his dad to come drive him to the hospital. At least that's one version of the story. In other versions, an ambulance pulls up in front of the school and a team of paramedics haul Jared out on a stretcher. And in another, there's blood. Gallons of it.

With each telling, it gets more blown out of proportion. By physics class the following morning, I hear some boys insist blood was squirting out of Jared's eyeballs. By psychology fifth period, Jared has Ebola. By English in sixth, he's dead.

"He's not dead," I assure Paige Sanchez. "I was there yesterday when it happened." I don't mention that I was the *cause*, but whatever.

"I heard—"

"He's not dead!" I snap.

"But—"

Mr. Campbell shuts us up with a pop quiz on the final scene of *Hamlet*, which I haven't yet finished, thank you very much. I have, however, seen the movie, so at least I know the more obvious stuff.

Who drinks from the poisoned cup? Gertrude.

Who is first wounded with the poison sword? Hamlet.

Does Hamlet profess his love for Ophelia before or after her death? After.

Which, when you think about it, is *so* like Hamlet. Or in other words, *so incredibly stupid.*

But love and stupidity kind of go together, don't they? Like how when a person says he loves you, that person seems instantly dumber than they did just a minute before. I mean, loving someone—anyone—is dumb enough, but loving *me*? I am many things, but lovable isn't one of them.

So this Jared situation is…distressing. I feel bad for him, but I don't know what I can do about it. What am I supposed to make of his puppy-dog eyes and rock ballads?

I glance over at Charlie, who is hunched over his desk, tapping the end of his pencil against his bottom lip. My own pencil stalls at the sight of it. Those lips. I take a second to appreciate the curve of them, sighing—which is totally appropriate because they're 100 percent sigh-worthy. Soft and full. And a brownish-red that's entirely their own. They quirk up in a private smile and I almost gasp. Oh, Charlie Hunt, you'll be my undoing.

"Hmmmh." Mr. Campbell clears his throat. He's in my blind spot, and for a second I'm disoriented. As I turn toward him, he plucks up the quiz from my desk. "You ready to turn this in?"

"Um," I say. I still have three questions unanswered, but I'm pretty sure I don't know the answers anyway. "Uh-huh."

"Fine." He strides back to his desk, collecting papers as he goes.

Charlie glances over at me, his eyes brimming with mischief.

Does he know I've been lusting after his lips?

Perfect. Now *I'm* a red that's entirely *my* own. Or at least my cheeks are.

But maybe the embarrassment is worth it, because after class Charlie totally kisses me. We're hardly in the hall before he pulls me next to the wall and we're going at it like frisky lemurs at the zoo. I can't complain. I mean, lemurs gotta do their stuff, right?

The bell for gym rings, and we haven't moved. The hall clears out except for us and our kisses, which seem louder now in the empty hallway. Echo-y.

"Maybe we should—" He tilts his head in the *let's go* gesture, and I'm all in.

"We totally should," I murmur into his neck.

He grabs my hand and we jog together down the hallway, past the foreign language classrooms, past the art room, left toward the only doors in the school not monitored by the front office, and then out into October. The cold air hits us face-first. Without our coats, the chill seems brutal, but the doors behind us only open one way, and we can't get back in the way we came. Even so, I don't regret it. I feel more alive than I have in forever.

This time, it's me pushing Charlie against the side of the building. Kissing him too hard, letting my hands trail down his chest. Shameless. It's like I've been underwater. All this time, underwater. And now I just remembered I need air.

He pushes up my shirt and his palm is on my bra and I don't pull away. Instead, I press closer, running my hands across him, standing on my tiptoes so I can deepen our kiss.

"We should—" he says, panting. And this time the *should* means *stop*. He drops his hand and my breast feels suddenly cold, exposed.

"Yeah…" I say, thinking *Nooooooo!* I pull down my shirt, step back, pivot away from him.

"Hey," he says, touching my shoulder, turning me back to face him. He gives a sideways nod toward a loading dock on the far side of the school, where some drama kids are hauling a big fake tree from the back of a truck. "It's okay. They didn't see us," he says. "I know a place we can go."

I rub my arms for heat. "Is it warmer than here?" I ask.

"I'll keep you warm," he says, kissing my chin, and I feel the breath of his words on my neck.

Foolish

full now and foolish with feeling foolish with him he is all that i'm feeling there is no thinking only skin and touch and lip and neck and wanting wanting his hands shoulder the muscles in his back the scar there are not words for his foolish scar thin and pink above his hip and when he tugs a quilt from the back seat and holding my hand leads me down a path in the trees when the hill of dreaming boulders rises before us when we climb first up and then down into a rocky nook shaded by shrubs and sheltered from wind there is no question in the light shining through leaves above us no answer for the bird calling whit whit whit and please bird please don't let this be love but i'm already foolish so foolish for him

Interlude

"If I made a lipstick from your lips, I'd call it *Dusk*." I turn over on my side, prop my head up on my elbow. The ground below us is hard, and something knobby pokes my ribs, but together in the burrito of the quilt, we're warm.

"Dusk?" Charlie laughs.

I touch his lips with the tip of my finger, pluck the bottom one like a guitar string. Kiss him leisurely. "Maybe *Red Fox*," I say. "Maybe *Mischief*."

"That's not a color." He pushes aside a strand of hair that's dangling in front of my face and tucks it behind my ear.

"Lipstick names are weird. You know what I'm wearing right now?" I look down at his neck and chest, marked here and there with smears of red. "Well, you're wearing most of it by this point."

He laughs.

"It's called *Interlude*. But at home, I also have *Fortune Cookie*, *Last Wish*, *Forbidden*, and, let's see, *Cozy Couch*. Lindsey says they must open a book at random and point. I mean, who wants to put *Cozy Couch* on their lips? But it is a pretty color. Kind of a glossy lavender."

He leans in and kisses me.

"If I were to name a lipstick after you," he murmurs against my cheek, "I'd call it *Kissable*."

"Really?" I ask, laughing.

"Really," he says.

We lie, side by side, watching the sky above us soften to a dusty not-quite gray.

"We should head back," Charlie says. "I didn't bring a flashlight, and I'm thinking getting lost in the woods isn't on your to-do list for any given Tuesday."

He stands and helps me up. We get ourselves together—"parent-ready," as Lindsey calls it. With my thumb, I blend in the lipstick on his neck. "Now it just looks like one of your bruises."

We're halfway back to the car when I remember. "Oh! I wanted to tell you. Your flowers! I put them beside my bed so they'd be the last thing I saw when I went to sleep, and the first thing I saw this morning." I know it's corny, but whatever.

He stops walking, and since I'm holding his hand, I stop, too.

"Okay, so there's been some kind of—I don't know. Anyway. I didn't get you flowers."

"What do you mean—?"

But of course what he means is exactly what he said: He didn't get me flowers.

So, if he didn't, who did?

Who Did?

1. Jared

Possible, especially given the whole love-song and sparkly-eyes stuff. But what about *It's not your fault*? I hadn't given him a concussion yet, so he wasn't letting me off the hook for that. Was it because I didn't stay for his song? Because he knew something was up between me and Charlie?

2. Mystery Dude

A secret admirer might be cool.

A secret admirer who leaves passive-aggressive notes is not.

3. Someone with the Wrong Address

The woman in the blue house across from us might have done something really, really bad...?

4. Right Address, Wrong Addressee

They could be for my mom, I guess. I showed her the flowers, but not the note. Maybe it would make sense to her. I could ask.

But if I showed her the note and it *wasn't* for her, she'd probably freak. Like call-the-cops freak or something. Because even though she acts all *la-la-la everything's awesome*, I know she was shook. I've heard her talking with my dad, *That boy—we never saw it coming. How did we not know?*

Now her worry—the fear of all she doesn't see—is like a piranha, darting around the edge of everything, little nip by little nip, eating her away.

5. Lindsey?

I'm grasping straws here, but I mean, Lindsey does some weird stuff sometimes.

Official

Thursday after school, my parents drive me to the Midland County Courthouse. It's weird having us all in the same car, weird sitting in the back seat, weird that I'll soon be talking to a total stranger about a boy I hardly knew who wanted to kill me. I don't unclench my teeth for the entire ride, and by the time we get there, the tension in my jaw could snap a pencil in two.

My father leads the way through security and then down and around the courthouse hallways to a brown wooden door with a see-through window. Old-fashioned letters in milky paint spell OFFICE OF THE COMMONWEALTH'S ATTORNEY.

"We're here to see Mr. Hayes," my father tells a young redheaded man at the front desk. He asks us to sit, which we do. Maybe it's nerves, but the waiting room air tastes stale to me, like something underground. A crypt with a coffee table and last year's magazines.

After a minute, the redhead calls us over and leads us single file down a hallway, then ushers us into an office lined with thick wooden bookshelves.

There, a grim, gray-haired man glances up from his computer at a desk in the middle of the room.

Waving us over, he stands to shake my father's hand. "Appreciate y'all coming in. Have a seat." His drawl is exaggerated, like he's been cast as the Southern Gentleman in the high school play. Clasping his hands together, he looks directly at me. "As you know, I've asked you here because it's probable we'll need you to testify at the sentencing for Kyle Paxson."

Hearing this serious man in his serious office and his serious suit speak Kyle's full name seems messed up, as if the very act of it makes Kyle and his murder somehow "official." Like it's been processed and pasteurized and wrapped in cellophane—the moral equivalent of fake cheese.

The bearded man proceeds to ask me questions, basic stuff about Kyle contacting me and not-so-basic stuff about our relationship, if you could even call it that.

How did you meet Kyle Paxson?

You were in the same grade?

So he was a senior when you were a freshman, correct?

Did you two ever date?

Did you consider him a friend?

But he had your phone number?

Did he ever call you?

Did you socialize with him?

And at these parties, did you talk with him or give him any special attention?

How would you characterize your association with Kyle?

What about after he graduated?

Anything besides these casual sightings at a party or the mall?

Did you ever purposely meet with him?

But you did see him shortly before the murder, correct?

And that was when?

Where were you at the time?

How would you describe that encounter?

What did he talk about?

You say you were in a parking lot. Did he see your car?

And what kind of car was that?

This was a new car, correct?

Did you have any other contact with Kyle after that time and before July 11?

But he contacted you on July 11, the day of Jamie Strand's murder?

What exactly did he text?

And you took "stuff" to mean drugs?

Marijuana?

Were you surprised to hear from him?

How did you respond?

When you heard that Kyle was arrested for Jamie Strand's murder, what was your response?

Did you think it could have been you?

Did he attempt to make any contact with you after the murder?

Has he tried to contact you in any way since the time of his incarceration?

Either directly or by a third party?

Are you sure?

It's unnerving. Before the murder, Kyle was just some guy. Over there. Where I wasn't particularly looking. He wasn't linked to me in any way. Now all these useless questions, all my useless answers, are like pencil lines on a dot-to-dot, bringing hidden connections into focus, drawing us both on a single, gruesome page.

I must have zoned out because my mom pats my knee. "Is that all?" she asks the lawyer.

"I believe so," he says. "We're trying to establish, you understand, a pattern of behavior here. To prove that the defendant showed premeditation, and that he poses a future threat to society. We'll be seeking a capital sentence." He turns to me, his face full of bottled sincerity. "You've been very helpful, young lady."

I know that "capital sentence" is just his lawyer way of saying death. And though Kyle deserves to die for what he did, the thought that I could somehow be "helpful" in bringing about that end doesn't give me even an ounce of relief.

One More Name for the List

6. *Kyle*

What exactly did that lawyer mean when he asked if Kyle had tried to contact me?

It's not your fault

That wasn't...I mean, there's no way he could possibly... Right?

The Unexpected

We're in the parking lot after school Friday, I'm perched beside Charlie on the hood of his silver Honda Civic, and there's a mole on his chin I've never noticed before.

How could I have missed that mole, I wonder. Not that it's huge, but I've been looking at his face a lot. Staring into his dreamy chestnut eyes in hopes they'll somehow transport me to a place far, far away from this town.

"Your eyes," I breathe, thankful they're there to help distract me from everything I'd rather not think about— first and foremost being that annoying knot in my brain that keeps wondering about those flowers.

And Kyle.

And if somehow he could have managed their delivery from his prison cell.

And what would that even mean? Is the note an apology...or a threat? Or just some deranged plea for forgiveness?

Logical me: *You're being absurd.*

Actual me: *Someone killing Jamie Strand seemed absurd, too.*

"So, I've been thinking," Charlie says, stroking the length of my hair. "I haven't taken you on a real date. Yet."

"Yet?" I ask.

"Um, would you? Go out with me? Tonight?"

He looks so sweet, a little nervous, even. I can't help but tease. "I was thinking I might spend tonight, you know, drinking vinegar, eating crocodile," I say, half quoting a line near the end of *Hamlet* that Mr. Campbell wouldn't shut up about. "But I guess a date would be good, too."

"I'm taking that as a yes."

"It's a yes," I say. "But wasn't last night a date?" After the lawyer thing, I'd met up with Charlie for a jog, and since I needed to blow off some serious steam, it was more a race than a jog. And afterward... "I mean, there was kissing involved."

"Last night was...exceptionally nice, but I want to take you on a real date. Where I pick you up and we, I don't know, do date stuff."

"So for this 'date,' what should I expect?"

He grins. "The unexpected."

When he picks me up at six, I'm wearing a short black skirt over black leggings and a red sweater. Even though the colors are all wrong and there's no glitzy *S* stitched on the sweater, I always think of this as my Supergirl outfit.

I'm also wearing my best version of a smile. I've decided to give myself the night off. I've been so worked up about

Kyle and the trial and the mystery flowers. And really, I could spend all day and night thinking about it and be not one inch closer to knowing what the hell happened or is happening or will happen. It's all impossible.

So I tucked the note under some papers in my desk drawer, just in case, and I threw away the flowers. Gone. Out of sight, out of mind.

Tonight, I promise myself, there is no Kyle, no upcoming trial, no horror story lurking in the bushes. There's just me and Charlie.

"You're—*man!*" Charlie exclaims before he even gets through the doorway. Then he checks out my shoes. Red, open-toed four-inch heels. "Wow!"

He frowns. "Double wow, but you should maybe bring some backup tennis shoes," he adds, with a secretive smile, "just in case."

"Okaaaay," I say, suspicious.

"Uh-um." My mom clears her throat behind us. "Hi! You must be Charlie."

For a second, Charlie has that deer-in-the-headlights look, but he recovers, gives a stiff smile, shakes my mom's hand, and lies, "Good to meet you."

He then travels back in time to the 1950s, where he trains with a team of crew-cut gents, and, without a wrinkle in the space-time continuum, reenters his present-day body. "I'll have her back early, ma'am," he says.

Mom gives me a curious look. "Why, thank you, young man," she says.

She turns me to face her and gives me a hug, like I'm leaving for boot camp. "I love you," she whispers in my ear, quietly enough that Charlie can't hear. "You have your spray, right?"

"Mom!" I complain, breaking the hug. They gave me the cans of pepper spray—one for my backpack, one for my purse—after Kyle. And yes, they're still at the bottom of each bag, with orphaned pens and tubes of ChapStick.

"Keep your cell phone on," she says, then mouths behind Charlie's back, *Text me*, as I pick up my running shoes from the basket by the door and scoot out.

When we get to the car, Charlie sprints ahead and opens the door for me. Before shutting the door, he leans in and kisses my cheek. I'm not sure if all this is because we're on an official "date" or if he's still in 1950s mode.

He climbs in, and before starting the car, turns to me and holds out his two closed fists. "Pick one," he says.

I tap his left hand. He opens it to reveal a folded bit of paper. He unfolds it and passes it to me. "Hungry?" he asks.

Drawn in pencil is a simple five-point star.

"I don't understand," I say.

"It's where we're going," he says, as he pulls away from the curb.

"What was in the other hand?" I ask.

He crumples the still-folded paper from his other hand and tosses it into the back seat. "The road not taken," he says.

194

Distance

Charlie takes the back roads into Roanoke, and then even deeper back roads out of it. Before I know it, we're heading up a mountain, long and winding, and Charlie passes the time by singing off-key.

"Whoa-ooh-ooh-ooh, the sun and your armpits..."

Make that: singing *wrong lyrics* off-key.

"Are you going to tell me where we're going?" I ask.

"It's a surprise," he says.

I know, I *know* I'm totally safe and there's nothing to worry about, and this is fun, right? Surprises are supposed to be fun. And flowers are supposed to be beautiful and teenage girls are supposed to be alive. But with every mile, I feel a slight tick of unease. And of course Charlie is *not* Kyle, he's *not* going to kill me—but there it is, regardless, that tick. Because once you know someone wanted to rape you and bash your head in, you can never *not* know it.

The woods on either side of the road blur red and orange in my periphery as we twist our way up the mountain.

"Hey, you all right?" Charlie asks.

"Yeah," I say. "It's just, I'm...I'm not a big fan of surprises, I guess."

"Okay," Charlie says, all business and transparency. "We're going to the Star."

I give him a blank look.

"You know, Mill Mountain Star," he says.

"Oh," I say. "Of course! The Star." Roanoke has this huge, tacky, lit-up star on the top of a mountain, which is kind of strange but kind of awesome, too. "Cool. I haven't been there since I was a kid."

"I made a picnic," he says. "There's a basket in the trunk. I figured we'd either set it up there or on the roof of that closed-down grocery store west of town. That's what's on the other slip of paper."

"You have a very interesting definition of 'date,'" I say, laughing. "I like it."

"You want to know what I packed?"

"Packed?" I ask, confused.

"For the picnic. Do you want to know what's in the basket?"

"Nah." I tease, "You can surprise me."

"So that surprise is okay?"

"You know," I say, "I've always found consistency to be highly overrated."

"Absolutely," he agrees.

When we get to the overlook, it's starting to become the

time of day that isn't quite day. Dusk. I smile, thinking of Charlie's lips.

A low, shadowy, luminous sky hangs over our heads. The electric star on the mountain is not yet lit, but street-lights have started twinkling on below. In the distance, the city spreads before us, a tiny toy village.

"It's beautiful," I say.

"Do you ever think, when you're down there, doing just regular stuff, someone might be up somewhere, look-ing down. And you're just a speck to them. Just part of the landscape?"

I consider it. "Not really. Do you?"

"Sometimes," he says. "It's strange, how distance changes things. What can seem so huge, so important when you're right in front of it—the farther you get, it's like nei-ther of you exist."

We watch as day morphs into night. When I squint, the highway below us becomes a silver stream of light.

"Come here," Charlie says. He leads me down a path in front of the Star, which is now lit in white. There's a bench on the other side of the path, but Charlie spreads a blanket at the foot of the star instead. He sits and pats the space beside him.

The ground is cold, but it's not a cold I mind. It's the cold of being alive and wanting some indefinable thing that may or may not be beyond your reach.

Charlie unpacks the basket, laying out a tub of

strawberries, two sandwiches in clear plastic wrap, a large bag of salt and vinegar chips, a clump of grapes, two big Starbucks brownies, and two large drinks—Dr Pepper for me, Coke for him.

"It's not really fancy or any—"

"It's great!" I cut him off. "It looks—yum! Thank you! Can I have my brownie first?"

"Would your mother approve?"

"Probably not."

"Then, by all means." He hands me one of the brownies.

His mention of my mother reminds me. "Excuse me for a sec," I say and shoot her a quick text.

At Mill Mountain in Roanoke. He packed a picnic!!! Am fine.

As we eat, a few families tramp past on the way to the parking lot. A white-haired couple ambles by; the wife, in a long fitted coat, holds her husband's elbow like they've just stepped out of a black-and-white movie.

"It was weird meeting your mom," Charlie says. "I hope I wasn't too...um..."

"Yeah," I say. "You don't really do parents, do you?"

"That bad?" he asks.

"You were...cute," I say.

"Cute?" He rubs his chin. "Hmmm. Maybe I should get all awkward in front of adults more often."

"Maybe," I say, like I don't mean it, and lean in to kiss him.

We feed each other strawberries.

If it wasn't me and Charlie, if it was some other couple I just happened to walk by, I'd probably find them ridiculous. But since it is me and Charlie, it's really, really sweet.

"I almost forgot!" He scooches two folded slips of paper out of his back pocket and puts one in each fist. "Choose," he says.

I consider his hands.

"It's surprise you don't like, right? Not chance," he says.

"No, chance is fine," I say, tapping his right hand.

"Let's see." He unfolds the paper and shows me a picture of what looks like a straggly mushroom. Or maybe a beret with a few strands of hair coming out.

"This you'll have to explain," I say.

"I will," he assures me, helping me up. "I'll tell you on the way."

Immortal

Mark Lee's cousin Ned works at the science museum and agreed to let us in after hours. Unlocking the door, he takes a nervous glance around, then waves us in. The front room is dark, all the displays switched off. "So no one will see lights from the outside," Ned says.

From a back office, a radio is blasting rock ballads.

Charlie takes my hand and leads me through the dimness. We pass a clear glass globe, a robot on a bike, and a huge plastic mouth.

"Power's still on in the back," Ned says, then leaves us, heading down a dark hallway toward the glowing rectangle of an open office door.

"Is he okay with this?" I whisper. "He's not going to lose his job or anything?"

"It's fine. He's working late anyway," Charlie says. "Mark and I hang out here all the time. Come on, there's something I want to show you."

In the next room, bright with lights, I hear the *shh-shh-*

shh of a stream, and squint. A little pond is in front of us, with a fake waterfall and real fish, turtles, rocks, and logs. Off to one side, a smaller room radiates with neon blue.

"In here," Charlie says, leading me toward the glow, which I find is caused by an atmospherically lit jellyfish tank that rises up one wall, arches over our heads, and then stretches down the opposite wall.

"I love it here," he says, letting go of my hand and lying down flat on the floor beneath the tank's arch. He pats the floor beside him, and I lie down, too.

"It's...quiet," he says, though in the distance the radio howls about beer and betrayal.

Three dozen jellyfish float above us, opening and closing the cloudy palms of their bodies in slow, mindless movements. It's almost hypnotic—lying on the floor beneath the tank, watching the white, spineless dance.

"There's a type of jellyfish that can live forever," I say.

"Wait. What?" Charlie says.

"It's true. My dad told me about it. They mature and reproduce, but instead of dying, they just turn back into a child. Then they do it all over again. They keep turning back over and over. If nothing kills them, they'll live forever."

"That's wild."

"I bet there's some scientist somewhere poking that jellyfish with needles right now, cutting it up, trying to create a pill that will make us immortal."

"I wouldn't want it," Charlie says.

I wouldn't either. I can't imagine going through high school in an endless loop. Having to learn it all again, having to *feel* it all. But I ask him, "Why not?"

"Who wants a life that can only end in killing?" he says. "It shouldn't be like that."

He must be thinking of Jamie. Her kind smile. Her broken body. Kyle's fists.

I watch one jellyfish bump into another, slowly bounce away, and knock into the side of the tank. The randomness of it fills me with a sadness I can't explain.

"I was with Mrs. Gardner when she was dying," Charlie says. "She's this old lady who lived down the street from us and I used to cut her grass. She always gave me five dollars and a slice of pound cake. When she moved to the nursing home, my mom made me visit her, you know, read the paper or talk about NASCAR. That lady could talk NASCAR all afternoon."

He grows quiet, like he's forgotten he was speaking, so I ask him, "You like racing?"

"No." Charlie laughs, surprised. "I don't *hate* it. But it wasn't really about that." He shifts, so he's lying on his side, propped on one elbow, looking at me. "She lost so much weight, week after week, till she wasn't much more than a skeleton. The last time I saw her, she didn't talk at all. I'm not sure she could. I knew she was dying, I *knew* it. It wasn't like—it wasn't like with Jamie. I could have said something this time. I could have said...I don't know... goodbye."

He flops on his back, stares up at the jellyfish. "But I didn't. I mean, I said bye when I left, but it was"—he makes a flippant gesture in the air above us—"just normal, like I'd see her again the next week. Even though I knew I wouldn't."

We watch the jellyfish dodge and sway. The back of Charlie's hand connects with mine and I shift my arm slightly so my palm rests in his. His fingers stroke the back of my hand, and it's like that touch is all that exists. Like his hand is talking to mine in its own language. I feel safe, and I close my eyes.

Mine

"It's like this." Lindsey spits her gum into a small square napkin. "You've been nowhere. Like you disappeared."

She sets her cup down on a table by the window. We're at the coffee shop in the old-fashioned part of town. Across Main Street, at the farmers' market, an old guy is packing up his leftover pumpkins into the back of his truck. It's past three on Saturday, and it's started to drizzle, so the other stalls have already cleared out.

I sit, keeping my eyes on the rain.

"You ignore me all week, then I get one text from you—ONE!—asking, of all things, about flowers. But when I ask WTH? All I get is 'I'll explain later.' So, it's later! Explain."

I'm not quite ready to talk about the other stuff, so I answer her question with another. "Where did *you* disappear to when you started hanging out with Robert?"

"That's different." Lindsey uses her coffee stirrer to carry a glob of whipped cream to her mouth.

"Different how?"

"I was justifiably pissed. You were being a butt."

"Hmm. You have a point." I take a big swallow of my warm chai tea and exhale. It's hard to argue when you're drinking chai.

"So to make up for it, you're going with me to Taylor's today," she says.

"Uh, what?"

"You are going. With me. To Taylor's. Today." She gives me her All-Powerful look. "Text Charlie and tell him you're mine for the rest of the day. He can have you back tomorrow."

"We're meeting up after dinner for a run," I say. "It's kind of a thing."

"Yeah, well, you'll always have Paris," Lindsey says.

"What does that even mean?" I ask, laughing. "Sometimes you're so freaking random."

"He's had you all week. Plus, it's raining. Plus, Taylor *needs* us. For support, you know. And this is so cool!" Lindsey's voice goes up in this excited way that lets me know that she knows I'm not going to like what she has to say next, so she's going to pretend it's thrilling and hope I play along. "She's going to do our hair!"

"Noooooo—"

"Yes! Just hear me out. She has to do these before-and-after photos for her beauty school project, so she's going to do it all. Cut and style. Makeup. Everything. It's going to be fun!"

"But—"

"Fun, dammit!"

"Arrrrr—"

"Fun, I say! FUN!"

There are times when Lindsey cannot be argued with. Times like now.

"And after, you're coming over to spend the night *for real*. And we're going to watch *Austenland* and talk girl stuff."

I've seen *Austenland* twice with Lindsey already. "How many times have you watched that movie?" I ask.

"Twelve. I stopped counting after twelve."

"You're possessed," I say.

"Yes, I am," she says. "So don't get in my way. Text the boy. Text him. Tell him you're miiiiine!"

"Okay," I say. "Girl stuff. Hair. Nails. Got it."

"Text!" She points to my phone like she expects me to do it this second.

So, sighing, I do. As I type, I remember Taylor's purple hair at the memorial for Jamie. I stop mid-word. "No dye, right?"

"Yep, no dye. You done?" she asks, pointing to the phone in my hand.

"Just a sec," I say, and resume typing.

"Send! Send!" she squeals, giddy.

"Geez, you're so hyped up," I say. "What is in that coffee?"

"Wondrous caffeine! Glorious caffeine!" Lindsey's arms are making outrageous gestures as she speaks, as if from the waist up she's waltzing. She almost accidentally fondles a large guy plugging into the outlet behind her chair.

When he leaves, I snicker, caught up in her irrepressible zeal. "You need to watch out," I say.

"Darling," she chirps, "the world needs to watch out for me."

"You're not wrong," I say.

"Oh—that text! I almost forgot. What was that all about? Flowers?"

So I tell her about the flowers on the porch and the note, how I was sure they were from Charlie but they weren't, how it must just be some random weirdness, right, but I'm not even done talking when the look on Lindsey's face gets frozen somewhere between just-saw-a-ghost and just-stepped-in-poo.

"Oh. My. God."

"What?"

"It's not your fault...."

She stands up, almost knocking over her coffee cup in the process, then sits back down, actually knocking it over this time. It's all but empty, so I just turn it right side up, and ask, more forcefully, *"What?"*

"I got—not flowers—a blue bear, a little teddy bear— same note—just a brown envelope, right? When was it? When did you get it?"

"Monday morning," I say, feeling my face go numb.

"Holy crap," she says.

"So you got the same note," I say, because I need to get

this straight, no misunderstanding, "the same note, but with a bear?"

She nods. "No signature. Nothing. Monday morning. It was outside my door when I went to school. But it was from Robert. He *said* so when I told him about it. He was like, *A sugar bear for my sugar.* And I was like, *What's not my fault?—you know, from the note?* And he was like, *It's not your fault you're so sexy.* And I was like, *Awwww!* But—but he sent *you* flowers? Like, *what?*"

"Is it possible," I ask, "that Robert was just taking credit? You know…lying?"

"Oh," Lindsey says, and I can almost see her mind putting it together. "Oh, yeah. Definitely. Robert would totally do that."

"So the flowers…the bear…they've got to be from the same person. But not Robert." Because really, there's a zero percent chance Robert Leuger got me flowers.

"Not Robert," Lindsey agrees. "But why? Why would someone do that?"

In a second, my list of suspects is whittled down to a single, horrifying name.

"Lindsey, what do we have in common, you and me—like, not just being friends, but you know."

"What happened to Jamie," she says, her eyes going wide as it hits her: "Kyle."

In the Stars

On the ride over to Taylor's house, Lindsey schemes. "We can't just come out with it. We need to scope out the situation. You know, go subtle."

Lindsey Barrow, the picture of subtlety. Right.

"I don't want to freak her out," she goes on. "It could trigger a relapse. And she was—God, she was a mess. So here's the plan: First, we chill. Then, while we're getting the makeovers, all casual-like, we slip in something about a delivery or a card or 'your fault' or something, and we see how she reacts."

"But if that doesn't work, we should just ask her."

"Maybe," Lindsey says.

"Yes," I say. I need to know what's going on. "That's Plan B."

"We'll see."

Forty-five minutes later, Taylor lumps half my hair in front of my face, shines a table lamp in my face, and snaps a picture with her phone.

"I look like a Muppet," I say. "A deranged Muppet."

"The 'before' is supposed to look ugly." She holds the phone in front of my face. "Ugly, right?"

"Aw, thanks," I say sweetly.

Lindsey, who has already undergone Taylor's "transformation," is on the basement couch next to Taylor's boyfriend, Kai, the guy from the memorial service with the real-fish T-shirt. Only now he's wearing a plain black tee under a quilted plaid overshirt. His lumberjack style makes him look surprisingly rugged, given the fringes of his hair are now frosted pink. A cherry Twizzlers dangles from his lips like the hero's cigarette in an old movie.

He and Lindsey are bent over his cell phone, watching YouTube clips of guys wrecking bikes. Taylor has given her a loose, layer-y cut with a bit of curl at the tips. The hair looks pretty good, though I can't say much for the makeover. Lindsey's cheeks are too red, her lips are too puffy, and her eye shadow has more glitter than a toddler at a princess party.

A loud metallic screech comes from Kai's phone. He laughs and offers Lindsey a strand of cherry licorice.

Taylor gestures for me to sit in the adjustable chair that's part of her "beauty station" in the corner. In front of me sits a three-mirrored gold-trimmed vanity strewn with dozens of bottles of mysterious gels, creams, and aerosol sprays.

Taylor shakes a bottle of something and mists it on my hair. "Ready?" she asks.

She bends down and peers at my face, scooching her lips up like she's considering the fate of a nation.

The basement is cold and smells vaguely of a hippie den. Or at least what I imagine a hippie den smells like. Chemical musk, patchouli, and the stale ash of past highs.

Spritzing my head with one hand, Taylor drags a comb through my hair with the other. I'm thinking how I can "subtly" find out if Taylor had anything show up on her doorstep last Monday. My best tactic is probably just to ask her, despite what Lindsey says, but when I open my mouth to find the words, Taylor starts in on a monologue that would rival *Hamlet*.

"So I told you guys I got that job at the Scissors Kick, right?" She's speaking loudly enough that Lindsey can hear from the couch. "I'm just answering phones and doing cleanup for now, but once I get my license, that'll change. I really think I'm in a good place. Which is weird, but if what happened, you know, if that hadn't happened . . . it's like it all led me here." She puts down the comb and spray bottle and starts clipping at my hair.

"Everything happens for a reason," Taylor continues. "It was written in the stars. I mean, if I hadn't gone through what I went through, I might never have met Kai. I might not have gotten that job."

I look hard in the mirror at Lindsey's reflection, willing her to look back at me. My eyes ask the mirror, *Are you hearing this? Because,* what?

Lindsey looks up from Kai's cell phone. She smiles at Taylor and nods. Like she's *okay* with all that?

"It all makes sense, you know," Taylor continues. "How everything happens."

"But—but—" I blurt, jerking my head out from Taylor's scissors. "Just because something happens doesn't mean it happens *for a reason*. Bad stuff happens, then good stuff happens, then more bad stuff happens with a little good tossed on top." I am talking too fast, too loud. I crane my neck up to look at her where she stands, scissors still open like a bird's beak. "But come on, it's not like putting a cherry on a big pile of crap magically turns it into an ice cream sundae. It's still a pile of crap topped with a cherry."

Taylor's face is unreadable, but I go on anyway.

"I just mean, we don't have to call the bad stuff 'good' just because something good happened after it. Like if..."

If Jamie had to die just so you could go to beauty school, what kind of ass-backward star chart is that?

"What?" Taylor asks.

If Jamie died so I could be with Charlie... No, I refuse to think it. I never asked for that trade.

"It's not like there's some big plan," I say out loud—*too* loud. "And if there is, it's pretty messed up, right?"

"Hmmm," says Taylor.

Hmmm? Is that all?

In the mirror, my hair makes a limp frame around my face. Taylor picks up a wet strand and starts chopping again.

I shut my mouth and let Taylor spritz and clip my hair, crinkling the ends and flipping it this way and that. Then, without pausing, she sets in on my makeup, grabbing a tube of liquid foundation from a metal tray on the vanity.

"Close your eyes," she commands. I am smoothed and dabbed and patted. "Look up," she orders as she draws a line on my lower lid. "Now straight ahead...now down. Mouth open...mouth closed."

I keep quiet during all the poking because first, I know Lindsey wants me to behave, and second, it's impossible to talk when someone is painting your lips.

Finally, Taylor stands back. "Perfect," she breathes.

In the mirror, I seem—*not me*, but a prettier, more put-together version of me.

"I thought a loose pageboy cut would suit you, right? What do you think?" Taylor asks.

"It's great." I say. "Really. Thanks." And it's not a lie. Even the makeup is pretty—not too heavy, mostly pinks and browns.

I've never had bangs before, and if I had less on my mind, I might obsess over how they feel on my forehead.

But my mind is full to bursting. I get that Lindsey doesn't want to mess up Taylor's progress or whatever, but I need to know what's going on. And if Taylor is being targeted, *she* needs to know it, too.

"Photo time!" Taylor squeals. She's generally not the squealy type, but this must be a special occasion. "Kai, will you do it?"

"Sure." Kai stands, points me over toward the single small basement window. The others watch as Kai makes me tilt my face this way and that, snapping pictures. "Got it!" he announces, holding out the photo for a grinning Taylor to see.

"You're amazing!" Lindsey says. She gives Taylor a hug.

"Thanks," Taylor says. "Oh! I almost forgot!" She walks over to a small side table near the basement door. Opening the drawer, she pulls out a small stack of Scissors Kick coupons. "Give these to your friends," she says, handing me and Lindsey three each.

But it's not the coupons I'm looking at. It's the open drawer, and what's inside. A clear cellophane bag full of strawberry candies—all wrapped in bright red and green. Just like the wrapper I found on my porch weeks ago. About fifty of them in a tidy little bag, tied up with a silver ribbon. And beside it, a small tan envelope.

Edge

"Where did you get that?" I point to the bag.

"You want some? A friend left them. I kind of botched...
well, anyway, she knew how bad I felt. She was really sweet
about it."

"Left them? Like at your door?"

"Yeah," she says. "I don't really like them. You can have
the whole bag if you want."

"No," I say, my stomach turning. "No way."

"We should sit down," Lindsey says, taking Taylor's hand, leading her to the couch. "We need to tell you
something."

"What?" asks Taylor.

I let Lindsey do the talking.

She tries to make it as non-creepy as possible, but by the
end, Taylor is clearly on the edge of freaked.

"He's still in jail, right? Tell me he's still in jail."

"He's still in jail," Lindsey says. "We'd know if he
wasn't."

"But how is he doing it?" Kai asks.

"No clue," I say. "Maybe it's someone who knows him from prison? Some guy who's out now, and he wants to... I don't know, mess with us for kicks." *Or murder us in our sleep. Either one.*

"It could be someone who knows him. From before," Taylor says. "Does he get to have visits?"

I look to Lindsey. She shrugs. "I guess so."

"He wasn't close to many people," I say. "I don't know anyone who would visit Kyle."

"Well, there was that one guy," Taylor says. "He thought Kyle was so cool. And when Jamie, you know... he was all talking shit, like Kyle was set up. Remember? What was his name?"

Lindsey and I shrug in unison.

"You know," Taylor says. "Big guy—always hitting on cheerleaders. Plays that weird plastic horn at pep rallies."

"Holy crap," says Lindsey.

"Holy crap," I say. "Todd Firebaugh."

Lifetime

"I know where he'll be tonight," Lindsey says. "Todd."

We left Taylor five minutes ago. She was freaked, but Kai said he'd stay with her, and when we left, they were cuddled up on the couch, the shell of him around the shell of her.

"Keep going straight," Lindsey says.

We're on Main, and I'm coming up to the turn that leads, eventually, to Lindsey's apartment. "Why?" I ask as I pass her turn.

"We should go," Lindsey says. "We should tell Todd we know what he's doing. The sick bastard. And he can either leave us the hell alone or we're calling the cops."

"No way, we shouldn't tell him. Have you ever even seen a Lifetime movie? You don't warn the creeper who's stalking you that you're on to him. That always ends badly."

"Seriously? Lifetime?"

"Don't judge. It's great when you're PMS-ing." I drive past what my mom calls the Fast Food Belt on Main Street.

It's pretty much at the edge of town. Soon, we'll hit a few outlying neighborhoods, the retirement home, the brick-yard, stuff like that, then the road will open up and we'll be in the country. "Where are we going anyway?"

"Tony's hunting cabin. He's having another bonfire. Jamal is going to be there, and Todd has started latching himself onto Jamal. He's like a friggin' shadow."

"Who's Jamal?"

"You know. Tight end Jamal. Football. The whole team'll be out there."

"Robert, too?"

"Yeah. He's so good to me. When I told him I needed to hang with my girl tonight, he was totally cool with it. With everything that's going on, though, I'm glad he'll be there. We can use the backup."

"I'm not sure we should even go," I say.

"But we can't just run and hide! I want to see Todd. See what he's up to. Plus, a bunch of the cheer squad will be there, and they always know what's going on. Todd's mess-ing with us, and we need to know what we're up against—and if there's anyone else involved."

"Okay," I say, not sure if it's the best answer, but I keep driving.

Fire

Perched on a rock, I take a swig from a bottle of Dr Pepper and watch the fire flare.

Todd hasn't arrived yet, so Lindsey is off talking with a group of girls. "Getting info," she says.

Meanwhile, here I sit, cold hands making a nest for no bird. Even in my hyped-up state, there's something calming about a bonfire. The crackle and shimmy of the flames. The hypnotic orange. The way, unexpectedly, red-hot embers flash into the sky. It's a gorgeous distraction. Like life, like desire. A reminder of how we will all one day turn to ash.

Joe Pinsky, one of the muscle-heads from my gym class, lowers himself onto a rock beside mine. Sort of like an ogre squatting on a pincushion. His neck is as thick as my... well, pretty much as thick as any part of me.

"Yo, you're that girl that clocked that squirrelly guy, right? What's his name?"

It takes me a second to put together what he's saying. "Jared. Yeah. Thanks for the reminder."

Not only will I turn to ash, but I will be remembered as the girl who knocked out Jared Hilley. And broke his heart.

All week, I've dreaded seeing him—I mean, what do you say to a boy who thinks your eyes are made of glitter? But he hasn't been around. Which is weird, now that I think of it. I mean, I didn't hit him that hard.

"Your hair's different," the Neck says.

"Yes, it is."

"Wanna hook up?"

Well, that escalated quickly.

"Um, I sort of have—" a boyfriend? I don't want to be throwing around words like that. Charlie never called me his girlfriend. "I'm happy where I am," I change course. "Thanks anyway."

"Cool. If you change your mind, I'll be over there." He walks back to There, a picnic table where a cluster of his guy friends are playing Downer. From what I can tell, their version of the game basically consists of two rules: 1) the guy who drinks his cup the fastest wins; 2) when the first guy finishes, everybody else has to pour whatever's left in their cups over someone else's head.

A year ago, I would have been on that table, pouring beer on my own head.

Maybe I should have stayed there. Beer in my hair might be better than this—this gnawing worry that directly behind me, just out of sight, is some wannabe killer.

But even if I found a magical city where everyone's safe and happy and we all hold hands and sing, even if Kyle

220

and Todd and their type were forever on the other side of a huge, impenetrable ocean, I can't help but feel I'd still be at risk.

Because you carry the past inside you—the truth of it.

True or False: *Kyle wanted to kill me, too.*

True or False: *My existence will always be a footnote in the story of someone else's death.*

True or False: *That "someone else" was much kinder than me. She would have done more with her life. She probably loved Charlie better.*

True or False: *It's not fair—what happened to her, what happens to all the lost girls, all the bodies dumped in the scrub by the side of the road, all the lonely, bashed-in skulls, it's not right, it's not fair—and what the hell am I going to do about it?*

A log low in the fire collapses, buckling down, spraying a constellation of sparks into the air. Lindsey returns from the hive mind of girls on the porch.

"You learn anything?" I ask.

"He's not coming," Lindsey says. "Jamal has some kind of stomach crud. No Jamal, no Todd."

"Let's go, then," I say, but as we start walking toward our car, a red truck pulls down the drive and parks.

"Robert!" Lindsey chirps. She takes off, skip-running toward the truck, then falters to a stop.

Robert emerges, followed by Brianna Cole, wearing Robert's coat. He drapes himself around her, hand on her butt as they stroll toward the fire.

Yorkshire Pudding

There's this thing my mom cooks called Yorkshire pudding, though it's not pudding at all. More a type of flaky bread-ish thing. When I was little, she'd turn the oven light on and call me in to watch it rise. It puffs up and up, sizzling in the muffin tins. But if you make a loud noise or open the oven door too fast, all the puff suddenly deflates.

That's what Lindsey's face looks like when I catch up to her—her eyes rise and rise and then go flat, as if she's not quite there, not seeing what she must be seeing, as if the door opened too fast and inside she's falling.

A low, animal sound comes from her mouth, soft at first, but it builds into an indecipherable wailing. She balls her fists and takes off in a run toward Robert.

He halts mid-step, but Brianna, clueless, keeps walking. The two of them come undone. Lindsey passes her a moment before she reaches Robert. With both palms, she pushes him hard. Big as he is, he takes a step back.

"You bastard!" she screams.

He stretches his neck in a cocky sort of what-about-it gesture, then grabs her wrists and holds them up around her shoulders. He's saying something I can't hear. She jerks her head away, yanks her hands free. "Keep telling yourself that," she barks, then pivots away from him.

Head up, shoulders squared, she walks toward me.

I go to her, put my arm around her. "Let's go," I say.

"Yeah." She nods.

She is not looking at me, and I know her well enough to know that she's not looking at me because she doesn't want to crumple entirely. Not here, not yet.

Popcorn

Lindsey and I spend Sunday morning in a listless cloud of loud music. All the diva heartbreak songs. Each time I try to ask her how she's feeling, she mumbles, "I don't want to talk about it," and sticks her head under a pillow.

Meanwhile, I'm stuck in her room, doing homework with Todd's creepy blue bear. It's there on the desk—just an ordinary stuffed bear, like something you'd get from a claw machine. While Lindsey lies there, curled up next to the wall, I scoop it up with a tissue and shove it in a drawer. I don't want that thing looking at me.

By noon I'm hungry and in need of distraction. I wander to the kitchen. Lindsey's kid sister, Veronica, is reading a textbook at a card table set up in the corner.

"Hey," I say, leaning against the counter. "Is your mom around?" I'm not asking because I want to find Mrs. Barrow, but because I don't want her to walk in while I'm poking through her kitchen.

"At the mall."

I open the cabinet with the cereal and pull out a box of raisin bran. "What are you working on?" I ask.

"Homework," she says, which is ninth grader for "Leave me alone."

I pour some milk and go sit on the living room couch with my bowl and my sad little spoon.

After fifteen minutes of flipping channels, I take my bowl back to the kitchen, rinse it out, and return to Lindsey's cave of doom.

"I should have let you gooooo…oh, oh, ooh," she half moans, half sings with the music. "I didn't know…oh, oh… that in your heart, you already said goodbye…goodbye… gooooodbyyyyye…."

I plop on the bed. "You need to get out of this room," I shout over the music. "You need food," I continue. "You need air!"

Lindsey stays buried in her heap. Sighing, I curl up beside her. The mascara and eye shadow from yesterday have migrated south on her face. The smudges make a sort of shadow-face, a smeary mask. Her lipstick, bleared with sleep and tears, halos her mouth with the ghost of red.

I rub her shoulder. "You know I'm not good at this," I say. "Just tell me: You want me to stay? You want to be alone?" I sound like her cheesy lyrics. *What am I supposed to do-oooh-oooh?*

She opens her mouth, I suppose to answer, but all that comes out is a hiccup-y whine.

"Awww." I pat her head and sit up. "You need to eat," I

say. Where are my mom and her muffins when I need them? "I'm getting you some toast, and I'm putting on *Austenland*, and we're not going to let some good-for-nothing jerk bring us down."

Lindsey pushes herself up to a sitting position. "You're right," she blubbers. "It's just—" She collapses again.

"Toast!" I say. "I'll be back with toast."

It takes another fifteen minutes to lure her to the living room couch, where she picks at her toast and we watch thirty minutes of *Austenland*, then twenty minutes of *The Avengers*, and then nothing because it turns out *Austenland* reminds her too much of Robert, and somehow *The Avengers* reminds her too much of Robert, too.

I wish I had some magic word that could make her feel better. Make the love of her life not a cheating mound of dung. Make Todd Firebaugh go lock himself up in a monastery somewhere.

The whole thing with Todd is super weird, and I want to talk it out, but I know Lindsey isn't up to it right now. So, my questions pile up like unwashed socks: Why is Todd doing this? Did Kyle tell him to? Does Kyle even know? What do they want? And why *It's not your fault*? Is he letting us off the hook for something we've done . . . or something that he plans to do to us?

Holy crap.

"Popcorn?" I hand Lindsey the now almost-empty microwave bag.

"I thought—I thought he was The One." She puts the bag down on the coffee table and lays her head in my lap.

"I know." I stroke her hair. "But is there even such a thing as a One? We want to believe there's this one perfect person out there, someone who's just for us, but it's...it's kind of like saying there's a single perfect family to be born into...or a single city where we're meant to live...or one perfect piece of popcorn."

"What about Charlie?" Her voice is gruff from crying.

"Yeah, he's—" I think about it. I should take my own advice, right? "He's amazing. Smart. Sweet in ways I wouldn't have expected. But I bet he thought Jamie was his One. And now...There's no guarantee. There's no person who can be your everything. I mean, look at Robert. In all the world, out of the billions of people, there's got to be more than Robert Leuger—"

"Can we talk about something else?"

"Sure," though I don't know what else there is to say, except maybe to ask the question that's been poking my brain all day. "What are we going to do about Todd?"

She sits up. "We can't just ignore it. Maybe we should confront him. I see him at lunch. We could..." She shrugs. "Something?"

"We need to know what we're dealing with. Do you keep in touch with Blair?" I ask.

"Blair Mattern? Not really."

"You have her number, though?"

"Yeah," she says.

"We should check with her. I mean, I'd like to know, did she get some weird delivery?"

"I'll ask." Lindsey wipes her swollen eyes, reaches for her phone, and types out a message.

A minute later, her phone buzzes.

"No delivery," Lindsey says, typing some more.

Another buzz.

"I told her what's going on. But guess what, her sister is dating a guard at the jail. She's going to ask if anyone's been visiting Kyle." Lindsey types as she talks. A buzz. More typing and buzzing, and then, "Oh, wow!"

She hands me the phone. The message at the bottom, forwarded from her sister's boyfriend:

> Far as I know that douche had 3 visitors. Lawyer, grandma, some guy named Tony. Maybe Todd?

The words go blurry and I realize my hand is shaking.

So, everything at the party, those creepy notes, the "gifts"—that must have been all Kyle.

"We should tell someone," Lindsey says.

"Yeah," I say. "But who? The police? What do we even tell them? That some high school guy sent us flowers and a bear?"

Lindsey gives me a gutted look.

"The police are just going to act like we're stupid, Linds.

I can hear them now." I mimic a police voice, *"That's nice, little girls, but we have real work to do.* And then, then we'd have to tell our parents, and my parents are just going to freak."

"But we've got to do something," Lindsey says.

"Yeah," I say. "We do."

Owlette, Taco, War

Monday, we're still trying to figure out what to do about the abject horror that is Todd Firebaugh.

Meanwhile, life goes on and I deal with everyday horrors instead. Third period, for example, I run into Jared.

I'm delivering a form to the office for Mr. Harrel, and there he sits on the long brown couch across from the secretary, his phone in hand.

And here's the weird part: When the dreaded moment arrives and I'm wondering where to hide, he acts like nothing ever happened.

"Hot stuff! Check out your hair!"

"You're back!" I say, overly perky, thinking, *I am so not ready for this.*

"You seen *Graveyard Burn*—that movie with the zombies, you know, at the doll factory?"

"Umm...?" I say.

"This guy on Twitter is trying to tell me it's better than *Dance for the Slayer*. The one where they invade the prom.

Which is an absolute classic." He holds up his screen, as if the idiocy of the guy on Twitter is something best communicated by the mere presence of his phone. "It's just bullsh—" He stops himself, glancing at the secretary. "I mean, come on."

I've been pulling out my hair, trying to figure out the right way to let Jared down easy, but there's apparently nothing to let down. Besides his disappointment in @Dude66.

"How are you feeling?" I ask. "With the accident and all?"

He knocks on the top of his head with his knuckles. "Doc says soon I'll be good as new."

"I'm so sorry," I say.

He looks at me blankly. "What for?"

"'Cause, you know, your head."

"Ah," he says, clearly still confused, "yeah."

"'Cause I hit you," I clarify.

"Oh!" He raises his eyebrows, bemused. "You hit me?"

"Not like that!" I say. "Don't you"—I hesitate, not sure I really want to bring this up—"don't you remember?"

"Hmmm." He clicks his tongue stud against his teeth, thinking. "Nope."

Now I'm the one who looks blank.

"There's a good chunk of time I've totally lost," Jared goes on. "Doc says it's normal with a concussion."

"Whoa," I say.

"He made me stay at home all week. And get this, I couldn't do anything. No Internet, no video games, no texting, no TV. He said I had to 'rest my brain.' I could listen to music and stuff, though. So that was all right."

It feels like the conversation has ended, so I make that "huh" sound—the one that means I have nothing left to say. I walk the few feet to the desk and hand Mr. Harrel's paper to the secretary. Her "Thanks, sugar!" is sweeter than a glazed doughnut.

"Hold up," Jared calls as I head out. "You'll see Charlie later, right?"

"Yeah."

"Would you give him something for me?" He starts sifting around in his backpack. "It's here somewhere."

Jared pulls out a mat of crumpled notebook paper, stained brown from what looks like coffee. Then a wadded paper cup and the remains of a fast-food bag. He keeps digging.

"Don't worry about it," I say. "You can give it to him in gym."

"I won't be there." Jared stops, looks up. "That's why I'm here. They're moving me to Coach Anderson's seventh period." He dives back in his backpack, poking around. "He's in a health rotation, and Doc says no physical stress for a while, so I'm—ah! Got it!" He pulls out a roughened-up paperback and places it in my hands. A black cover with MARTIN TRUNDEL at the bottom in big white letters, and above: THE RULES OF ANT LIFE. "Charlie left it at my house."

"Hmm." I say, flipping through the first few pages. It's

broken up like poetry. Strange words stand out: *owlette, taco, war.* I pick a few lines at random and read them out loud:

> *In the beginning was a gun that dreamed of*
> *swallowing a mango pit.*
> *In the beginning was a mango pit that*
> *couldn't keep the hair out of its eyes.*

"Deeeeeeeep," I say.

"Yeah." Jared laughs. "Charlie…" He drifts to silence.

"What? Charlie what?"

"It's kind of embarrassing."

"Sure. Okay," I say. "But if you don't tell me, I'm going to spend the rest of the day imagining every embarrassing thing two guys could possibly do with a book of poetry."

"Stop!"

"I can't help it. That's just how it is."

"He was reading it to me, all right!" Jared says. "You know, 'cause I couldn't do anything. I was bored. It was no big deal."

"Charlie visited you while you were out?" I ask.

And of course he did. Like he did for his dying neighbor. Like he would for anyone. Because that's who he is.

And just like that, the part inside me with all the romantic goo suddenly goes warm.

"We hung out some," Jared says.

"That's like…like…" I realize *sweet*, the word I want to say, would embarrass Jared even more. "Cool."

"You guys have been hanging out, too, right?" he asks. And if I didn't live through last Monday, when he gazed up at me and declared I was so beautiful that my eyes glittered, I might not have heard the tint of mustard yellow in his voice. Because if yearning's a color, it's definitely yellow.

"Yeah," I say. "Listen, Jared—"

"That's awesome," he says, and it sounds like he really means it. "You're happy, right?"

I nod.

"Then awesome," he says. "Fantastic."

"Fantastic," I echo, making my voice light. "I'll see you around," I say, then leave.

Distance

Sometimes I think I'm the only person at Midland High who doesn't have a regular lunch table. I guess I'm what you'd call a floater. Which is also what you call little bits of food that backwash into someone's soda bottle. Or poop that won't flush. So yay me.

I choose a table that's mostly empty due to the choir field trip to Washington, DC. Just me, my obsessive thoughts, my baked potato, and two guys in country-boy T-shirts. One, a dog on a tractor. The other has a big flag and literally reads COUNTRY BOY, AMERICAN MADE.

As I eat, I pull out the book Jared gave me to pass to Charlie and flip through it again. It's mostly bad behavior—drinking too much, living in squalor, cursing a lot, a bunch of weird stuff. And occasionally something heart-stopping and true.

I imagine Charlie reading those poems. No, even weirder, reading them to Jared. Jared in a sickbed, a cold cloth on his forehead, the blue light of his unused laptop flickering in the corner as Charlie intones line after line in that droning voice people use for poetry.

I'm not sure when Charlie found the time last week to go get all bromantic with Jared. Maybe after my ten thirty weekday curfew? It's not like we're joined at the hip, but except for this weekend, we hung out a lot. I texted him a few times on Sunday, but I didn't hear back. Charlie's normal response-to-text ratio is pretty lacking, though, so I'm not worried.

I want to tell him in person anyway about Lindsey's creepy bear and Taylor's creepy candy and Todd cozying up with Kyle all creepy in jail.

I poke what remains of my potato—looking forward for once to English class because I know Charlie will be there. As I rise, I feel my bangs brush my forehead and I wonder if he'll like my new hair.

So when Charlie blitzes in a second before English class starts and sits *not* in the desk beside me, but in the only other empty desk three rows away, I'm—I guess you'd say surprised. Then, when I'm looking right at him and he stares ahead, as if Clarissa Coleson's back is the most interesting thing in the world, I'm confused. And when he just keeps staring ahead all through Mr. Campbell's lecture on the absurdity of evil in *Heart of Darkness*, no matter how obviously I try to catch his eye, I'm some weird combination of hurt and sad and someone-just-stole-my-rainbow pissed.

Not that he doesn't get to stare at Clarissa's back if he wants to. Fine. Fine, right?

Yeah, it's fine. But I get to feel what I feel, too. The last I saw him, he didn't want to let go of my hand. And now, what? I'm invisible? How does that work, exactly?

Plus I *need* him to help me figure out this stuff with Todd. How did I get in the place where I *need* him at the exact moment he is for no reason whatsoever on another planet?

Arrrgh!

By the end of class, my anger has become a regal thing. It wears its own crown and demands subservience.

Even so, I take my time packing up, intentionally not slamming my notebook into my backpack, but placing it in slowly, with exaggerated care. There's a sliver of sanity that whispers, *Maybe I don't know the whole story, maybe I'm imagining things, maybe Charlie will come up to me after class and take my hand and walk me to gym like he did every day last week, maybe he's just tired or distracted, maybe there's something else going on.*

But by the time I zip up my bag, stand, and shoulder it, Charlie is already gone.

Moons

In seventh period, it's more of the same. He's intense. He's brooding. I don't exist.

We end up on teams across the gym from each other. At some point, Joe Pinsky clobbers the volleyball. It slams down and bounces into the far court, near where Charlie is positioned. I'm closest to the back, so I run to get it. But Mark Lee, for no reason, blocks me off.

"Our ball?" I pant, hand on hip.

"Hold on," he says, giving me a sit-stay look, and goes to knock it toward me with his foot.

For the rest of class, Mark remains a moon in an oddly shifting orbit—solidly between Charlie and me.

In the shower, I try to hold on to my anger. Because anger is also an orbiting rock, burning at its core, and I want it to keep me from any other feels that might be rattling around in space.

Afterward, I text Lindsey, and she texts back that she picked up a shift at Big Lots after school.

> How's it going?

> sucks

> Yeah. Sucks.

> Need a ride?

> no moms car finaly fixed

> Sure you ok?

> trying not to freak ... keeping busy

It's good advice: Keep busy. I have nowhere to put all my anger and fear and pre-chewed confusion, so I do what I always do when at a loss. I gear up for a run.

As I double-knot my shoes, I wonder if I should risk it, you know, running alone, with Todd out there and his weirdo plans.

But Todd would have to catch me first, and he's pretty slow.

Plus, damn it, I get to have this. I get to go out and run

in the world. For a half hour after school, I get to listen to nothing more than the river birds and an occasional car passing in the distance. I get to set off like a flame, burning hard, leaving behind whatever unanswerable questions can't keep up.

Unfortunately, at the moment my unanswerable questions—about Charlie, about Todd and Kyle, about Lindsey and Robert and Life—are every bit as fast as me.

did I do something wrong?—thup, thup—*make something of nothing?*—thup, thup—*what am I not seeing?*—thup—*what does he want?*—thup, thup—*is someone watching us? am i safe?*

I run harder, deciding it's all stupid anyway. Stupid that I thought I might get to feel something. Stupid that I wanted to be alive in this world without someone messing with me.

Anger is stupid. So is Charlie's face. So are the trees.

I slow to a walk. Walking is stupid. Two kids on bikes zip past me on my left. Stupid and stupider.

Then I pull my cell phone from my jacket pocket and do something truly stupid. I text Charlie.

> Is something wrong?

No answer.

> Because it kind of seems like something's wrong.

I wait two minutes, counting in my head as I walk to make sure it's a full two minutes.

> Let me rephrase that. Why am I pissing you off?

Two more minutes.
Three.

> No, let me rephrase that. Why are you pissing me off?

Thirty seconds.

> No, no. Screw you. That's what I really mean. Go screw yourself.

Two seconds.

> The End.

The Plan

The bright blue sign above Lindsey's head reads SMOOTH
MOVE: EXCEPTIONAL SMOOTHIES AND CONFECTIONS, and
underneath, for no apparent reason, MAKE YOUR LIFE A
WORK OF ART!

She takes a slurp of her almond-banana smoothie and
confesses, "I've been keeping an eye on Todd."

"Seriously?"

She nods, taps a finger against the table. "Like at lunch
today. I was just watching him, trying to see if he was
watching *me*."

"And was he?" I ask.

"He didn't *seem* to be, but maybe he's just...subtle."

"Todd Firebaugh is the least subtle person I know." I
think back to the tight, perfect loops in the notes he left
us. *It's not your fault.* "I'm surprised he can even write in
cursive."

"I think we should spy on him."

"What?!"

"Everywhere I go, I'm like, *Is he following me?* I checked under my friggin' bed last night before I could fall asleep. It's messed up. And on top of the whole thing with Robert...God, I'm coming unhinged. I need to *do* something. We should follow *him* for a change."

It sounds like it should be a joke, but I'm pretty sure she means it. "Okaaaay," I say. "That's pretty extreme."

"Why?"

"Because...how do you even do that?"

"Easy." She leans in. "Here's the plan. I'll drive my mom's Chrysler tomorrow, so he won't recognize us. Then we hang in the Sheetz parking lot after school. Anybody coming out has to pass that way, and when he goes by, we pull in behind."

"Are we wearing fake mustaches, too?"

She brushes off my snark. "Hats, yes. Mustaches, no."

"I don't know, Lindsey. This could go—"

"I'm doing it. Whether you come with me or not."

I sip my mango smoothie. I know that tone. She's not giving this up.

And there's no way I'm going to let Lindsey do something like that alone.

"Okay," I say. "Whatever. I'm in."

Invisible

Lindsey, it turns out, wasn't kidding about the hats. She has a dark purple knit beanie with a pom-pom for me and a black velvet baseball cap for herself.

"It's like I'm invisible," I say, tugging the beanie over my hair.

"I got you Strawberry Lime." Lindsey hands me a frozen slushie, then points to a bag of barbecue potato chips on the floorboard. "And look! Snacks!"

We both got out of seventh period early—me by telling Coach I had to go to the bathroom fifteen minutes before the end of gym, and Lindsey by skipping government altogether. We're parked behind a delivery truck, but we still have a good view of the road. It isn't long before the line of after-school cars snakes by.

"That's him!" Lindsey pulls out into the flow of traffic, positioning herself a few cars behind Todd's red Mustang.

We follow him down Main, right on Fourth, and left on Garfield. As the streets become less busy, Lindsey slows to leave more distance between us and Todd. When he pulls over in front of an old brown bungalow, Lindsey drives past, then circles the block and parks a few houses down on the opposite side of the street.

We hunker in our seats and wait.

And wait.

And wait.

I open the chips, take a few, and hand the bag to Lindsey.

"So we just sit here?" I ask, crunching. "Forever?"

"Yeah," Lindsey says.

I've had time to count the wooden fences (three) versus chain link (five), mailboxes with decorative covers (two) versus black metal (ten), bare yards (eight) versus yards with trees (four). I've had time to contemplate the likelihood of life on other planets and the perpetual lack of ketchup packets in the school cafeteria and the top ten names for puppies (from #10, Artemis, to #1, Griffindog).

"Ugh." I pull off my hat and comb my fingers through my hair. "How do cops do this?"

"It's boring, but at least we know he's in there, right? If we're watching him, he can't be watching us."

I eat another handful of chips, then wipe the orange dust on my jeans. "Do we have any real food?" I ask, checking my backpack. I come up with two squished granola bars and hold one out for Lindsey, but she doesn't notice. Instead, she's sitting up in prairie dog mode, eyes focused on the bungalow's front stoop. I glance over and there, maybe thirty feet away, is Todd in a bulky gray jacket, heading down his front walk.

"Oh my God," she squeals, squeezing my knee.

It's weird how the sight of a guy strolling to his car can make my stomach suddenly feel like a Mentos dropped in carbonated soda. For a second, it's like I'm back at Matt Graybill's party, Todd's hands on my body, his weight pressed against me.

"Okay, be cool," Lindsey tells herself, though she might as well be talking to me. She yanks the brim of her hat down and purposefully slouches in her seat. "I'm going to wait for him to turn," she says, her hand hovering near the ignition switch. Half a block away, Todd's Mustang veers onto a side street that leads back to Main.

"Are you sure we should be doing this?" I ask.

"No," she says, then flicks on the engine and follows him down the street.

We trail Todd down Main, past the edge of town. He turns right into a weird little strip mall. Lindsey turns left instead and parks in the lot of Twin Acres Motel across the street.

Todd pulls up to the pump outside the Fast Gas convenience store at the far end of the strip. The other places look super sketchy, like they're fronts for something else. Except for Luann's Nails and Midland Tactical Supply, they don't even have business names on their signs, just what they do in big letters and a phone number below. MASSAGE and TATTOO and PIZZA.

"Can you see what's going on?" Lindsey asks.

The way she's parked, her view is obscured by a mangy

shrub, but if I press my forehead against my side window, I see the strip mall perfectly.

"He's at the gas pump," I say. And after a minute, "He's walking into Fast Gas."

What's weird, though, is that when he goes to pay, the checkout woman reaches under the counter and pulls up a plastic bag full of something. She rings up his gas and hands the bag to him, like it's something he just bought, only it's not. He went straight to the counter—not getting anything—then pulled out a wad of bills and handed them to her. So, what's in the bag?

Something else weird: She doesn't give him any change.

"What's going on?" Lindsey asks.

"Good question," I say, then describe what I saw.

"That's taking skeezy to a whole new level," she says.

"I know. What are we doing, Linds? This is such a bad idea. Maybe we should just—"

"He's *leaving*!"

I squint at the parking lot. No red Mustang.

Lindsey backs out, then turns left onto West Main.

There's a white truck and a green sedan between us, but ahead is Todd and his strange plastic bag.

"What do you think's going on?" I ask. "What's this have to do with Kyle?"

"I don't know," Lindsey says. "That whole exchange was super dodgy. Some kind of payoff or something? Maybe drugs?"

"Holy crap! Remind me why we're following this guy."

"It's keeping my mind off Robert."

"Are you kidding me?" I say loudly. And then, in case she somehow didn't hear, "Tell me that's a joke."

"It's a joke," she says, though we both know it's kind of not.

I don't want to obsess on Charlie's crappiness any more than she wants to obsess on Robert's—but it's not like I'm ready to throw myself under a bus just to avoid the subject. And this kind of feels like throwing myself under a bus.

"*Plus*," Lindsey says, "we need to know what he and Kyle are doing. Last time, I was—" She pauses, takes a loud breath. "Last time, I had no idea what was going to happen. I had no—I can't go through that again."

It makes a weird sort of logic. As risky as it feels to be out here, following Todd, it might be riskier to sit at home, pretending we're safe.

It's starting to get dark, and Todd's brake lights flash. "He's turning left," I say, pointing.

We're pretty far out of the city by now. There are a few outlying neighborhoods, some trailer parks, and then mostly curvy country roads. The road Todd turns onto doesn't look like it gets much traffic.

"Hold back," I say. "Don't let him see us."

Lindsey idles in the median for a minute. By the time she turns, Todd's car is out of sight.

"I don't want to lose him," she says.

"There's nowhere to go but straight," I say—though

straight is a relative term. The road itself rises and dips with every swell of the land, curves around every hill.

We drive maybe five minutes, but it seems like forever.

"We're in the middle of nowhere, Lindsey. Maybe we should head back."

"Let's just keep on for a little," Lindsey says.

I try to text my mom, thinking at least she'd know where to start looking if this goes south, but my service doesn't reach out here.

After another minute or so, we see the Mustang, not on the road, but parked outside a junky trailer. In the yard, abandoned kids' toys, a metal ladder on its side, the carcass of a washing machine.

There's nowhere to pull over that wouldn't be conspicuous, so Lindsey drives by. Then, past the next curve, she pulls into a driveway and turns around.

"I saw a place back there, on the other side of the trailer, where we can park."

She drives back the way we came, past the trailer, and then veers onto a grassy patch beside the road.

"What now?" I ask.

She stares ahead, considering. "We walk." She switches off the car. "Veronica's softball stuff is in the trunk. She's got three or four bats."

"Bats?"

"You know, in case we need to defend ourselves."

"I'm betting the people in that trailer have shotguns, Lindsey. What's a bat going to do against that?"

"They're not even going to see us," she says. "We'll keep at a distance, stay hidden."

"Okay," I say. "That is officially the worst idea ever."

"You got a better one?"

"We go home, make sandwiches, and watch TV."

"Yeah, no." Lindsey pops the trunk and slides out of the car.

I pull the knit hat back over my head, open my door, and join her.

Bats in hand, we walk toward the trailer in the gathering dark. *This is stupid*, I tell myself, *so so stupid*, and yet my feet keep following Lindsey.

When we get near the trailer, we cross the street and clamber off the road, into the woods. We make a wide circle around the property and, keeping to the trees, approach from behind.

Through a window, we can see Todd at a table. There's a bearded guy across from him. They talk and drink. The bearded guy leaves the room. He comes back in with a package that he hands to Todd, who stuffs it in his jacket. Lindsey clutches my arm like we just got to the good part in a movie.

"Definitely drugs," she whispers.

They both leave the kitchen, and for a minute we're just watching the yellow glow of artificial light on a cluttered kitchen table.

Then we hear a car rev to life, and the sound of it driving away.

Criminals

Lindsey squeals, "I can't believe we did that!"

"Shhhhhh," I say, though I don't know who's going to hear us out here. We're slogging back through the woods. It's not totally night yet, but it's darker under the trees, and the glare from our phones helps light our way.

"That was unreal," I whisper. "I think we may be criminals."

"Superheroes, you mean."

"Isn't looking in someone's window illegal?"

"Not if that someone has been stalking you and is heading up a drug ring!"

"I don't think that's how laws work."

After a minute, Lindsey asks, "Are we lost?"

I stop and glance around. Every tree looks pretty much like every other tree.

"I don't know. Are we?"

"I thought we'd be at the road by now," she says.

"This is the way we came. I'm sure of it," I say, though I'm only half sure.

I lean my bat against a tree and check my phone to see if I can find where we are, but I still don't have a signal.

"Are you getting service?" I ask Lindsey.

She checks. "Two bars!"

"Pull up your GPS," I say. "Where's the road?"

She props her bat against her leg, taps at her phone, and squints. "Got it!" she says, then points in a direction about forty-five degrees to the right of where we'd been heading.

"Thank you, O Great and Powerful GPS!" I pick up my bat and we set off again, our feet rumbling through dry leaves.

"It's just ahead," she says, and after a minute more, we break through the edge of the woods, onto the roadside.

"Yes!" I have never been so relieved to see a black stretch of asphalt.

"Holy hell!" Lindsey stuffs her phone in her pocket and grips her bat with both hands in swinging position.

I look to where she's staring. Down the road, just ahead of where we parked, sits Todd's red Mustang.

Suddenly, being back there lost in the woods doesn't seem like so bad a thing. The door to the Mustang opens, and Todd emerges, roughly the size of a bear.

"Um, um, Lindsey." If my heart could pound its way clear out of my chest, it'd be on the road by now, gasping like a fish on dry land.

"What the fuck, people?" Todd yells, crossing the road toward us.

Lindsey swings her bat. "Back off!" she shouts.

"Whoa, whoa." Todd holds out his hands in a *settle down* gesture.

Following Lindsey's lead, I raise my bat. "Stop!"

Todd takes another step to get clear of the road, then stops on the curb about ten feet away from us, hands on hips. "You following me?"

"Oh, really, you don't like being followed?" Lindsey asks. "Well, maybe you should have thought of that before you started stalking us!"

"Stalking you?!" His outrage seems genuine, but maybe he's just a good liar.

"We know about you and Kyle," Lindsey growls.

"*What* do you know?" Todd takes a step closer.

"Stand back!" I jab my bat in his general direction.

"You and Kyle think you just get to mess with us. But we're not—"

"Wait, wait. You think—" He rubs his face, amused. "You think *that's* what this is about? Messing with *you*?!" He laughs like he just heard the best joke of all time. "I couldn't give a solitary shit about either one of you. I wouldn't waste my time."

"What about 'it's not your fault'? And that nasty bear? And the candy? The flowers?"

"Bitch, please! You're off your fucking nut."

"You really don't know, do you?" I ask.

"Know what?" He spits out the words, and for some weird reason, it's his anger that convinces me. This is no act. He's clueless.

"Look, everything's cool," I say. "We made a mistake. We should all just go on home and—"

"Where you think you're going?" he says. "Not after what you've seen. And you—" He points at me. "You spit in my face and shit. You got it coming."

"I will cut you," Lindsey snarls, which doesn't make much sense in that she's holding a bat, but it still sounds scarily badass.

It might be panic or rage or too little food and too much stress, but I am *not* having it. "WILL EVERYONE CHILL THE HELL OUT?"

In one motion, both Lindsey and Todd swivel their heads toward where I stand.

I say it slowly, pointing for emphasis, and with as much authority as I can muster: "We are *not* going to mess with you. And you are *not* going to mess with us. We didn't see *anything*. We don't know *anything*, and we don't want to. Far as we're concerned, you'll never see us again. So we're done here. Like you said, you don't need to waste your time."

Todd's face is scrunched up like he's trying hard to convert what I'm saying into English. It's then that a green minivan passes us on the road, slows to a stop, and backs up to where Todd is standing. The passenger window rolls

254

down and the driver, a woman by her voice, shouts out, "Y'all all right? Need me to call someone for you?"

"We're good," Todd says, but Lindsey yells over him, "Yes! That would be great! Could you do that?"

She runs behind the van to the other side of the road, and I follow. Lindsey bellows, keeping eye contact with the driver, not taking a breath: "Our battery is out, it just up and died, I think I have jumper cables in the back, maybe you could give me a jump, or you know, call someone, that would really help a lot, and..." The whole time she's talking, she walks backward toward the Chrysler, and motions for me to do the same. "Maybe you'd have more luck than I did, let me see, I know I put my phone somewhere...." She climbs into the driver side. I climb into the passenger seat. Lindsey starts the car. "Oh, look," she yells over the engine, "it started, we're good." She gives the van lady a thumbs-up and peels out.

Driving way faster than is legal, Lindsey steers us toward home.

Never

Between yesterday and today, it's like a hundred years have passed.

But in that time, my secret life as a spy left me with one certain truth:

"I am *never*," I tell Lindsey, "*never ever ever* doing anything like that again."

"Yeah." She settles into the oversized beanbag chair in my room. "I don't know what got into me. This whole thing—the weird packages, and then seeing Robert with Brianna—it has me on edge."

I might call it *over* the edge, but whatever. I collapse onto my bed. "On the bright side, we now know Todd wasn't the one leaving us 'presents.' We can cross him off the list."

"Why was he visiting Kyle, you think?"

"Maybe he was...being nice?"

"Yeah, that sounds exactly like the Todd Firebaugh we know," Lindsey says. She sits up, leans forward. "Here's what I think. Kyle's been in jail, right? That place is full of dealers. Maybe one of them needed someone on the out-side for deliveries and stuff. So Kyle contacted Todd and set him up for a job. Meanwhile, there's some guy behind bars who's pulling all the strings."

"Wow," I say, considering. "You watch a crap-ton of cop shows, don't you?"

"Knowledge is power, baby."

"Have you seen Todd since yesterday?"

"At lunch. It was weird," she says. "I mean, it *wasn't* weird, which made it weird. I walked by him, and he just kind of nodded, like, *Hey!* And that's it. Like, what the hell? We're *buds* now? I don't think so."

"Maybe he thinks you're tough. Oh my God, Linds. The sight of you with that baseball bat." I start giggling. "I'm taking that with me to the grave."

Lindsey laughs. "I told Taylor what we did, and she was about to hyperventilate."

"I bet. But at least she knows what we know."

"Right," Lindsey says. "Which is...what, exactly?"

"Well, we know that Todd didn't deliver those notes... and whatever he's up to with Kyle, it doesn't have anything to do with us."

"But we still have no idea who *did* deliver that stuff," Lindsey says.

"True. Maybe it was just some—I don't know—someone's idea of a joke? I mean, we haven't gotten any-thing else...."

"If we do, though," Lindsey says, "if something else

happens, we're going to the cops. This is getting way too real. No more bats in the woods."

"No more bats in the woods," I agree.

"What about Charlie?" she asks. "Is he still giving you the silent treatment?"

I sigh.

"It's like he dropped off the face of the earth," I say. "It's been, what"—I count it out—"five days, and not a peep." After my ill-conceived stream of rage-texts, I texted Charlie twice. One an apology. One a meme of a ridiculous dog on some guy's head. Then I deleted his number from my phone so I wouldn't end up like one of those screenshots from the crazy ex.

No return texts, no calls. And in class? He's pulled his hood back up and ceased to notice me.

To be fair, he's ceased to notice anything. Period. The hermit crab retreats into his shell.

It's not surprising, I guess. Even so, I am surprised. Not the good surprised either. But the one where I discover a knife I never saw before sticking out of my chest.

Wow! That's a big knife. Where did that come from, anyway? Oh, and gee, it smarts!

I remember Charlie on that first night, outside Bobby's Barn—how he asked, *Will it hurt to find out?*

It turns out that was a pretty crappy question. Because it *does* hurt. Like a mousetrap to the tongue. But all over, inside.

"God, this trial!" I say, eager to talk about anything else. "I just wish it would get over with."

The three of us—Lindsey, Taylor, and I—have met individually with both of the lawyers at this point. The defense attorney, Mr. Wirtz, is a younger, beardless version of Mr. Hayes. Same questions, less obviously southern, and slightly more smarmy.

"It's amazing," I say, "to think how much power those lawyers have. If you suck at your job, some innocent person could die."

"Can you imagine having to *defend* Kyle, though?" Lindsey asks.

"That would be the worst. I mean, you're sitting there with a guy you know killed someone in this horrible way, and your job is to help him get away with it. Really?"

"I don't know how they live with themselves," Lindsey says. "I'd rather sell crackers and shower curtains at Big Lots for the rest of my life. At least I could go home and know I've brought some joy into the world."

"Well, people do love their crackers and shower curtains."

Next Day

Another restless night, and it's Charlie Hunt's fault. How, I wonder, can someone be so present by the sheer force of their absence?

So I decide: I'm not doing this. I simply will not hurt anymore. And if that means I don't feel anything else, so be it. I tell whatever's in me that's all pissed and confused and achy over the lack of Charlie Hunt to shut the hell up. Then, brick by brick, I build a soundproof wall between me and it.

In English Friday, I raise my hand to debate loudly, if not exactly logically, the relative merits of Conrad's use of God imagery in *Heart of Darkness*. I flirt with the thick-necked guy in gym. And when I trip over my feet while missing a volley, I make a spectacle of my own great sense of humor.

So while I'm out on my evening run, is it any surprise that I'm numb when Charlie turns up by the river, like something snagged on a tree branch after a flood.

"Hey!"

I know the voice, look back, and there he is, in the woods beside the path.

"Wait up!" he calls.

I turn around, jogging in place, and let him catch up.

Then I stop cold, hands on knees, breathing hard, glancing up.

"What?" I say, disgusted at my heart for its rebellious little flip.

"You should keep walking," he says, "so you won't cramp."

I straighten and fall in beside him.

"I kind of disappeared, I guess." His voice is low enough I have to strain to hear him over the water.

"Whatever," I say, meaning, *Hell yeah, you did.*

The wind picks up and a smattering of leaves whoosh down, beautiful and doomed.

"Sorry," he says.

"Sorry?!" I stop, face him. He stops, too. "For what?" I say.

"You know," he says.

"I don't know anything," I say.

"For—" He gives a frustrated sigh. "I had a rough weekend. A rough week."

"Yeah? Me, too." I stare laser beams.

"I was kind of a jerk."

"You think?"

"Kind of," he says.

I start walking in the opposite direction and after a second, he half jogs to catch up.

"No, really," I snap. "I want to know, what exactly are you apologizing for? Why is it, after ignoring me all week, you suddenly feel the need?"

"That was…bad, I know. And like I said, I'm sorry. The last thing I want to do is hurt you—"

"Oh, don't worry. You can't hurt me."

"—but I was—"

"You were *what*?"

Charlie putters to a stop, rubs his temples. "I'm sorry. I shouldn't have come." He begins to back away, and the bottom drops out of my rage, leaving me grasping.

"What happened?" I ask, and it comes out as almost a groan.

He stops, but doesn't answer.

"Tell me," I say. "Why…?"

"It came back." He shrugs, shakes his head, walks off the path, down toward the water. I follow.

"It all came back." Crouching, he sorts through the pebbles at the water's edge. "I thought I was done, you know. I was finished feeling like that. So, so—" He waves his hand out, like trying to push some invisible something away. "After I dropped you off last Friday, when I went home, I was restless. I was *happy*. I climbed up the tree house out back. I just wanted the air. I wasn't thinking." He scoops up a handful of pebbles, stands, picks one out, and skims it at the water. I count the skips—*one, two, three, four, five, six*—almost to the other side of the river. "I wasn't

262

thinking. It was her...where we...and her sweater was there, from before. There were bugs...her sweater...I kept thinking..."

His face pales, like I'm seeing it underwater. Wordless, I place a hand on his shoulder.

"So." The pebbles drop from his fingers, clattering to the ground. "This is me. Fucked up as ever." He gives me a wry smile. "I was trying, but..."

"Hey, hey," I murmur.

His eyes—sleepless, hunted—say what he can't.

Whatever hell I've been through this past week, it's been nothing compared to his.

"I'm sorry," he says. And this time, I have no choice but to believe him.

I sneak my hand in his. There's still grit from the rocks on his palm.

"I'm glad you're here," he says, giving my fingers a rough squeeze. "I hope I didn't—I wish—I mean, it's been over a year, I'm supposed to be—"

"You're not supposed to be *anything*," I interrupt. "It's not like there's an expiration date on any of this." I sigh. "It's messed up, but *you* didn't mess it up. It's not on you."

He turns to face me, full-on, taking my other hand in his, like he's making a solemn vow.

"I started feeling things," he says, "with you. Things I didn't think I'd feel again. And I lost myself in it, it was—I guess, a relief. But I won't ever, I won't ever—"

"You love her. It's okay."

"It's not," he says. "It's not fair to either of you."

"Fair?" I drop his hands, walk toward the water. "When did you expect anything to be fair?" I nudge rocks into a small pile with my toe. "I don't expect you to forget her. I don't expect anything."

"But you should, you deserve everything—"

"Just stop there!" I humph. "No one deserves *everything*, Charlie. Don't put me on a pedestal just so I'll be out of reach. Because that, *that* isn't fair."

"It's not as easy as—"

"Oh, come on, why not?" I'm looking at him now. His full lips slightly open, the almost imperceptible cleft in his chin.

"What?"

"It doesn't have to be hard."

I go to him, raise myself on my toes, and press my lips lightly against his, quick and matter-of-fact—like a handshake, but with lips. "What's easier than that?"

He kisses me back, ragged and searching and full of long, white urgency. Not like a handshake at all.

"I can't promise I'll be able to put all that behind me," he says.

"I know," I say. "You have stuff. Everyone does. Just don't shut me out."

"Okay," he says, but he still seems wary. "I can't promise I'll be the person you want me to be."

"No promises," I agree. "Got it. And for the record, I want you to be *you*. I want you to be my friend."

"Hmmm." He scratches his chin, and smiles in a way that changes everything—my mood, his mood, what can happen between us. "Do you kiss all your friends that way?"

I snort—and the sound of it surprises me. I'm not sure if it's nerves or relief, but I feel a little-kid restlessness jolt through me.

"Just the ones with your lips," I say, moving my face closer to his, as if I'm going in for the kiss, but instead I give him a quick grin, pull back, and skip away down the path. He follows, and my skip turns into a sprint.

"Hey!" He laughs, following fast, and before I can blink, we're running again.

Eighteen

November 5. Charlie is eighteen today. My age. The age Jamie was when she died. All three of us the same.

The same, except Jamie will be eighteen forever.

When a person dies, they're frozen in time. Frozen at who they were when they died.

So Jamie is frozen in goodness. She is always and forever the girl who makes time for the loser, misfit kid. *Want to hang this afternoon?*

Should it tell us something that Kyle thought an offer of pot would appeal to me, when all he asked of Jamie was a sympathetic ear? Yet, she is the one who answers his text, spends her afternoon beside him in that field while he rattles on about his problems. She is forever Charlie's adorable girlfriend. Older than us, at least then, but with a little-girl innocence about things like boys with crowbars.

I see her sometimes in that field, Kyle's boot coming down at her head. I can't know what she was thinking, but I wonder.

Was she angry? Confused? Did she try to fight back? Was she so scared she could only scream? If she'd had jujitsu training would she have made *him* cry for mercy? Would she have had any mercy to spare?

I can believe she forgave him. I can believe she was, at the moment of her death, the same girl she'd been all her life. A pure heart. If there was time for such things, she probably forgave.

Of course, she never had the chance to find out the kind of person she could become once she knew her life was disposable. There wasn't time for anger and fear to settle in, become part of her skin, of her breathing. She never walked the halls and saw her name on the boot of every boy she passed. She didn't even know she was a target. That some miserable asshole jerked off at the thought of his hands squeezing her neck until she went limp.

Jamie. Forever eighteen.

Charlie seems totally okay with the whole birthday thing. I don't think he's done the math, and I'm not about to bring it up. Ever since his reappearance by the river, he's been his old self. Charming, funny. Fine. He hasn't cut out. There have been some moments when he seemed sad, maybe, but nothing major.

When Halloween came, for example, he said he was maybe coming down with something and asked if I was okay going without him to Desiree Ballou's party. Which of course I was. Lindsey and I made a pretty awesome Wonder Woman/Vampire Queen duo, though she was more of a Vampire-Pirate Queen because she insisted on spicing up the black with a pink bandanna and a necklace made out of skeleton keys.

But afterward, Charlie never actually got sick. Maybe it was just a false alarm. Maybe he needed some alone time. Or maybe he was busy mourning his dead girlfriend.

Sometimes when we talk, there's a fogginess I can't cut through. I haven't told him yet about Lindsey's blue bear and Taylor's strawberry candy—or how Todd visited Kyle in jail and how Lindsey and I stalked Todd. I'm pretty sure he'd just go off and do something stupid involving his fists slamming into Todd's face. Plus, bringing it up now, after all this time has passed, just seems stupid.

Charlie said I should go out to dinner with his parents for his birthday, but I'm not about to set myself up for an hour of uncomfortable chewing, followed by who knows what—cake, communal singing, balloons. I don't particularly enjoy celebrating my own birthday, and that's with presents.

When I met them last week, I might as well have carried around a big neon sign reading UNCOMFORTABLE GIRL WHO LIKES KISSING YOUR SON.

Hello, Mrs. Hunt. Hello, Mr. Hunt. Smiles, smiles. Yes, thank you for the iced tea.

They were the kind of couple my mom would call attractive, but to me they just look like long-faced people in cardigans with identical brown-shoe-polish hair. Sometimes I think adults are from another country. The Land of Back

Aches and Broken Dreams. I drank my tea and tried not to make eye contact.

So I text Charlie that I'll see him *after* his birthday dinner. He says he'll come by for me around nine.

Between now and then, I have my own plans. There's something I need to do without him around.

Climb

At a quarter after six, I cruise by Charlie's house. His silver car is still parked out front by the curb, but his parents' minivan isn't in the driveway. Just in case, I park my Bug down the street, a throbbing blue thumb on an avenue of well-manicured fingers.

I check to make sure no one is looking, then shimmy around the chain link gate beside Charlie's house. Scooting down a narrow strip of grass, I slip into the Hunts' backyard. A large tree sprawls out in the far corner, where their fence meets the Strands'. Slats nailed in the oak's trunk make a sort of ladder leading up to a simple wooden platform, like a deck.

The sun has set, but it's not yet dark, and the branches make black veins in the sky. I slip across the yard and begin to climb.

The platform is farther up than it needs to be. I go fast, wanting to remain unseen, my hands gripping the rough slats.

I crane my neck back. Another four slats and there's a small hole in the floor of the tree house that I climb through. Pulling myself up, I kneel on the floor.

The boards are damp and now so are the knees of my jeans. I rub my hands, brittle with cold. I'm not sure why I've come.

Wet leaves, an old paperback of a Star Wars novel, a yellow plastic flashlight, and a pale blue lump of fabric.

Jamie's sweater.

Still on my knees, I crawl closer and inspect the lump. The fabric is sour, like something that's gotten wet, then dried stiff in the slow heat, then gotten wet again. A small bloom of mildew accents two splotches of whitish goo. Bird stuff, probably. A queasiness rises in me as I watch a dozen or more black bugs scuttling across the sweater's surface, vanishing into the folds.

Is this why I came? To see what Charlie had seen. To see what sent him back.

It's not my place, I know, but I pick up the sweater anyway. I stand and, with force, shake the bugs off. They make a random *put-put-put* as they smack against the wooden rail of the tree house. A few are flung against my jeans leg and one by one I flick them off.

The sweater was pretty once—a light, summery V-neck with a dainty crochet ruffle down the front, where the buttons meet. There's a hole near one shoulder, and another at the waistline in the back. I take a leaf and scrub across the splotch of bird crap, trying to rub it off, but I only smear it around.

This was worn by a living girl, I tell myself. Charlie would have touched it. Unbuttoned it, maybe. Pushed it off her shoulders.

I look at my hands—wet, dirty, cold—then carefully fold the sweater, trying unsuccessfully to press out its wrinkles, and place it back where it had been.

But that isn't right either, is it, just leaving it there on the rough boards? A small blue package of grief.

I think of all the people who wrote to Jamie in the funeral home guest book. *You're with the angels now*, and *Your life touched us all*, and a hundred other words that essentially say the same thing: *Your existence had meaning*.

Because we all want to think we have a purpose, right? That we're here for a reason. But if Kyle had gotten me instead, if I was already dead, what would my great purpose have been?

Is it pitiful that I don't know? That I haven't figured out yet why I was put on this earth?

So kill me now, and there's no answer. No reason. But I bet people would still write on my page, *Your existence had meaning*. Because they want to believe it so badly. We're all desperate for something so senseless to make sense.

Jamie should have had an entire lifetime to figure out why she was here, what she was doing. She should have been able to grow up—to grow *old*—before needing to make her beautiful mark on the world.

My cheeks are cold and damp. It's only when I brush the wetness with the back of my hand that I realize it's tears. I'm not a crier, but something like a sob escapes my mouth. I don't know what makes me sadder. The waste of Jamie's life. Or the impossibility of ever letting her death go.

The Sweater

I take it with me. It won't fit in my jacket pocket, so I tie its
arms around my waist as I climb down in the dark.

Pucker Up

Charlie texts me at 8:50 to say he'll be about a half hour late. I plop on the bed with a sigh of relief. Since I got home, I've been running like a gerbil on a wheel—showering, dressing, doing my hair and makeup, wrapping up Charlie's present.

Jamie's sweater, stiff and sour, is sprawled on the trunk at the foot of my bed. I'm not sure why I brought it here. I have a bad habit of picking at scabs.

I roll over. Beside the sweater sits a useless purple stuffed frog Sander won at the Midland Fair and, on top of the frog's fat front feet, the Martin Trundel poetry book. It occurs to me that I should have returned it by now; I'm not sure why I haven't. Forgetfulness in general? Or the specific desire to forget all the weirdness with Jared?

At any rate, Jared's been back in our gym class for a week now, and there really hasn't been any weirdness, anyway. We say hi. He jokes in that mildly goofball way of his. I gave him a ride home on Thursday. No drama, thank goodness.

I pick up the book, too, and stuff it in my purse.

Then, because I have fifteen extra minutes, I start fooling with my makeup again, so by the time I finish, it's way too much of everything.

Before blotting, I make a kiss-face and text Lindsey a selfie.

> Pucker up, beyotch!

RED!!! I like red.

Baloons are red.

> Why yes, they are.

clownnoses!starberries. Tricks are red.

Robet's truck is red. lol

> Are you drunk?

no

Are you high?

...

It's TUESDAY.

I am too.

What?

Where are you?

with very nice boy named max.

He has a cat in his room but no one is

spposed to know.

What?

hidden cat. Like Ann Frsnk.

He is peeing

Lindsey, what's going on?

cat not peeing. max peeing.

Who is Max?

I am lovely.

Max has a tattoo around his arm.

It is keltic. And beuatiful. Boutiful.

The hell. I all words re

Where are you?

> Im stil young and pretty.
> Fuk Robert

> Where are you? Tell me
> your address.

> Shhhh

She attaches a picture of a furry gray blob with ears.

Downstairs, the doorbell rings. I hear the floor creak where Mom goes to answer it. I yell down the steps, "GIVE ME A MINUTE, 'KAY?"

I dial Lindsey's number.

"Helloooo." She sounds airy. Definitely high.

"Hey, where are you, honey?" I ask.

"I'm right here."

"Okay. Um, where did you meet Max?"

"He came to the store." Her voice lowers to a whisper. "He's a college boy."

There's only one college in town, but I make sure. "Midland?"

"He has a lava lamp."

"You're in his room?"

"Yep."

"What's the building called?"

"Something someone president. I don't know. The cat's on me." Lindsey's voice goes up into baby talk. "Who's a pretty kitty?"

"What room are you in?"

"Twenty."

"You remember exactly? Twenty?"

"Because Max is twenty. It was soooo funny."

"Okay. Should I come get you?" I ask.

"Shhh." And then, like she's talking to someone else, "Hey!"

"Is that Max?" I ask.

"Yeah." She giggles.

"Hey, Lindsey, could you hand the phone to Max for a sec?"

"Whaaat?"

"Just give him the phone, okay?"

I hear some muffled discussion and then a male voice. "Hey?"

"Um, hi," I say. "I'm Lindsey's friend. She sounds a little out of it."

"You could say that," Max says. He laughs, but not in a crass way. I try to take that for a good sign.

"Are you...um, yeah, this is a little weird, but..." I keep talking, trying to find the right words. "She's on something, right, and—"

"Super skunk! Fucking awesome!"

"Okay, so maybe—" I start, but he doesn't hear me.

279

There's the sound of the phone clattering, and then Max's voice. "You starting, wildcat?"

Then Lindsey giggling. Then raspy kiss sounds, a couple *baby*'s, a thump, and the line goes dead.

I try to call back but go straight to voicemail.

The Creepiest Thing

When I get downstairs, Charlie is sitting in an armchair across from my dad in the living room that no one ever uses. I don't know who looks less comfortable.

Apparently it's *me*, because both my dad and Charlie say at the same time, "Are you okay?"

"Yeah." I paste on a smile. "Yeah, of course. Ready?"

Charlie stands just as my mom comes into the living room holding out a glass of ginger ale. Charlie looks like he doesn't know whether to take the glass, which was clearly meant for him. What is it with parents and their drink-peddling? I need to get out of this place. I take Charlie's hand before he can accept the glass and tug him to the door.

"See you guys later," I chirp, and we're out, heading to the car.

As I fling open the passenger door, Charlie holds me back. "Hey." He turns me around so I'm facing him. "What's up?"

"Let's just go," I say.

"Okay." He looks into my eyes. No fog this time. "You're really okay?"

I nod and give him a brief, reassuring peck on the lips. "Let's go," I repeat, and climb in the car.

He comes around, buckles himself in. "So...where do you want to go?"

"It's your birthday, you choose," I say.

"Okay. But first, how about you tell me what's bugging you?"

"It's that obvious?"

"Well, I do have eyes." He smiles and takes my hand. "For what it's worth, I have ears, too." He leans in, whispering, "They actually work pretty well for listening, you know, when people talk. You, especially. They especially like listening to you. They think you have a pretty voice."

"Your ears like me?"

"Don't make me say it again," he teases, then drops all teasing. "So, what's up?"

"I'm just—worried, I guess," I say. "I talked to Lindsey, and she's at some college guy's dorm. She's wasted and he's wasted and she's being reckless. But I don't even know where she is exactly."

"He's not, like, forcing—"

"No, not like that. Just—whatever. But the thing is, when I was being reckless, when it was me, I had *her* to look out for me. She was there. And me—I don't know what to do, Charlie."

"Call her."

"Her phone's off."

"Should we find her?"

"I don't know. Maybe?" If Lindsey is looking to get naked with some college guy, who am I to interrupt? It's not my place to go all judge-y on her. Even so, I can't help thinking this might turn out to be a huge mistake. Or worse. I don't even know this guy's name. He could do anything. He could get violent—

Okay, I'm probably being paranoid. But it can't hurt to check on her, right?

"Yeah, maybe," I tell Charlie.

Charlie starts the car. "So, how do we find her?"

"Look, it's your birthday. We should probably just—"

"No, really. My cousin Kayla goes to Midland. It's small, and she's pretty social. I bet she can help us. Do we have any clues? Anything you remember?"

"Let's see. The guy's name is Max. He's twenty. That means he's probably . . . a junior, right? He's in room twenty of a dorm that might or might not be named after a president. He has a secret cat. Um, yeah, that's it."

Charlie texts something into his phone, then starts driving toward the college.

When his phone bleeps, he hands it to me. "That might be Kayla."

It's not. It's Mark. I put it facedown on the seat, trying not to read it because, you know, I'd rather not be *that* girl.

The next bleep is Kayla.

> Sounds like Max Tieger. He's in Roosevelt. The one next to the tennis courts. When are you going to give me my frisbee back, little cuz? I miss that frisbee.

"We have a destination. She's in the dorm by the tennis courts," I tell Charlie. "And your cousin wants her Frisbee."

"Yeah, figures," Charlie says. "She's been harping on that Frisbee since I was eight."

"Must be a pretty special Frisbee."

"She just likes to mess with me," Charlie says. "Sometimes I wish..."

"What?"

"I wish I had a sister. You know."

"Really?" Both Charlie and I are the only kids in our families. Sure, I'd wondered sometimes what it might be like to have a brother or sister, but I'd never *wanted* one. It seemed like enough just keeping up with my own life, much less having to worry about some other little version of my parents' mixed genes running around town.

"What? Haven't you?" Charlie asks.

"No way! It's probably selfish of me—okay, it's *definitely* selfish of me—but I like having my own space. I like having a hairbrush that doesn't have any one else's hair clogged in it. I like not worrying about anyone touching my stuff."

"What, like this?" Charlie pokes my purse on the seat beside me. And again. And again.

"Are you trying to piss me off?" I ask.

"Is it working?" He grins.

"Just focus on your driving, okay."

"Bossy," he razzes me.

"Touchy," I razz back.

He snorts. "Maybe I don't need a sister. I've got you."

"Okay, for the record: *I don't need a sister, I've got you* might be the creepiest thing anyone has ever said to their date. Like, ever."

"Ewww." He makes a face. "You know what I meant."

"I'm still putting it on a trophy and presenting it to you on Shame the Boyfriend Day."

"Is that what I am?" He turns, pulling into the tennis court parking lot at the college. "Does that mean I'm your boyfriend?"

He parks, turns off the car. And in the silence that comes, I feel a blush rise to my cheeks.

"Ummm..." I say.

"What?" He pushes my hair back from my face.

"We should go check on Lindsey," I say, opening the car and bolting for the dorm.

I'm five steps ahead of him on the path, and when I reach the entrance, I yank the door handle, but it's locked.

"Well. What now?"

Charlie catches up, tries the door. "We wait," he says. "Someone's bound to come in or out soon."

I try Lindsey's phone again, on the off chance I can get through, but no dice. Three college girls pass through the grass on their way to somewhere else. I might be paranoid, but I'm pretty sure the one in the yellow dress gives me stink eye.

"Do we look suspicious or something?" I ask.

"We should make out," Charlie says.

"Well, that's an excellent suggestion," I say, meaning *not*. "Good to know you got your head in the game."

"Seriously." He gives me a nudge. "We have to wait anyway, and people ignore people who are making out. We won't look as suspicious as just standing around." He moves closer, pressing me against the brick wall beside the door. The warmth of his breath at my ear is like its own drug. "Plus, it's kind of amazing," he adds.

"What?"

"Kissing you."

Then he does. And yeah, it is amazing.

We break for breath and I give a contented sigh. "Someone should bottle your lips," I say. "Like make an elixir or something."

"*That*—what you just said there—is now officially the creepiest thing ever uttered on a date." His voice is low, teasing. "I pass my trophy to you."

"What!" I protest.

"Sorry, I don't make the rules. Lips in a bottle beat the imaginary sister thing."

"That is so not fair."

"Nothing I can do, lip-girl. It's not my decision to make." He nuzzles my neck. "But as long as we're turning body parts into elixir, I think I'll take your earlobes." He gives one a nibble, which simultaneously tickles and makes my insides flash with a blind, ambiguous need.

Just then, a boy with headphones and a long orange scarf pushes open the door from the inside. Charlie grabs the door before it closes, and, nodding to the guy, ushers me quickly inside.

"Okay." I shake my head clear. "Room twenty, room twenty," I mutter, checking down the hallway to the right. *Two, four, six...* and after two left turns and an accidental sighting of a half-naked guy coming out of the showers, *twenty.*

I put my ear to the door, trying not to feel so young and foolish, hoping I'll hear something that will tell me this is the right thing, that I'm not overreacting, that Lindsey needs me and I'm not a mother hen for being here. I can't hear anything, though, so I raise my fist and knock.

There's no response. I knock again and call, "Lindsey? You in there?"

When I still get nothing, I rattle the door handle. It isn't locked and the door sways open, making a painfully loud creak.

The room is small enough that I can see right away it's empty. Messy bunk beds, messy desk. A gray cat looks up from its perch at the windowsill. Lava lamp on the floor beside an incense burner. On the wall, hand-drawn cartoons on torn loose-leaf paper, a few stray photographs stuck through with pushpins, a world map, a not-great semi-realistic painting of Jimi Hendrix, an old movie poster with Marilyn Monroe and two guys in drag. In the nook by the door, smelly cleats and guy stuff.

But no Lindsey.

"Hey," Charlie calls to a guy passing in the hall. "You know where Max is?"

The guy shakes his head and keeps walking, but from behind us a voice calls, "Y'all looking for Maxy?"

We turn to find a big guy in flip-flops, hairy legs, trimmed beard, shiny shaved head. "He's in The Cave. He and that little honey badger." The guy pushes past us and into the room. He's large, so the room suddenly seems twice as small. "I'm Everett. Max's roommate. Charmed." He flops on the bottom bunk and extends his hand like maybe he expects us to kiss it.

"Nice to meet you." I take his hand and shake it, trying not to be as awkward as I feel. "What's The Cave?"

"A sandwich shop. In the basement of the student center. The food is nasty, but it stays open late, so."

"Thank you," I say, and start to leave.

"If you find Maxy, remind him it's open mic night," he calls after us, then laughs like it's some inside joke.

The Cave

The Cave is, as it turns out, not at all cave-like. Instead, I might think we wandered into an oversized game of Twister. Multicolored circles are painted in random order on bright white walls. A dozen round tables with matching padded stools, also multicolored, fill the white tile floor. In one corner, a counter is set up with a chalkboard menu behind it. In the other, a girl in ripped jeans and a green stocking hat howls and strums her guitar.

There are only twenty or so people in the room, so it's easy enough to spot Lindsey. She is a brilliant disaster, her hair dyed pale pink since I last saw her, thick blue eyeliner, mustard smudged on her cheek. She's wrapped around an unwashed, skinny guy that might as well have *trouble* tattooed on his forehead. He's holding her wrist with one hand, gutting a sub sandwich with the other. With his fingers, he digs out messy hunks of shaved meat and stuffs some in his mouth, some in Lindsey's. It's like a messed-up version of that thing where brides and grooms feed each other wedding cake, but grosser.

"Hey!" I walk up to her table and, without asking, take a seat. Charlie, quiet, letting me lead, sits beside me.

"Hahahaha." Lindsey's laugh is almost mechanical, a possessed windup doll. A few bits of chewed meat spray out. "What are you doing here?"

Step One, detach her from Max. Step Two, get her somewhere she can sleep it off.

"I need to talk with you," I say. "It's important."

"What? Why?" Her eyes, even through the glaze of the drugs, turn soft with worry. "Are you okay? Sweetie?" Here she is, worrying about me, bless her. It's like a person who just tumbled down a ravine asking the person passing if they need help up the trail.

"I just want to talk with you." I glance at the dirty-haired guy beside her. "Sorry," I say, standing, "I'm gonna take Lindsey for a while."

Charlie stands, too.

"Sure. Yeah," Max says, but he doesn't let go of her wrist.

I take Lindsey's other hand and tug her up. "Come on. We can talk out there," I say, gesturing to the door leading outside.

The guy still doesn't let go, but I think it's more because he's out of it than that he's actually trying to hold on. I tilt my head, silently asking for Charlie's help, and he reaches over and gently unplucks the stoner's fingers from Lindsey's wrist.

Together we pull her through the double doors leading outside. The air is cool. I wrap my arm around Lindsey's shoulder. "Hey, so what did you take?"

"What? What? I smoked some pot," she says. "What's up?"

"I'm just worried."

"Why? What do you think's going to happen?"

"Nothing, maybe. I don't know. You could get hurt. That guy," I say. "Do you *know* him?"

"Does knowing him even matter?" Her eyes get a blurry look. "We all *knew* Kyle." She starts to laugh, like that's the funniest joke in the world—then her eyes refocus on Charlie. Staring, she covers her mouth. "Oh God. Sorry. I didn't mean it like that."

Charlie blanches. Which is saying something for a boy who's normally pretty pale to begin with. "It's okay," he says.

But we all know it's not okay.

It hasn't been entirely okay for any of us, not for a long time. I feel tired with the "not okay-ness" of it all. Is it really my job to worry that every boy we pass on the street or smoke pot with in some dorm or sit next to in a coffee shop will hurt me or someone I love? Is that what it means to be a girl?

"Do you want to go back in there?" I ask her. "Do you want to be with that guy?"

Her eyes are weak-tea brown, drenched with an unfo-cused longing. She shakes her head.

"Let's get you home, then," I say.

Charlie rounds over to Lindsey's other side and gently takes her elbow in his. Together, the three of us walk across the beautiful, manicured college lawn toward the dark dome of sky.

Perv

We drop off Lindsey with her sister at Willow Ridge. Mrs. Barrow is out as usual, but Veronica is sprawled on the couch in the living room, her laptop open on the coffee table and a celebrity dance show blaring on the TV.

"I'm hungry!" Lindsey mumbles as she plops her bottom on her sister's feet at the end of the couch.

"Ow!" Veronica complains. "Get off!"

"Don't be such a party pooper!" Lindsey says sweetly, stretching her body out so she's head to toe with her sister.

"Get your feet out of my face!" Veronica barks. "Geez!" She sits up, snapping her laptop closed, then roughly pushes Lindsey's feet off the couch.

"And you want one of those?" I half whisper to Charlie.

He shrugs. I toss Lindsey's car keys to Veronica.

"Don't let her drive," I say. I found Lindsey's Toyota in the tennis court parking lot. Instead of leaving it parked at the college, I drove it to the apartments, and Charlie followed in his car.

"I'm not her mother," Veronica says.

"Just hold on to the keys until tomorrow morning, all right?"

Veronica glowers, but she pockets the keys. "Whatever."

"This is the funniest show," Lindsey half laughs, half mumbles. "Like, why are they dancing?"

I squat down so I'm face-to-face with Lindsey. "Charlie and I are going to take off now. You should get some sleep."

"Do you have any Doritos?" she asks.

"Nope," I say, "no Doritos. Go on to sleep, and I'll see you tomorrow, okay?"

"Okay."

Outside, Charlie and I walk to the car, hand in hand. "That was very patient of you," I say. "Sorry for screwing up your birthday."

"You didn't." He grins. "And anyway, it's not over yet."

"True," I say. "Which reminds me!" I reach around in my bag, grab the Trundel book, and put it in his hands. "Jared gave me this to return. Happy birthday from you to you! And then there's this." From my back pocket, I pull out a tiny wrapped package, a little bigger than a stick of gum, and place it on top of the book.

He takes the miniature package and holds it up to his ear to give it a pretend rattle. "Let me guess. An itsy-bitsy Yoda tie?" he says. "A mysterious key? A very small, very flat pair of roller skates?"

I shake my head, laughing at his randomness. "Not even close."

"A ticket to the moon?"

"Warmer," I say.

"Hmmm..." He carefully peels back the tape on the wrapping paper and tidily, like he's opening a tiny door, unfolds the wrapping.

"Oh, man!" His eyes widen when he sees what's inside. "You're kidding me!"

Next weekend, the Virginia Tech Student Union is bringing in Bax Wilcox, a singer-songwriter Charlie loves. It's only about a forty-five-minute drive, so I got online when tickets went on sale and ordered two.

"Happy birthday!" I exclaim, suddenly nervous. "I got two, so you know, you and Mark could go...or whoever."

He chucks my chin, lifting my face so I can't avoid his eyes. "Would you and me be an option?"

"Huh?"

"Would you go with me?"

"Sure, I mean, if you want me to."

"Yeah, I want you to." His lips are breathy on my cheek when he whispers, "Mark's a great guy, but he doesn't have your ears."

"Again with the ears, you perv."

"Um, excuse me." He steps back and waves his arms in mock affront. "You act as if my quite natural admiration for your ears is somehow *dirty*, which, you know, is a clear indicator that you *yourself* are thinking something way perv-ier than me. It's a classic case of psychological transference. But that aside, I wasn't even talking about your ears' physical perfection. I was talking about your ears' ability to hear and appreciate music. Mark is tone-deaf. And his dance moves—well." He grimaces. "Yours, on the other hand..."

Whisking me into his arms, Charlie slow-dances with me in the parking lot. A car near us backs out and putters by, but he doesn't stop swaying with me. "Thank you for my birthday present," he whispers. "So, it's a date?"

I go light-headed from the nearness of his arms, his chest, that boy-smell that is warm and musky and a tiny bit sweet, like an overripe peach. "It's a date," I say and nestle into his chest.

Heart of Darkness

Our grief is our signature, with everyone dotting the *i* in their own special way.

You might think one moment that all is lovely, that you're done with the emptiness, the anger, the tears, that you never needed them in the first place. You might think one curve curls into another, which curls into another—life spiraling forward in the corkscrew of destiny.

But then the pain returns, more certain than before. It doesn't make sense, and it doesn't ask for your permission.

Here's a nickel of truth for you: It's sometimes painful to be in Charlie's presence. Usually not. Usually, he's sunshine on my back, the sweet surprise of wind in my face. But then rain patters down, and the cloud descends, dark and swirling.

When Charlie stood before me by the river and told me what a mess he was, he was really saying something else. The words under his words. *Even when I'm distant, don't leave.*

And yeah, he's not ignoring me this time, for which I'm grateful, but he's not exactly *here* either. Sometimes he stares out with grim, glassy eyes, and I can only guess what he's thinking.

I don't have to guess, though, on Wednesday afternoon when the subpoena for Kyle's sentencing hearing arrives at my front door. Charlie and I are upstairs in my room, supposedly prepping for Mr. Campbell's *Heart of Darkness* test. In reality, we're prepping for the Bax Wilcox concert this Friday—lying side by side on my floor, one earbud in his right ear, the other in my left.

Charlie waits upstairs when my mom calls me down. Apparently, since I'm a legal adult, the guy from the court has to give the subpoena directly to me.

"Here ya go!" the guy says as he places the envelope in my hand. "Have a lovely day!" In his pink-striped oxford and two-toned dress shoes, he seems awfully chipper for a Messenger Boy of Doom.

"So, the date's been set," I say as I flop on my bed, open envelope in hand. "Two weeks from today. November twentieth." And then, in case he doesn't understand. "Kyle's hearing."

"I know," Charlie says, his voice small, like something on a faraway shelf.

"You know?" I ask.

"Yeah, Daniel got his yesterday. For the impact statement."

It takes me a second before I remember who Daniel

is—Jamie's older brother. The whole idea seems messed up, if you ask me. Her brother is supposed to stand up there in front of Kyle and talk about how he's been impacted by Jamie's death? I mean, of course, Jamie's death must have screwed him up, but—and I'm not trying to be cold here—why does that make a difference in Kyle's punishment?

Would Jamie's life be worth less if fewer people were "impacted"? I don't have a brother like Jamie, so would Kyle have been better off killing me? I don't get the math of it.

I've heard people say, when they find out about some violent thing done to a woman, "What if that happened to your mother or your sister?" And I always want to ask them, "But what if that happened to some ugly old bag-woman who drooled when she talked? What if no one loved her? Would that make it somehow okay? Does she only matter if she's someone else's sister or wife? What about *her*, just herself? Isn't that enough?"

For my part, the lawyer said we're there to show Kyle's state of mind prior to Jamie's murder. Lindsey and Taylor and me. I'm not sure if they're calling in Blair Mattern from Los Angeles or not. What are all of us supposed to prove, anyway? That Kyle was willing to kill whoever was most convenient? Joy.

After Jamie's murder, the school administration sent out an email to the entire student body with a link to a web article called "Tragedy in Your Community." They listed

Stages of Community Healing. I forget what the actual stages are, but I'm pretty sure for me so far it's gone something like this:

Stage 1: Freezing Out Friends
Stage 2: Drinking & Associated Acts of Stupidity
Stage 3: Hating Kyle
Stage 4: Pissed That I'm Not Over It Already
Stage 5: Guilty Because I'm Pissed
Stage 6: Pissed About Feeling Guilty
Stage 7: Seeking—?

That's as far as I've gotten.

Seeking—?

Question mark and all, because I'm not sure *what* it is I'm seeking. Justice? Safety? Maybe just to breathe without this *weight*. I don't know how else to describe it. Even in my happiest moments, there's something heavy in my chest. I hate what Kyle did, and I hate him for doing it. I hate that I don't get to skip out into the world with some misguided, carefree notion that people are good at heart and my own girl-ness is not a liability.

I'm not sure what the weight's made of, but if I had to guess, I'd bet it's one part anger, one part guilt, one part "horror," like that bonehead says in *Heart of Darkness*. Whatever, it just sits there, invisible, unspoken, between me and what might come.

There's a part in the novel where the main guy says,

"Your strength is just an accident arising from the weakness of others." In the book, he's talking about the way people have screwed over other people simply because they can. But that's not why I remember it. I remember it because I want to be strong.

It makes me wonder about what Kyle did. I mean, obviously he was *stronger* than Jamie. He took his physical strength and—his word—*bashed* her. But wasn't it really his weakness that was lashing out? He couldn't handle his life. He couldn't get out of town. He couldn't live with his own smallness and unimportance. He wanted to be famous, he wanted to rub his sad little brute self against the crust of the world and listen for the echo.

So if what I'm seeking is my own strength, is it possible—is it possible that in Kyle's wretched, vile, disgusting weakness, I might find, even by accident, some sort of strength?

Bird Outside

When Charlie picks me up for the Bax Wilcox concert, a jazzed-up version of Jared Hilley is riding shotgun. Since the car is a two-door coupe, Jared first has to climb out of the car and then squeeze into the back while I wait at the curb.

"Hope I'm not butting in," he says as he flops the passenger seat forward and pokes his literal butt in the direction of my face. "Charlie was kind enough to let me bum a ride. Bax Wilcox—DUDE! I'm amped!"

His long legs are folded way too tight in the back seat now and one knee is bopping up and down like it's on a spring. "This is okay with you, right?"

"What? Yeah! Of course," I lie, climbing in front and scooching up my seat to make more room for Jared.

I avoid eye contact with Charlie because I don't want him to see how disappointed I am. I'd been hoping this date might let me forget for a night about the upcoming trial and Kyle and *It's not your fault* and everything else that is sucky and scary and confusing in the world. I was hoping it might be, I don't know, *fun*.

"You got enough room back there?" I ask Jared. My knees are pressed against the glove box and there's really nowhere for me to go, so I'm hoping the answer is yes.

"Yes. Plenty of space back here for me and Mark."

"Mark?" I ask. I can't help it; I'm pretty sure I'm bug-eyed when I crane around to face Jared. I get no answer, so I ask again, turning to Charlie. "Mark?"

"Yeah." Charlie has the good grace at least to look uncomfortable. "You remember you met Ned, Mark's cousin? From the science museum? It ends up he won a ticket to the concert, but then he had to work, and he gave the ticket to Mark, and so we're carpooling. We're picking him up before we head out of town."

"Oh! Uh, cool!" I fake enthusiasm—but it's a genuine fake. I'm not trying to be sarcastic, though I'm afraid it might come off that way. And really, if it does, who could blame me?

It's not that I don't want Charlie to have time with his friends, I do. And already he seems less grim than he has for days, so that's a plus, right? But it doesn't mean I want to be stuffed into a car with the guy I kiss, a guy I kissed, and a guy who pretty much hates my guts.

I'm surprised when Charlie starts heading through the sketchy part of town on the way to Mark's house. At twilight, the river neighborhoods look old and cramped and quirky, but not in the good way. The house Charlie drives up to is small, with dingy lime-green siding and a dead bush beside the stoop. The porch light gives a weakish glow to the door, which looks like it was once a peach color, but is now chipped and blistery.

Mark has always seemed so polished, so perfectly creased. I can't imagine him walking out of that ramshackle door, but he does, looking as neat as ever. He's almost to the car when a short, thick woman appears on the stoop and calls him back to her. He turns, shoulders slumping in the way of the oppressed, and walks quickly back to the woman, who takes something from an apron pocket and presses it into his hands. He nods, puts it in his pocket. She reaches up to fiddle with his collar, but he pulls away and power-walks to the car.

I hop out and fold over the front seat, expecting him to climb into the back next to Jared, who has scooted to make room, but Mark just glares into space, irritated and clearly anxious to leave. The woman—his mother?—is still on the porch. I think about telling him to get in; I mean, really, why should I be the one in the back with Jared? But Mark's shoulders won't let me do it. The tense way they're curving in on themselves, like he's hiding some prickly thing under his shirt—he never stands like that at school.

Even if he isn't my favorite person, he maybe is Charlie's, and I don't have the heart to pick a fight with him in front of the woman, who is still standing on the porch, watching. So I keep my mouth shut and climb in next to Jared.

"I brought tunes," Jared says as Charlie starts to drive.

He passes his phone up to Charlie, who hooks it into the car's speakers. Bax Wilcox's gravelly voice wails:

> *I see your reflection*
> *When I first look through the window*
> *Bird outside, bird in*

"That guy's a freaking genius!" Jared fan-boys. There's not enough room for his knees to fit behind Charlie, so he's squeezed himself sideways in the car.

"Do you want to switch?" I ask him.

"What?"

I don't know if he didn't hear or if he's so into the music that he can't process a relatively simple question.

"There's more room over here," I try again, gesturing. "We should switch."

He bops his legs awkwardly, as if attempting to understand how we could possibly switch places in a space that's already so cramped.

"You scoot over here," I say, patting the middle part of the seat, "and I'll scoot over you."

Jared darts a look at the back of Charlie's head, then fixes his eyes on me. He gnaws his bottom lip, eyes my hips, and nods. He scoots over to the middle of the seat and his hand, by necessity, edges up against my thigh. I notice a slight tremor in the hand, and I regret saying anything. What does he think I'm offering? I should have just stayed put, but it's too late now.

I lift one leg over Jared's knees and put it down on the far side of the seat, then half standing, I chuck myself over him. It's pretty awkward, and yeah, for a second my butt jostles against his chest, but it's not even vaguely sexual. For the heat on Jared's face, though, you'd think it was.

Geez. Boys. What is wrong with their brains?

I try to play it off by talking about whatever random thing comes to mind.

"So I wonder how Bax Wilcox comes up with his lyrics," I say. "I mean, how does someone just come up with a song out of nothing? It seems impossible. How do *you* do it, Jared?" As the words are already spluttering out of my mouth, I realize how immensely stupid they are. The one song I know for sure Jared has written is about me. And what if that's it? What if he hasn't written anything else? So is it possible I've just asked him to tell me about what inspired that song? Oh no, please, no. "I mean—" I rush on in a classic attempt to cover awkward talk with *more* awkward talk. "—anyone. How does anyone do that? I mean, hypothetically speaking."

Jared grins, giving me a cocky come-hither look, like his hand never trembles and his face never blushes and he's certain I'm mouth-vomiting because I'm turned on by his mere presence. Ugh.

Why again am I not in the front seat? Charlie and Mark are up there having their own little boy-conference, which is impossible to hear over the music, and I'm stuck back here with the Hormone.

"Hey!" I poke my head in the space between the front seats. "What's the name of this song?" I half shout over the music, interrupting whatever Charlie and Mark were talking about.

"Um..." Charlie glances at Jared's phone, as he turns onto the highway on-ramp. "Infinity."

"Thanks," I say. How appropriate. Infinity. The length of this ride.

I look out the car window. It's just darkening into night, and the lights in town have that special glow. Beautiful, but we pass too quickly to take them in. Each one is gone in a blink, replaced by another, that is in turn replaced by another, until we hit the gap of mountains between towns and it's all dark hills against a not-yet-black sky.

If we're stuck here forever, I suppose we have to do something to pass the time.

"What's your favorite stupid joke?" I ask Jared.

"Um...huh?"

"It's a long ride, JJ," I say. "Tell me a stupid joke."

"Uh, okay." He strokes his chin-hair, considering. "You said stupid, right?"

I nod.

"Okay, then," he continues. "You asked for it. Knock, knock."

"Who's there?"

"Oswald," he says.

"Oswald who?"

"Oswald my chewing gum."

I laugh, probably more than the joke deserves, but that's kind of the point, isn't it? "Knock, knock," I say.

"Who's there?" Jared answers.

"Sherwood," I say.

"Sherwood who?"

"Sherwood like to have another piece."

He looks at me blank.

"Of gum," I explain. "Since you swallowed it. Another piece of chewing gum."

We both snicker. Thankfully, nothing kills misguided sexual tension like a bad knock-knock joke.

"Oh, oh," I say, remembering. "I got one. Knock, knock."

"Who's there?"

"Interrupting cow."

"Interrupting cow—"

"Moooooo!" I interrupt. I can tell the moment it clicks in his head, and we crack up.

The Awesomeness of Music

By the time we get to Virginia Tech, Jared and I are giggling like ten-year-olds over pretty much anything—drunk on bad jokes and loud music. Because even though Jared sometimes wears the air of Sleazy Country Boy, it's just air. Like a crappy cologne he doesn't have the sense to wash off. Underneath all that bravado and nonsense, I believe he's basically a smart and decent human being. There's goodness in him. He just doesn't know what to do with it.

"What have you guys been up to back there?" Mark asks as we spill from the car. "Sniffing glue?"

Apparently, references to glue sniffing are also funny, because Jared and I just keep giggling.

"Okaaaaay," Charlie says, taking my hand. "The concert's in Burruss, right? It's this way."

He leads us across the parking lot, between some buildings and across part of a vast lawn to the entrance of a huge, castle-like stone building. Inside the auditorium, the seats are assigned. Charlie and I are supposed to sit about halfway back in the middle section, Mark near the front, and Jared on the left side near the back. The opening act, a folk rock band, has already started. The seats are pretty packed, so instead of making people move to get to our seats, we find a few empty seats near one another toward the back on the left side. Two in front, which Jared and Mark take, and two behind for Charlie and me.

The warm-up band, which Jared tells us comes out of Floyd County, is good. Lots of adrenaline-pumping banjo and electric guitar and a little blond girl who couldn't be older than twelve playing the kind of fiddle you'd expect from a bearded coal miner. When Bax Wilcox walks out on stage, though, the real party starts. Everyone stands and whoops and holds up their cell phones to take pictures.

Before long, the music shifts something in me, breaks it loose. Even though there isn't room to dance, I'm dancing. Charlie's dancing. Jared, in front and slightly to our right, is dancing. Even Mark is flailing about in a jerky kind of way. We're all singing along, though the loudness of the speakers makes it seem like Bax's voice is coming out of our mouths.

The sound, heat, lights, our bodies—everything is about *being*. It's all life and breath and making noise. All sweat and sensation. All love for humankind. The college girl on my other side bumps hips with me, but I don't mind. We're in this together. I'm almost *too* alive. When Bax howls out about the baby his girlfriend lost, I howl, too, like I was the lost baby. When he shouts about the fire of love, I feel it ignite in my chest.

Charlie leans down and kisses me and I want to drown in it right here and now. Because it's so passionate and so perfect, and I know what waits on the other side of that kiss.

This feeling—the rise and surge of it—is too much to be contained by everyday.

And I know, I know that one minute, he'll be everywhere, all in my head and on my lips and against my skin. I'll be the stars he sleeps under at night. Intense like that. And the next day, without warning, he'll be so distant I have to use a telescope just to find his eyes.

And that's okay. I can't blame him. I'm not the one he mourns. I'm not the dream ghost with her perfect sawdust cupcakes and her grave.

But hear this, heart! Hear this, head! With Charlie's hand on my waist and his song at my shoulder, I'm not holding back anymore. I'm not going to regret a single dance, a single kiss.

Even if he isn't my One. Even if there is no such thing as a One.

Because there is such a thing as now. And for now, I'm alive.

That's not my fault. It's not my burden.

Lindsey

So you dumbledore that night?

Um?

Autocorrect, barge! I turned it back on
and this is what I get.

Your phone loves HP, Linds.

You can't stop the wizard love.

Do you remember that night
when we were at Matt's party?

Yes.

When was that?

A while ago. End of September?

Like when?

Will check.

September 20

Why?

Oh.

??

I need to talk.

We are talking.

No, for real. Come over.

Lindsey answers the door in her pajamas, eyes swollen. Her mom is home, back in her bedroom, but the apartment always feels crowded when I know her mom is here. Not that there's any less space, just more electrons bouncing off the walls.

"You want to go out to the coffee shop?" I ask, but Lindsey swipes her mouth with the back of her hand, like she ate something messy, or she's trying to keep a burp in, and then leads me back to her bedroom.

She curls on her bed, making room for me at her feet.

"What's up?" I ask her.

"I think something horrible happened," she says. "When I was at Matt's party, I was wearing those white shorts, remember?"

"I guess," I say.

"*I* remember. I love those shorts. I only wear those when I know I won't have my period. This I'm sure of, because you didn't really know me then, but in seventh grade, I was wearing a white skirt and I started my period and we had a substitute in Ms. Mosley's civics class, and she wouldn't let me go to the bathroom and I was bleeding through, and David Sirrine...was David Sirrine."

"That little turd."

314

"Yeah, well, now I only wear white if I'm *sure* I'm not going to start. So, that was the end of September, right? Which means it was over a month and a half ago when I had my last period."

"Crap, Lindsey, don't you keep better track than that?"

"No. It just, you know, it's pretty regular, but generally my life doesn't revolve around my menstrual calendar, sorry."

"A month and a half? Gah! You're not—" I lower my voice, aware that Mrs. Barrow is only two rooms away. "You're not pregnant?"

Lindsey doesn't answer. She just cradles a hand to her stomach and moans.

"Sweetie." I rub her bare feet and up her ankle and shin. "Oh, sweetie," I say, not really thinking about what I'm saying, just trying to make comforting sounds, as if I were talking to a sick cat.

"N-nooo." Lindsey shakes her head and pushes herself up. She puts her hand on mine, stilling it. "It's not that."

"You're *not* pregnant?" I ask.

She shakes her head.

"Then what?"

"I think I *was*," she splutters. Bending forward, drawing up her knees. "I started bleeding this week, but it was, you know, weird. Too red, and the cramps were pretty bad. But I just thought it was my period. Like maybe late, but it was more spotty. I didn't really think about it. But then, last night, it was—different, a clump. And I knew something was weird about it. It was, you know, not normal, kind of translucent. It was—I'm pretty sure it was—" She stops, takes a deep breath.

I lean in and give her a hug. Her shoulders shake as, noiselessly, she sobs. "Oh, Lindsey," I say, not sure why she's crying.

"I think I must have been—I didn't even know—I lost, I lost it," she whimpers.

"Uh—" I start to say, thinking, *It's not like you* wanted *a baby, right? At our age...?* But I'm getting better at listening to shoulders. I swallow my words, pat her back gently, and murmur, "It'll be all right."

That seems pretty feeble, though. *It'll be all right?* How the hell could I possibly know that? I have no clue what's coming—and whether what comes is all right or not isn't necessarily up to me.

Lindsey keeps weeping, like she's the one lost. Her sobs come out muffled against my shoulder, hiccup-y, but still way too intense. The arm of my shirt is damp now with something, and I'm not sure if it's snot or tears.

I switch to "Shhh, shhh," though I'm not sure that's any better. Isn't that like telling her to shut up?

"It was—was—I didn't even know—and now it's gone." She draws out the *go-o-o-o-ne* like a country singer.

"Shhhhhhhh." I'm saying it for real now because the last thing I need is for her mom to come in.

I have to ask. "You would have wanted it, then—a baby?"

She pulls back and squints at me, like I'm the too-bright light on the other side of a dark room.

"I don't know." Her voice is careless. She tries to work up a smile. "Maybe not."

I give my head the tiniest shake. The shake that says, *You don't have to put on a smile for me when your heart is ingesting itself.* The smile slips from her wet face like it was made of oil.

"It's probably hormones," she mumbles, going back into the hug.

"It's okay." I pet her hair. "It'll be all right."

Kyle's sentencing starts this week—with Lindsey and Taylor and me scheduled to testify on Wednesday morning. Whatever this sadness is, I know it's the last thing Lindsey needs right now. I rock her gently, and wonder how we're going to find the strength we need to stand up there and face our would-be killer.

Eve

The night before I have to be at the courthouse, Charlie stays late in my room, door shut. My father is uncharacteristically okay with this. Perhaps the catatonic-squirrel vibe I've been giving off for the last couple of days has convinced him that I'm better off with company—or maybe he's just convinced I'm currently incapable of carnal relations.

Lying down, I curl on my side and Charlie curls around me, a question mark in a question mark. The small lamp on my bedside table casts a dim cone of light that doesn't fully reach either one of us. He fiddles with my ear.

"When he killed her," Charlie says, his voice wavering between a whisper and a choke, "it's like he killed me, too. But I had to keep breathing. I was supposed to protect her, but I didn't even see it coming. And the worst part was— the worst part"—his hand stills, and I feel the tension in him, like he's made of electric wire—"she must have hurt so much. She didn't have to hurt like that."

I reach up and my fingers find Charlie's forearm. I pull

his arm around me, then trace the veins on his wrist. I don't know the words to say, so I just hold him and hope my hands can somehow speak how sorry I am.

"I hope he fries."

"What?" My hand stills.

"Kyle."

Charlie breaks away, sits up on the bed, leaning away from me, elbows on his knees. "He should suffer, like he made her suffer. *Worse*. It should be worse." He looks back over his shoulder, and his eyes make a flat space in the center of the room.

I've had the same thought. But how could anything they do to Kyle be worse? It's not like they're going to rape him and shove a crowbar down his esophagus. No matter what, they aren't going to bash his skull in and ditch him by the side of the road.

Yet, hearing Charlie say it out loud—hearing him *wish* Kyle dead—seems cold. Like *he's* the killer.

I've known all along what this trial is about. But I've been focused on my part, having to see Kyle again, having to stand there and speak. I've tried to block out everything else—what comes tomorrow, or the day after tomorrow, when they decide whether Kyle lives or dies.

"You think he should be executed?" I ask Charlie.

He looks at me like there can only be one answer.

A life for a life.

A jagged sort of logic. What Kyle did can't be undone. What other end could it come to?

I shift toward him. "Is that what Jamie would have wanted?"

He turns so I can't see his face and shrugs. "I don't know. She was—I can't say what she would have wanted." He sighs. "But it might have been better for her if she hadn't been so nice."

I curl back into my question mark, facing the wall. Close my eyes.

All this year, I've been playing what happened over and over in my head. Like one of those times, I could make it different. I could do something or not do something, and it would all be changed. The fourteenth time, or the twenty-fifth or ninety-eighth time, it miraculously wouldn't have to end that way.

But there's no redoing the past.

And this—the idea of killing Kyle now—it seems...I don't know.

I feel Charlie's fingers at my temple, brushing back my hair.

"Go to sleep," he says softly. "I'll see you in the morning."

I reach up and tug on his finger. Just a little tug to let him know I'm still awake.

"She had such small hands," Charlie says, his voice distant. "Sometimes when she touched my face or something, I could hardly feel it. She was that gentle. And he crushed her. Ten bones in her right hand were broken. I read the report. Ten bones in that one little hand."

His fingers slip away then, and I hear the door open and close behind him.

Dawn

It is her hands I dream of. She wets sand, scooping large globs of it into a heap, pressing and pushing to shape it.

A seagull lands by her knee.

What are you making? I want to ask her, but I know she will not hear me. I am nowhere in this dream. Unseen. Invisible even to my own dream-eyes.

I hold up one translucent hand, and through it, I see the sun rise.

Ready

"Want to head over, jelly bean?" My mom pats my back, smooths my shoulders.

"We'll be early," I say.

"Might as well," my dad says. He closes his laptop, stands, and stretches. He usually seems so distant, like he's thinking about a perplexing chemical reaction, jewel-colored liquids fizzing in his brain, even when he's guzzling down artichoke dip across the booth at Red-n-Mac's. But now he peers at me too closely, with a vague sort of tender regret. Like he did when I was four and a big kid at the playground called me a name I didn't understand.

Charlie went to the courthouse first thing this morning, but I don't have to report there until ten thirty. I took the entire day off school anyway, though, and have already eaten a bowl of cereal, a yogurt, and three and a half muffins. Not smart, since the last thing I need is to puke up a bunch of curdled raisins in the middle of my testimony. But I was up early, showered, and dressed by seven, and there was nothing to do but eat and stress and tug at my mom's pantyhose, which keep slipping down my hips.

In addition to the hose, I'm wearing my mom's skirt, jacket, and one-inch pumps. All uncomfortable and all periwinkle blue.

I text Lindsey a picture and she texts back a mirror shot of herself in a black-and-white pinstripe blouse, cute black capris, and killer heels.

We're decked out like old-fashioned stewardesses. It seems weird that we're dressing up to see the guy who wanted to kill us. But whatever. Society.

My parents have both taken the day off work, and I take a second to thank my lucky stars that I got them in the birth lottery, not Mrs. Barrow who, from what Lindsey says, is out of town again.

When we get to the courthouse, we check in and are told to wait on the benches in the hallway outside the courtroom.

People in suits walk by every so often, carrying folders. No cell phones are allowed in the building, and I didn't bring a book, so I now have even more time for stressing and tugging my hose. Nothing to eat, though, so there's that.

When Lindsey comes in alone, I meet her at the doorway with a hug. It's like a reunion, even though I saw her yesterday in person.

She's added a black bandanna-kind-of-thing around her neck and some muted red lipstick.

"You look good," I tell her. "They said we'll have to wait a while."

"I thought as much, which is why I brought these." She draws a beat-up pack of playing cards out of her back pocket.

"You're on," I say.

She's been more herself this past week. A bit subdued, but I can tell she's trying. Looking for a miraculous spot of turf where she's not self-destructive and not high and not sad.

We find an empty bench down the hallway where we can spread out the cards between us.

"Rummy? BS? War? Crazy Eights? What's your poison?" she asks.

I know better than to play BS with Lindsey. She's told me before I'm a horrible liar, and even though I think I'm decent, she can always spot the fib.

"War," I say, because I know we don't really need to pay attention to play such an easy game, and I want to talk.

We shuffle and deal. I take her three with a jack. She takes my queen with an ace. "How are you doing?" I ask her.

"With what?" she asks.

"With...everything." I gesture vaguely to indicate... *vagueness*.

"Well, in particular, *this* sucks," she says, smiling philosophically, laying down a ten. "But it's always sucked, hasn't it?"

"What about the other thing?" Since Sunday, Lindsey and I had talked *around* her miscarriage rather than actually talked about it. But I know she knows what I mean.

"Better." She takes my four and lays down another ace.

I hope for a low card, turn over an eight.

"I was..." She pauses, trying to find the word. "Shocked. Maybe that made it worse? Or maybe just more confusing."

I push the cards toward her pile. "I'm sorry. You know, that you had to go through that."

"Me too." She's looking at me full-on now, and her look is a lacy landscape cut from paper. Beautiful, but too fragile. "Everything I thought. You know, Robert and all that. I had all those big plans. It was a fantasy. But now, it's like it *wasn't*. I just didn't know it wasn't."

We leave the cards abandoned between us. Lindsey shifts so her back is against the wall. She stares at the door to the records office across the hall. "There was something real there," she says. "Some*one*. Someone I could have loved."

I take her hand and squeeze it. It's still like she's talking a foreign language. But I didn't understand it before either, when she was all hyped up on Robert, and the way I responded then—well, I screwed that up.

I guess it doesn't matter if I get it or not. It doesn't matter what *I* think or how *I* feel. What matters is that she thinks what she thinks and feels what she feels—and my job as her friend is to take the time out from my own bullshit long enough to actually *hear* her.

Taylor Avril, who has come here with her mom and Kai in tow, walks down the hallway with new hair. A silver pixie cut that makes her look a little like a middle-aged woman on a yogurt commercial, but cuter.

"You guys up for this?" she asks. She looks as nervous as I feel.

I shrug. Lindsey nods. Taylor checks the clock on the wall.

"Ten twenty-nine," she says.

I take a breath, like the next minute might change everything and I want to be ready. But the minute passes: 10:30. 10:31. 10:32. Taylor's mom sits on a bench across from us and digs in her purse, while Kai and Taylor stand in the nook beside the water fountain and breathe in each other's faces.

Eventually, around 10:43, a woman in a pantsuit tells us things are running later than expected. "Hold tight, hon," she says to Lindsey in that southern way of making everyone, even strangers, her baby. "They'll be calling you in one by one. Just keep your ears open, there." She points to a speaker above a doorway and moves on down the hall.

Lindsey and I finish our game of war, which she wins, though she doesn't rub it in like usual. My mom walks over and smooths my hair. She tries to play it casual, but I think she just wants to touch me. "How's it going?" She nudges my chin up so I have to look into her bright eyes. The smile she gives me is the one that means I'm her baby and always will be, that I am beautiful and brave and she would do anything to live the next half hour for me, but she can't so here's this smile instead.

"Okay," I say. "Good."

She lets go of me and squeezes Lindsey's shoulder. "Let me know if you girls need anything."

Like how about another life. One where the biggest stress I have is what to order from the cabana boy.

By 11:10, we're laying down cards in our third game, and except for the *thwap* of the cards on the bench between us or the shuffle of some random thirsty soul to the water fountain and back, it's turned quiet in the hallway. Too quiet; tomb-like. My nerves might as well be stretched out on some medieval torture device.

That's when the speaker crackles, "Taylor Avril, report to Courtroom Four, please. Taylor Avril, Courtroom Four."

The Whole Truth

They call me in after Taylor, but before Lindsey. At the entry, I walk past a line of framed portraits, men in high collars from a hundred years before. The courtroom is not too large, with about eight rows of benches in the back, a big desk on a platform in front for the judge, and tables on each side for the lawyers.

There aren't many people. A few reporters with their notebooks, Jamie's family, a few girls who must have graduated with her, some old people, and Charlie. He's at the back, on the left side, eyes down, hoodie up. I'm not sure I'd notice him if I wasn't looking for him; he sits still and blends in, a chameleon, as if he's become part of the bench.

He's been here all morning, hearing them say who-knows-what about Kyle, about Jamie, about the heart of darkness that makes someone shove a crowbar down a girl's throat. He doesn't look up when they usher me to the little wooden box in the center of the room where I'm supposed to sit in a green upholstered chair and tell the truth, the whole truth, and nothing but the truth.

I raise my hand, say "I do," take my seat, and state my name.

I am trying not to look on the side of the room where Kyle, a blurred bit of orange in my periphery, sits between his lawyer, Mr. Wirtz, and a middle-aged woman in a gray pantsuit.

The lawyer on the other side of the room, Mr. Hayes, begins. "You remember me, correct? Now I'm gonna ask you some questions, but I want you to look to the judge when you answer. Will you do that?"

I nod.

"Where'd you go to high school?"

"Midland."

"Did you know Jamie Strand?"

I nod again.

"Answer out loud, if you would, and speak up so everybody can hear you, okay?"

"Okay," I say, my voice echo-y in my own ears. "I knew who Jamie was, but she wasn't in my classes or anything."

"She was one year ahead of you in school?"

"Two years," I say.

"And Kyle Paxson? Did you know him?"

"Yes."

He makes me tell it all, how I met him in algebra when I was a freshman and he was a senior. How he had my

number from a group project we did. How I saw him sometimes after he graduated, but never really thought of him as
a friend.

"When did you last see Kyle in person?"

I tell them how I saw Kyle outside the Hardee's, about a
month before Jamie was killed. I was walking toward my
car when he came over from the Advance Auto across the
street, where he was working at the time.

"And what did you talk about?"

"We didn't say much. I asked him how he was doing.
He said he was working, that things were getting rough at
home, you know, with his grandma. He said he was thinking about moving to Florida."

"And he saw you with your new car?"

"Yes, after we talked, I got in my car. He saw me in my
car before I drove away."

"Did Kyle contact you at any point after that?"

"Just once."

"When was that?"

"July eleventh last year."

"You're sure of the date?" he asks.

"Yes, I'm certain." It's not like I could exactly forget.

"How did he contact you?"

"He sent me a text. He said he wanted to hang out."
It's so weird to me, talking about all this while Kyle is over
there, the unseen orange blur in this very room. I keep
my eyes forward, focused on the judge, who is younger
and thinner than I expect a judge to be—blond with a

caterpillar mustache. From where I'm sitting, a circular brass emblem on the wall behind him seems to frame his head like a crown for baby Jesus.

"Did Kyle offer you anything?" the lawyer asks.

"What do you mean?" I ask, then I remember. "Like drugs? I guess. He said he had stuff."

"And you took that to mean marijuana?"

"Yeah." It feels so weird admitting this in front of a judge.

"And how did you respond?"

"I didn't," I say. "I didn't respond."

True, but is it the whole truth?

"And that was July eleventh, the day Jamie Strand was murdered?" he asks.

"Yes."

"How did that make you feel—knowing he'd contacted you out of the blue, trying to see you on the very day he went on to murder another girl?"

"Horrible," I say. "Like it could have been me." I'm trying to hold it together now, trying not to think about Jamie, bruised and battered, wrapped up in a dirty tablecloth.

Trying not to look at Kyle.

But then, because my eyes apparently have their own will, I do. I look full-on at the immobile lump of him.

Kyle sits, head angled toward the judge, shoulders sloping off in a curve. The mild pudge of his belly. His shaved head and dark glasses. His bland, stupid face. Vacant eyes. Less scary than pitiful.

Not that I pity him.

"I felt…I felt…What he did to her," I say, still looking at Kyle, "it was so cruel. She didn't deserve it. No one deserves something like that."

I turn my eyes back to the judge. "But I guess it doesn't matter what you deserve," I say. "When I heard what Kyle had done, I knew it could have been me."

The randomness of Jamie's murder has always disturbed me, but killing Kyle now, if he gets death, that's the opposite of random. He absolutely deserves it. And all this process, the judge with his robe and gavel, the lawyers with their files, the lurking bailiff and the portraits of dead men peering down from the walls—all of this is as intentional as it gets. It will be calm, measured. A metal gurney and a needle in his arm where the poison seeps in.

But—for all its calm—will it be so very different in the end? Will his death undo anything? Bring Jamie back? Bring justice to our unjust world?

An eye for an eye?

But his blank eyes cannot equal her bright ones. There is no evening this scale.

"I'm sure he would have killed me if he'd had the chance," I say. "But killing him now…"

"No further questions, Your Honor."

Answers

But there are further questions. At least for me.

I tell my parents I'm fine, to go on without me, that I want to wait for Lindsey. But as much as anything, I just need a minute alone to breathe. I can almost feel the zillion microscopic questions buzzing through my body

"You sure?" Mom asks.

I give her my *I can handle myself* smile. "I'll catch a ride with Linds."

My dad leans over, tucks my hair behind my ear. "I was proud of you in there."

"Thanks, Dad," I say, though I'm not sure what there was to be proud of.

With them gone, I watch the door to the courtroom, clearing my mind, waiting for Lindsey to walk out.

But when the door finally opens, a stream of people shuffle through. Everyone must be breaking for lunch. First some old people come through, then the reporters, then more old people.

One, a lady, I swear I've seen her somewhere. Her tan coat is unbuttoned, and her pale blue blouse matches a flower tucked into her coat's lapel—a small blossom, unnaturally blue. She's carrying an old-lady bag that's the same color, and her gray hair is topped with a little black hat.

She passes me on her way to the water fountain, but then stops and turns back, her black flats clicking against the floor tiles. Coming close, she leans down as if sharing a secret. Her breath is warm and yeasty, her lips determinedly red. There's a tiny crumb of egg caught on her chin-whisker.

"He was trouble, that boy. But what he done, that's what *he* done. And he'll be the one paying for it." Her voice rises, no longer a whisper. "You girls, you ain't to blame. I ain't either. I done my best, what with his daddy. I raised that boy best I could. None of us could've known what he was gonna do. And what happens now, if they kill my boy, he got no one to blame but hisself. Like I told you and them other girls, it's not your fault."

"Like you told me?"

Her eyes lock onto mine. "That's right." She points a bony finger in my face. "And I meant it. You remember that."

Then before I can blink, she passes on down the hallway. And...*what*? Who *was* that?

When Lindsey comes out of the courtroom, my head is still whirling.

"Charlie's with the Strands. They went out the back

way. There's this other door the lawyers use.... Um, are you okay?" She waves a hand in front of my face. "Sweetie?"

"Oh my God, Lindsey. Oh. My. God. The old woman... you remember at Jamie's memorial service at the start of the school year?" She looks blank, but I go on anyway. "We saw her in the stands. All alone, it was weird, remember? Well, she was just *here*. And get this.... She said that she had told me and the other girls that it's not our fault. And she was wearing a flower on her coat, like one of the little blue ones in that bouquet I got. She's gotta be the one who sent us that stuff."

Lindsey looks as confused as I feel.

"And I think—I think she's Kyle's grandma."

Swings

I text Charlie to meet me at the coffee shop that evening, but he doesn't show and he doesn't text back. After twenty minutes, I leave and drive by his house, and then the river. No Charlie. No Charlie's car.

I go back by the coffee shop, but his car isn't there either. Instead of going in, I park and walk over to an empty playground in the alley nearby. It's supposed to be for the Baptist Church, though I don't ever see anyone playing in it.

I sit on a swing and drag my feet through the mulch.

Today shook me up. Having to answer all those questions right across from Kyle while he sat there like a lump, emotionless. The old woman with the dyed-blue flower on her coat, just like ones she left on my porch. Her pointing that bony finger in my face and telling me it's not my fault if Kyle gets the death penalty.

And that's his *grandma*. The person who puts you on her knee and plays pat-a-cake. The one who's supposed to love you best.

Was she like that all along, so harsh and detached, or did what happened *make* her that way?

It couldn't have been easy to have a boy she raised go out and kill someone. And before that, didn't Kyle's dad shoot himself?

If I feel guilty about what happened to Jamie, what must she feel? If there's any feeling left after all that.

After Lindsey dropped me off, I skipped the rest of the school day, stayed curled up in my bed—but in my mind, I was there—there without being there—beside Charlie on that hard courtroom bench, listening to each painful word.

And for what? What good does all that pain do?

I'm not saying we don't learn from pain, but that's just a coincidence. All those sweet little life lessons might be pain's by-product, but they're not its purpose. Pain is its own purpose. And in general it's a purpose that deeply sucks.

I saw somewhere that in pop songs the word most commonly associated with *pain* is *love*. Which makes sense, I guess. Love can hurt like nothing else.

Or maybe it's just that *all* pop music is about love. If I did some research, I might find out that the word in pop music most commonly associated with *dog* is *love*, too. The word most commonly associated with *toothbrush* or *bridge* or *door*—all *love*. Whatever.

I think about texting Lindsey to come get drunk with me. I'm sure we could find someone who would buy us beer. But I know it's a bad idea. Plus, that's the last thing Lindsey needs. The last thing I need.

Instead, I swing—pointing my feet skyward as my heart plunges to my shoes. The air is cool, and I'm washed with the dizzy feel of coming and going, going and coming, reaching out to my limit, only to be jerked back. I close my eyes and mutter Zen bullshit in my head. *Become the swing. Let the swing become you.*

The air shifts, and I feel a soft, wet chill sift down on my face, the only exposed part of me.

"Hey."

I stutter to a stop, opening my eyes to find Charlie, hoodie up, the picture of rain.

The Obvious

"Hey." I start with the obvious. "It's raining."

"Yeah," Charlie answers, plunking down in the swing beside me. "Ironic."

"What?"

"The day Jamie was murdered was sunny, beautiful," he says, twisting his swing around, the metal chain clinking over his head. "And today—when we're finally getting some justice—it's like this." He turns a bare palm up to catch a few drops, which glisten silver under the streetlamp.

"Justice?" I ask.

He stops turning and digs his heels in the mulch. The tension in the chain over him creaks.

"It'll happen. It has to. He's going to pay for what he did—no one could hear that and not—" He shakes his head, falls silent.

I don't know what to say, so I sit, unmoving, in my swing and watch his hand as it grips the chain.

After a half minute's silence, I ask, "When will they have a verdict?"

"Who knows? There's more tomorrow."

"You're going to go?"

"Yeah."

"Is that—are you sure that's a good idea?"

"What?"

"I just mean, that's got to be the worst. Do you really want—"

"Want?" He growls. Like actually, wild-animal *growls*. "Jesus. I owe her that much, don't you think? She had to *live* it. The least I can do is sit there and *listen*. That bastard, that bastard—so yeah, it's the worst, but—don't you get it?" He lets go of the chains and sinks his head into his open hands. "I wasn't there for her. I couldn't protect her. I didn't even know it was happening."

I am wet now. The rain, soft as it is, has drenched me. I put my hand on Charlie's curved back. He looks up, eyes stripped. "I *have* to be there," he says.

"I'm sorry," I say, and mean it.

"For what?" he asks.

"Everything," I say. "For everything."

When Charlie stands, the swing chain clangs like an awkward conversation.

"I need some air," he says, walking away, though we're already out in it.

Days

The hearing isn't finished on Thursday. Or Friday. I go to school, text Charlie that I can see him if he wants. If it'd be helpful. If he'd like to talk. If he needs a run. If...anything. He doesn't text back.

So, I give him space.

I look for Mark Lee in gym because, what? I'm going to ask him if he knows how Charlie is? Yeah, that's my sad little plan. But Mark Lee isn't there on either day. I'm hoping that means he's been in the courtroom with Charlie. Where I can't be because of the whole testifying thing. I'm hardly President of the Mark Lee Fan Club, but I'd consider a trial membership if it meant Charlie didn't have to go through this alone.

Meanwhile, I watch from the sidelines as the paper and local news channels report on the case—new details floating to the surface like pond scum. They don't use my name in print, hallelujah. Or the names of Lindsey, Taylor, and Blair, who apparently was called back into town to testify.

We're just "a series of girls Paxson approached prior to the murder with offers of drugs and money in exchange for sex."

Not exactly. But thanks anyway, local news.

There's stuff about Kyle's bad childhood, his psych evaluations, job performance, outbursts at school. Like we're playing #10RandomFactsAboutMe.

Then come new bits about the murder itself. How Kyle rode in the back of a squad car, directing police to the site where he murdered Jamie, and then to the road thirty-five miles away where he dumped her body. His little behind-the-scenes tour.

Charlie has got to be lost in all kinds of awfulness right now, but by Friday I just want—I don't know, a sign that he isn't lost for good.

> You ok?

Then, in roughly forty-five-minute intervals:

> You ok?

> Really. Are you ok?

> Okay??????

Then, when he still doesn't answer, I send random emoticons, because why not. It's not like English was working, anyway.

Charlie finally texts back after midnight.

Yes.

It's better than a "No," I guess, but just by one letter.

Would it help to talk?

No.

He responds right away this time.

No offense. Just not up to it.

Maybe after this blows over.

Which seems unlikely. When is this likely to "blow over"? Should I set my alarm for The End of Time?

Ok.

343

Then I grumble and toss my phone onto the carpet.

My Saturday comes and goes in a funk. I try to do homework and ignore how quiet my phone is. I try to forget Kyle's face. His nothing face. Faceless un-face.

By Sunday, I'm tired of my own head. Charlie texts, but he basically says the same thing: *Not yet.* So I haul myself out of bed and meet Lindsey at the mall. There's a sale at the huge makeup store she loves.

"It was so weird," Lindsey says, pawing through a bin of eyeliner. "I mean, God."

"Yeah," I say. "Did you look at him?"

"Ugh. He looked awful. All pasty and out of it."

She picks out a teal eyeliner from the tub, and we walk over to the eye shadow display. "So Charlie is still..."

"Yeah," I say. "He just—needs time to process."

"That has got to suck." She dabs her finger on a sample of a swampy green color and rubs it across her lids.

"I guess it's like he's living through all of it again."

"I meant for you," she says.

"Oh," I say, "yeah, that too."

"How are your parents taking it?" she asks.

"Pretty low-key," I say, though the truth is that my parents have been on high alert all week. On the Parental Freak-out Advisory Scale, I'd say they'd rank a solid Code Orange. They keep asking me how I feel, and telling me they're here for me if I need to talk. But I know it bugs Lindsey that her own mom is so out of the picture, and I don't want to make her feel any worse.

"Oh, hey! I forgot!" Lindsey's voice goes up, genuinely excited. "I'm doing this online certification so I can teach at the summer camp. And Miss Mirabelle says if I work full-time next year, the church has this thing where they can help pay for classes, you know, for like an actual degree."

"Linds! That's awesome! Are you going to do it?"

"Yeah. I think I want to." She plays it off, keeping her eyes on a makeup display with a dramatically posed It Girl, but her voice sounds almost shy. "I think I want to study special education. There're a couple kids at the daycare and, man, they're...I mean, they have to work so hard, just to do the most basic stuff—telling you they want more juice or whatever. But when they do, when they get it—it's like, huge. I just...I just love them."

"Wow," I say. "That's, that's—you know, you never cease to amaze." I reach over and squeeze Lindsey's hand. "You'll be so great at that."

"Well, who knows?" she says. "I hope so!"

"Definitely," I say. And she will. Though I can't imagine why she would want to teach anyone, ever. I mean, you'd have to be a saint.

Saint Lindsey: ripped jeans, a flirty tee with a vintage Harley-Davidson logo, and a silver bracelet with a charm that reads QUEEN BITCH.

"Hey, can I ask you something?"

"Sure," Lindsey says.

"If you had to decide," I say, "I mean, if it were up to you, would you give Kyle the death penalty?"

"Well…" She pauses, pumps some Mango Magic lotion from a sampler into her palm and wipes it up her forearm, considering. "I honestly don't know." She sniffs her arm delicately. "I'm glad it's not my decision to make."

This World

As it turns out, the trial is still dragging on the following Wednesday, the day before Thanksgiving. It's colder than it's been all fall. A gray-mist day.

We get out of school early, just after noon. I don't know how Charlie has been handling all his absences—if he got excused or is taking penalties for the skips. I don't know, in fact, how Charlie has been handling anything.

Instead of going home, I drive to the greenway and hike back up the hill where Charlie took me on our first run. Where I asked him what he'd do on his last day on earth.

This could be Kyle's last day, I think, as I make my way up the dirt path—even though I know the court doesn't really work like that. If he gets death, it would take years—maybe decades—before he's executed. I avoided sleep all week, so I've had lots of time for reading up on things like the death penalty. Not to mention the birthing habits of tiger sharks, Bigfoot sightings, the history of early sound recordings, top criminal justice programs, and the relative salaries of movie stars.

The air is chilled and brittle, and the mist makes a silvery wall that retreats as I climb, perpetually fifteen feet in front of me. I hike quickly, with only a few noisy birds for company. By the time I reach the top of the hill, I am gulping cold breaths, giving myself a sort of brain freeze in my lungs. I bend over, cupping my gloved fingers in front of my mouth to warm the incoming air.

Dizzy, I lean on the long log of the horse jump and gaze out at the mountains beyond. They seem to pose, wrapped in a shawl of mist, majestic and serene.

This world. This preposterously beautiful world. You'd think we could live in it without killing each other.

I spy two deer on the edge of the meadow; they hold my gaze, frozen for a moment, then bolt into the woods. Wind rips across the grass, gusts through bare branches, singing its surreal melody. Anthem for the lost.

This world. This world, so much more than we deserve.

Over

Charlie is sitting on the edge of my front stoop when I get home.

"Hey." I cross the last few steps to the door. "My mom didn't let you in?"

"I didn't knock," he says, standing. "Your car was gone." He looks thinner than usual—his face pale, smudged by dark hollows. For whatever whacked reason, I find myself thinking of a worn gym sock turned wrong side out.

"It's good to see you." I smile, and the smile feels odd on my cheeks, I suppose because I haven't been smiling much.

I lean in for a hug. Charlie's arms encircle me, and even in the chilled air, even with his eyes blurred into another hemisphere, I feel warmer than I have for a long time.

"You want to come in?" I ask.

"I was hoping maybe we could go somewhere."

"Yeah, sure," I say. "Where?"

"I don't know, for a walk or something," he says.

He looks like he hasn't eaten for days.

"You want a sandwich before we go? A muffin? My mom's muffin production has been in overdrive. She's probably in there baking pumpkinseed muffins as we speak."

He tries to smile, and his smile looks as clumsy as mine felt. "No, thanks."

I want to ask him about the trial. If it's really over. What happened. But the time for all of that will come.

"How are you?" I ask.

He shakes his head. "You know."

I don't. But yeah, I can guess.

We walk under the bare limbs of trees. Wood fire from someone's house scents the air like we're in a cave, or one of those fancy hiking-gear stores. The fog from earlier has lifted now, and in comparison, the street has an exposed look.

"How about you?" Charlie asks. "Have you been okay? Sorry I couldn't..."

"No," I say, "I get it. You needed time. I just wish—"

"What?"

"I wish I could have been there for you." I take his bare hand in my gloved one. "I wanted to be."

"Yeah," he says. "I know you did."

We pad down street after street. When we come to the railroad tracks down near the river, instead of crossing, Charlie stands on the iron rail, balancing on the balls of his feet. He drops my hand and holds out his arms, like he's testing the wind, then cranes his neck up. I stop in the gravel between the ties and look up at him, haloed by a stark November sun. His hood falls back and his dark hair flecks with red in the light.

The sight of him—such a raw, beautiful mess—feeds a hunger I didn't even know I had. He closes his eyes, then opens them and steps down.

"It's over," he says. "It'll never be over. But it's over."

"Over?"

"They gave him life," he says.

Whoa.

And that's—I don't know what that is. My eyes open wider and my throat clamps shut. The street behind Charlie goes blurred, too bright, unreal.

I feel, for a second, like I'm hovering an inch over my body, not quite *in* it.

Here I've been reading and thinking and talking—like I had to prepare for some looming moment when The World would ask me where I stood on the death penalty in general and the death of Kyle Paxson in particular. I had to be ready.

But it turns out I'm not ready for this. Because it's not Kyle's death that I have to resign myself to. It's his life.

"Three life sentences," Charlie says as he crosses the tracks, heading toward Low Water Bridge. "One after the other."

"What does that even *mean*?" I ask, following Charlie onto the bridge's curb, which people use as a walkway, though it's just wide enough for single file.

"It means there's no fucking justice. That's what it means."

"But—"

"It means he'll live to be an old man in a little cell, safe and sound, while she—while she—" He pounds his fist on his leg as he walks. "That son of a bitch!"

"But *three*? Why?" I ask. "Do they expect him to live—"

"No. God." Charlie lets out a frustrated huff. "It just means he's never getting out." We're halfway across the bridge now. He stops short and grips the railing, staring out over the water. Below us, the river rushes on its endless pilgrimage to somewhere else.

"He's not getting out," he says. "But he's not paying for what he did either. Not really. Not enough."

I don't know what to say, so I stand beside him and watch the water's glassy, urgent flow.

"The things he did to her. You wouldn't believe. I swear I wish I had a gun. I would have taken care of him myself."

"Holy shit! Charlie. What are you saying?"

He hurls the words over the bridge, a message in a clouded, cracked bottle. "I should have fucking killed him when I had the chance."

A Jeep slows as it passes, blasting country music through closed windows, cowboy wailing, bass line thumping.

I search Charlie's face for some sign that he's still there. Still the Charlie I know. His eyes are drained—but the glossy trail of a tear snails down his cheek.

I slip off my glove and wipe his cheek dry, then guide his face so he's looking fully at me.

"Who *are* you?" I ask. He doesn't answer, and my hand drifts from his face. "Seriously. Who are you, Charlie?"

What I Mean

If someone slaps you, turn the other cheek.

That's what I remember from Sunday mornings in the stale basement classroom of the First United Methodist Church. *Turn the other cheek. Our Father, who art in heaven. The meek shall inherit the earth.*

The meek, who I imagined as a family of meerkats. Our father, a golden-robed Santa Claus. And slapping, which was something I saw two bikini-clad girls on TV do.

It makes about as much sense now as it did in elementary school. If someone slaps you, give them more places to slap? *I think you missed a spot.*

Kyle's sentence does *feel* like turning the other cheek, though. Sort of. I've watched enough Netflix to know that prison isn't a stroll in the daisies. It's horrible and scary. You're basically kept in a little metal cage. But what Kyle did was so much *more* than slapping. When he was done with Jamie, there was no cheek left for her to turn.

So yeah, Charlie's angry. But his whole *I should have killed Kyle myself* thing is ... well, horrible and scary, too.

"You don't mean that," I say.

"Don't tell me what I mean." He slants his head away, staring back at the water.

"Come on, Charlie." I put my hand on his shoulder.

He shakes my hand off. "Go! Just go." He turns his back and walks away.

I stand, stunned, as he slouches across the other half of the bridge and down the sidewalk, farther and farther, turning from a boy into a blurred gray silhouette.

After a minute, my hand begins to sting with the cold, and I slip my glove back on.

Then I follow him. Because I know he's hurting. Because I'm afraid of what may happen if he's alone. Because, God help me, there's a pit in my stomach, a dense swirl of wanting, that vibrates with his voice, even when that voice says *go*.

When I catch up to him, he's halfway down the second block, passing little frame houses that look like they were painted with a kindergartner's watercolor set—yellow, then green, then yellow, more yellow, then pink, purple, blue.

"Charlie," I say, and when he doesn't respond, "CHARLIE!" Like shouting his name in the middle of the sidewalk will make him remember who I am.

A woman unloading grocery bags from her carport across the street shuts her hatchback and yells, "You okay, hon?"

I'm not sure if she's talking to Charlie or me, but I answer, "Sorry! Yeah, we're fine!" I smile and wave to show, *Look, normal, see!*

"All right, then! Y'all be good!" She waves us on. "Enjoy your Turkey Day tomorrow!"

"You, too!" I answer, my voice falsely bright.

Charlie pauses, waits for me to catch up. Not necessarily because he wants to, but what else are you supposed to do after a middle-aged woman yells at you in the street?

As soon as I'm beside him, he takes off again, and this time I keep up. We walk fast—arms and legs pumping, like we're in training for some sort of Angry Pairs Power Walk 5K. And then out of nowhere, he pulls to a full stop at the curb in front of an old fire station. "Look," he thunders, "I don't even know where we're going!"

"Okay," I say softly, wondering what I'm agreeing to— that we're walking aimlessly or that he and I are through?

"*Okay?*" he asks.

Since he's standing there in front of me, a stationary target, I take him by the wrist. I slip my gloved hands down to cover his bare ones, trying to warm him. "This is so messed up. I can't imagine what you've been going through, Charlie. Hearing all that stuff. It makes me sick. It *is* sick. But what you said about Kyle. You can't for real—I mean, *what?*"

Charlie lets out an exaggerated breath. "He just soaked it all in, like this is what he's been waiting for, to get attention, all eyes finally on him. And they sit there in their suits, looking at pictures of Jamie's body, mangled and—*God!* They hear what he did, and then it's like—it's like, don't you think *we* should have a say in what happens? The people who knew her and loved her, shouldn't *we* get to decide?"

He takes his hand out of mine and points to his own chest. "*I* knew her. *I* loved her. *I*—"

Then his face clenches like a fist and he's sobbing, crumpling into my shoulder, and I'm hugging him fiercely. "I know," I say, "I know," but all I know is that I need him to get through this. Tears stream down my own face, brash and cold. I need him. I need him like my own worthless lungs.

Thanksgiving

"Well, I, for one," Mom says, "am going to sit here sipping my sweet tea until I fall over in a sugar coma."

"Good plan!" my dad agrees, rising from the table to clear our dirty dishes, still laden with half-eaten food. "I'll be in the kitchen. Let me know if you need me to dial nine-one-one."

"You guys are weirdos," I say, and with his free hand, my dad ruffles my head as he passes behind me on the way out of the dining room.

"Remember," Mom says, "we weirdos *made* you, so keep that in mind."

"First, yuck. And second, I need a nap." I rub my full belly like an old man.

When I start to rise from the table, though, my mother touches my arm, pulling me back. "Hold up," she says. "I want to talk with you."

"We've been talking," I say, sitting back down. For the past forty minutes, we've talked nonstop about just about every ingredient of every dish my parents cooked. The dill in her green beans, the horseradish in his mashed pota-toes, how moist the butter rub made the turkey. (And can I take a moment here to express how gross I find the word *moist*—especially when my mom says it?)

"True, but I want to—well, you heard about the sentencing?"

"Yeah, sure," I say, keeping my voice *I'm okay you're okay* neutral.

"So, how do you"—and here my mom has the good grace to look at her crumpled napkin instead of giving me one of her soul-searing stares—"*feel* about that?"

"Ugh," I grumble. "It's Thanksgiving. Could we not?"

"I want to know. How are you?"

"Good. Fine. I'm great," I say.

And now she goes ahead and does the soul-thing with the eyes. "Really?"

"Really," I say.

"It's just you've seemed a little off these past few days."

And this is a surprise? "I'm fine," I say. "It's been, you know, whatever."

I sit there in her laser-vision for a half minute more. "So can I go?"

"Yes, go," she says, then calls after me as I break for my room, "but I'm here if you feel like talking."

"Thanks."

And yeah, I guess that is something I should be thankful for. My parent's Code Orange. Better than them not caring at all.

We used to do that when I was younger—go around the table on Thanksgiving and give our list of *thank-you*'s. As a kid, that pretty much meant Mom; Dad; Juniper, my baby doll; food; grandparents; my latest library book; going to the park; and pie.

I stretch out on my bed, feeling full and sleepy, and wonder what would be on my list today.

I'd keep Mom and Dad, and, despite the fact I hardly see them due to living several states away, my grandparents. Pie still ranks up there, of course. And some obvious additions:

Lindsey.

Charlie.

The fact that I'm alive. Even when life is, to misquote *Hamlet*, a quintessence of crap.

The grace to forgive myself for being alive in the first place.

Open

Clack!

Clatter! Clack!

Reluctantly, I open my eyes, still half fogged by my turkey-induced snooze-fest. *What—*

Clack!

Definitely not a normal room-sound. I roll over and check my phone for the time. 1:38 AM. And five messages. All in the last ten minutes, all from Charlie.

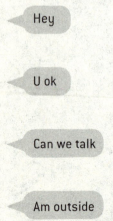

Hey

U ok

Can we talk

Am outside

U there

Clack!

The clack, I realize, is something hitting my window. I haul myself out of bed and peer into the darkness of the backyard. There's only a slice of moon and the neighbor's deck light to see by. I squint. On the lawn, a rectangular glow lurches back and forth like a buoy.

Are you in my yard?

The glow stops waving.

Yea

Coming. Wait a min.

Barefoot, in fuzzy pajamas, I sneak down the steps. Crossing the house, I'm careful to be quiet. As I creak open the mudroom door, I can make out the figure of Charlie about ten feet away beside a hydrangea bush.

"Hey," I call in a hushed voice.

He pockets his phone and jogs over. "Hey." At the doorway, he pats my hair, tangled and frizzy from sleep. "You're sooooo pretty."

"Wow," I say. "Thanks?"

Nestling his face in my neck, he sniffs. "Your hair smells like flowers."

His stinks of stale beer.

"What's up?" I hold him by the shoulders and step back, so I can see his eyes. "Did you drive here?"

He scrunches his face, like he isn't sure how to answer the question. "I—I left my car...somewhere?"

"Okay," I whisper, leading him into the house, "you gotta be quiet. My parents are asleep."

"Okay," he whispers back, but it's the type of exaggerated whisper that is louder than normal talk would be. "Where are we going?"

Which is a good question, actually. My room is down the hall from my parents' and the den is right under them. Way too much chance of being heard in either place. Instead, I take his hand and guide him to the basement door. I flip on the light, then mouth, "This way," leading him down the steps. I figure there's a couch in the exercise room where he can sleep it off, with any luck undetected by the parentals.

When we get to the bottom of the steps, Charlie pulls me to him, kissing my neck, then ear, then cheek. "Ummm, gorgeous."

"You're drunk," I say.

"A bit." He gives me a sweet, wolfish grin. "But you're still gorgeous."

Smooth. "Are you hungry?" I ask. "There are tons of leftovers—" And he's busy nibbling my neck again.

"All right, big boy," I say, "let's get you somewhere you can sleep it off." I peel him away from me and, awkward, like I'm dancing with a mannequin, shuffle him past the unused treadmill and stationary bike and over to the couch.

I sit; he lies down, puts his back on my lap, head on the pillowed arm of the couch.

"Hey, you." He takes my hand and rubs the back of it against his unshaven cheek. It's prickly, but comforting in a weird way.

"Why are you so far away?" he asks.

"Close your eyes," I say.

"Hey, I know," he says, like this incredible idea arrived out of the blue. "We should totally make out. Am I right?"

I laugh, because *geez*.

"Close your eyes," I say again, and this time I cover his lids with my free palm. "Are they closed?" I ask.

"Um-hum."

"Good." My hand drifts down to his cheek. He starts to reach for me, but I gently shake him off. "Keep your eyes closed," I say.

"Kinky." He smiles, eyes shut, hands still roving.

"No one likes Drunk Handsy Dude," I say. "Be still."

"Kinky *and* mean."

"I gotta be me," I say.

He laughs, a soft little snort, and lets his hands fall by his side.

I push his hair back from his forehead. There are scratches, I see now, on his face—ones that weren't there yesterday. Chapped lips. A bruise on his cheekbone. I check his hands, a few gashes there, too. Like he's been caught in briars. Out who-knows-where.

I bend over and kiss him on his lips, tenderly, like a prince in a fairy tale. Sleeping Beauty probably didn't have beer breath or five-o'clock shadow, but still. "Now, sleep," I say, straightening.

"I'm not sleepy," he says.

"Too bad." I run my fingers through his hair.

"Tell me a story," he play-whines.

"About what?"

"Something awesome," he murmurs. "About a turtle. Turtles are cool."

"God, aren't they!" I say, and not just because it's two AM and my semi-drunk, semi-sweet, semi-homicidal boyfriend is in the basement of my parents' house. It's not just middle-of-the-night logic, but an empirical fact: Turtles are the coolest.

"A turtle story. Hmmm...Once upon a time, there was a turtle princess. She moved really slowly, but that just meant she had time to think things through. And she wore this beautiful tiara—"

"A tiara?"

"Hush, yes, she's a turtle princess, and she wears a tiara that is magic. With magic emeralds and stuff. But then this mean wizard comes and is all, *I'm going take your shell.* Which is a really sucky thing for him to do. But she zaps him with her magic emerald. And then...Okay, I'm not making sense." I yawn. "You tell the rest."

"And the wizard—the turtle tries—" Charlie sighs. "The turtle princess zaps the wizard into another dimension and she lives happily ever after with her hot turtle boyfriend?"

"Hmmm," I say. "Seems a bit suspicious."

"The end." But then his voice shifts. Serious. "Hey, you know what we were talking about yesterday?"

Like him wanting to kill Kyle? "Yeah," I say. I peer at his face, hoping that he will tell me something, but his eyes are still closed.

"That was...I don't even know what that was. I guess I was...angry."

Understatement of the Year.

"I'm—it's hard to—" he says. "But I didn't mean it. You know I wouldn't do that."

"Yeah?" I say. "Good."

He sits up, eyes open now, and even through the haze of alcohol and exhaustion, it's there: a blur of pain.

"I just want—justice, you know." He takes my hand and holds it. "I want him to pay for what he did."

"Yeah," I say, "I've been thinking about that. It's like—" And I've never quite gotten my thoughts this close to words before. "I don't even know if justice is a *thing*. If it's possible. Killing Kyle, that doesn't bring anyone back. When he—last year—I knew, like really *knew*, someone could take my life, and there was not a thing I could say about it. Sure, I can try to avoid it. I took self-defense. I carry pepper spray. But if someone wants to kill me—well."

I drop his hand, because I need both of mine to get this out. "So, I got drunk. I swallowed everything wrong in the world. All the fear and hate, I was full of it. God, I hated him so much." I stand, walk over to the stationery bike, mindlessly flip its pedal with my foot. "And I hated myself for being afraid. But no matter how much I swallowed, there was more. That crap was eating me up. But you helped. I know that wasn't the plan or anything—but you did. You and Lindsey. Jared," I say, then add quickly, "as a friend."

I turn to face Charlie. "So now, now, yeah, I still don't get to *decide* to *not* be killed today. But I can decide that I'll do my best to live. And it's not up to me if Kyle goes to prison or dies on a table. But I *can* do something. You guys have shown me that. I can fight it. Because I'm, you know, I'm worth—" Just saying it, I feel the blush rise in my cheeks. Sure I can be selfish and mean, but that's not all I am. There's someone there worth loving, too, right?

"What?" Charlie stands now, too. "Fight what?" His face is a moon-bleached island. It occurs to me that it's probably not the best idea to be hashing all this out with him half drunk in the middle of the night. But you don't always get to choose your moment.

I walk to him, take his hand again. "That hate. I have to let go of it," I say. "I think it's the only way I can let go of *him*, of Kyle. It's the only way I can get myself free of it."

He tilts his head like a dog that hears something that can't be heard by humans. "So how you doing that?"

I know he's not going to like what I have to say, but I can't *not* say it. "I'm going to forgive him. No, I *do* forgive him. Not for what he did to Jamie—that's not mine to forgive. But I forgive him for what he tried to do to me."

"What the fuck?"

"Look, I don't expect—"

He jerks away his hand. "You don't expect what?"

"I don't expect you to understand—"

"UNDERSTAND? That you FORGIVE him! No, I don't *understand*!"

"Keep your voice down," I grumble.

"I came here because I wanted to see my girlfriend—my *girlfriend*—and this is what I get!"

"Your 'girlfriend'! Are you serious?" I'm insta-mad now, and I'm yelling, too. It's not like I didn't know what he wanted—I mean, I'd have to be blind—but still. "So what I feel doesn't matter. I just need to keep my mouth shut like a good little 'girlfriend' while you—"

"Her left ear had been beaten off her head. They still haven't found it. Did your boyfriend Kyle tell you that?"

"Are you—?"

"Oh, and get this! In the car, when they arrested him, you know what they found? A brand-new crowbar. Just like the one he used on Jamie. He was heading to the beach, and he was going to do it *again* to some girl there. He had a duffel bag with duct tape and a crowbar, and this is new, a big-ass hunting knife."

"What?" *That* hadn't been in the papers.

"Yeah. So you go ahead and 'forgive' him? But what are you going to say to the girl he cuts—"

"He's in jail. He's not—"

"You don't know! You can't tell the future."

"I have—"

"*What the hell?*" We both turn to find my father, naked except for boxers, baseball bat in hand, at the bottom of the basement steps. He glares at us like we're actual intruders.

"Dad..." I say, not sure what to follow those words with.

"Charlie was just leaving," my dad growls, pointing his way upstairs.

"Yes, sir," Charlie says. He takes the steps two at once. And by the time I get upstairs, he's gone the way he came, in the dark.

Search

forgiving is
   forgiving is **hard**
   forgiving is **not forgetting**
   forgiving is **forgetting**
   forgiving is **easier than forgetting**

forgiveness is about
   forgiveness is about **freeing yourself**
   forgiveness is about **the forgiver**
   forgiveness is about **you**
   forgiveness is **about not the other person**

reasons to forgive
   reasons to forgive **me**
   reasons to forgive **student loans**
   reasons to forgive **your boyfriend**
   reasons to forgive **yourself**

i forgive you because

    i forgive you because **i love you**

    i forgive you because **god forgives me**

    i forgive you because **nobody's perfect**

    i forgive you because **i love you poems**

to forgive is to

    to forgive is to **suffer**

    to forgive is to **suffer lyrics**

    to forgive is to **set a prisoner free and discover**

    to forgive is to **be forgiven**

Door

It's Saturday morning, and I'm at Charlie's front door. Because if I'm making myself forgive Kyle, I can surely make myself forgive Charlie. Charlie, who is *not* a homicidal sociopath.

"Your friend is here, Charlie," his mom calls toward the back of the house, and then, while we wait for him to appear, asks me a series of questions that have no answer except "yes, ma'am."

I didn't text Charlie in advance, but decided to go with a stealth attack—a decision I question when he finds me in the living room with his mom, inspecting her collection of miniature porcelain shoes as I confirm the fact that I did indeed have a lovely Thanksgiving with my family.

"Hi," I chirp enthusiastically, as if I don't see the *hell no* all over his face.

He gives me the tight-lipped guy-nod.

His mom looks from him to me, back to him.

"I, uh—that thing—I was—hi," I say, feeling the stupidity of my babbling twice, once as it passes out my mouth and then again after it makes the long journey to my ear holes. Geez. Throw me a bone here, Charlie.

He wipes his hands, which are dark with grease, on a white rag draped over his shoulder. "I'm in the garage," he says, and turns back the way he came. For a second my breath catches in my throat, but then he calls over his shoulder, "Come on."

I follow him through the kitchen and into the garage. I haven't been here before and I'm surprised to find a workshop with car parts everywhere. The half-gutted body of a 1970s hot rod is planted in the center, surrounded by clumps of gears and tools that unfold in each direction, like the petals of a complicated metal flower.

"What's all this?" I ask, gesturing in the general direction of the car.

"My dad likes to tinker," he says. He picks up a greasy piece of machinery about the size of a rabbit and starts fiddling with it.

"You, too, huh?"

"Yeah. Good for thinking."

"You've been thinking?"

"Let's cut to the chase." He puts the oily robo-rabbit on a counter. "What're you doing here?"

"Maybe I've come to do my duty as your 'girlfriend.'" It's not my intention to snark, I swear. It just spikes out.

"Yeah." He sighs, shakes his head. "I'm sorry. That was

rude of me, the other night. And wrong. I don't think of you that way."

"Hmm," I say. "How *do* you think of me, then?"

He wipes his hands, comes close. "You're—"… *beautiful? … smart? … amazing?* "—fierce."

"Wha—"

"You are the one," he says, his voice packed, "you're the one I want to be trapped with in an avalanche because I know you'd just keep digging."

Which means what? I'm a three-legged terrier with the efficiency of a backhoe? *Um, thank you?*

"You're—you're—" He rolls his hand in the words-won't-come gesture. "Hell, I'd want to be trapped with you, avalanche or not."

Kind of creepy, but his eyes soften as he says it in a way that makes me go soft, too.

"You know how I feel about you," he says, tucking back a stray strand of my hair.

"Maybe," I say. "Maybe not."

His fingertips linger at my ear. I smell the grease on them, and it's like some kind of irresistible pheromone. I press my cheek against his palm, catlike.

"Is your dad still mad at me?" he whispers.

"Probably. But he'll get over it," I say. "Are you still mad at me?"

"I'll get over it, too," he says, then pulls his hand away. I feel its absence on my cheek like a physical thing. "You are wrong, though. That guy's a monster. And forgiving him.

That's a little easy, don't you think? That's the kind of stupidity that got Jamie killed in the first place."

"Ow." Because what do you say to that?

"You know you can't just forgive him," he says.

"No," I say, "I don't *know it*. And it's not easy, it's—"

"We shouldn't be fighting about this," he says.

"So I should just agree with you, instead? Problem solved?"

"I'm right." He shrugs, like it's the end of the story.

"I'm not saying you're not right, but being right isn't always—the right thing," I say, painfully aware of how stupid that sounds.

"I don't forgive him. And I don't, I *won't* forgive myself."

"Well, that's a plan," I say. "I'll make sure to visit you in the asylum. Mark my calendar for this time next year?"

"Oh, come on."

"I'm serious," I say. "If you can't forgive yourself, you're not going to—"

"I don't *want* to," he says. "I already—I already—I'm not going to forget her."

"Forgiving doesn't mean forgetting." When in doubt, quote Google. "It just means you let go of the hate."

"But I *do hate* him. I will always hate him."

I feel like picking up the rubber mallet on the counter and throwing it at the wall. Hard. *I'll show you forgiveness, damn it!*

Deep breath in. Deep breath out. Repeat after me: *I am not the feelings police. I am not the feelings police.*

Because seriously, who am I to tell Charlie he doesn't get to loathe the guy who murdered his girlfriend? It's not like I didn't spend a year of my life with a little bag of hatred in my gut.

The question for me now, I guess, is, *Can I live with that in him?* Do I have the strength to be with Charlie—to do what I need to forgive—when I know he never will?

Short Answer

I don't know.

Long Answer

I really, really don't.

Box

How do you know you've forgiven someone? Is saying it to yourself enough? Do you have to tell the person you forgive them? Are there rules?

Because on the outside, forgiving Kyle is not so different from *not* forgiving him. I'm not planning a trip to the county jail where I'll murmur into a black phone wired to the wall as we peer at each other through two-inch Plexiglas. There won't be any handwritten letters stuffed in small blue envelopes. No visiting-day cake. To be honest, I have no intention of ever speaking to him.

The only difference between me now and me then is I said I forgive him. Both to myself and out loud in the world. I committed to it.

Maybe later it will become important to track him down for some deathbed confession. But for now, just me knowing is enough.

Does that mean I'm okay with what he did?

No.

Does it mean I want to be his best friend?

No.

Does it mean I got rid of my little sack of hate?

Kind of.

I tied it up, tossed it down, and set the thing on fire.

That's how I feel inside, too—like something that's been through a fire. All the same molecules are there, but they're altered versions of themselves.

It's Sunday morning, and the house is quiet. The light in my room is delicate—an eggshell of light. I go to my closet, stand on my tiptoes, and slip a box down from the top shelf. I place it on my bed and open it, knowing what I will find.

And yes, there it is—the soft blue sweater from the tree house. Jamie's sweater. A few weeks ago, I cleaned it by hand in my bathroom sink, laid it out to dry, folded it neatly in a shirt box I had left from last Christmas, and tucked it away in my closet.

Because what else was I supposed to do with it?

I knew I couldn't give it to Charlie. Not after it messed him up so much. That would just be mean.

It's not mine to keep, though, either. So it just stayed there, in the limbo of my closet space.

But now, it occurs to me there is something else to do with it. Someone else who might want it.

I leave a note for my parents on the kitchen counter, put the box in my backpack, and drive.

Every Girl

"Yes?"

I'm suddenly aware of the huge empty space in my stomach. Because one, I didn't have breakfast. Two, I hate talking to people I don't already know. Three, Charlie is one door over and I don't want him to see me here. Four, I'm about to return the sweater of a dead girl to her mother and, really, how is that sort of thing done?

"Hi," I say, and then in one big breath, "I'm a friend of Charlie's, I didn't really know Jamie, but you were her mom, right?"

"Yes, I am." She is a tall woman, with chocolate-brown hair, in a brown-and-purple floral dress and unzipped knee-high dress boots. I know her by sight, but only from a distance. Up close, she looks beautiful, despite the lines under her eyes and the gray at her roots. "Oh, of course"— she points her finger vaguely, like she's shaking something loose—"from the courtroom…and you're Charlie's sweetheart." She smiles, and it's a lovely smile. Jamie's smile.

"Um, maybe?" I say. "I, uh, I found—I thought you might, I didn't know if you would..." I start to rummage in my backpack.

"Why don't you come in?" she says, backing into the foyer as she swings the door wider. "I was just getting ready for church. Would you like some coffee?"

"Um, no thank you," I say, walking inside.

She sits on a decorative white metal stool at the edge of the living room and bends down to zip up her boots. She points to a bench in the foyer. "Have a seat. What can I do for you?"

"I'm all right," I say, still standing. "I just wanted to give you this." I wrangle the box loose from my backpack. "I found it in Charlie's tree house. I'm sorry." I hand the box to her. "I didn't know if you'd want this or..."

She opens the box. "Oh!" The sharp *oh!* of recognition. This scrap of her lost life.

She runs her palm across the surface of the sweater, takes it out of the box, and holds it to her cheek. But then there's that smile. Her eyes welling up with tears, and that wrenching smile.

"I gave this to Jamie for her seventeenth birthday."

"It was outside," I say. "There're some stains I couldn't get out."

She holds the sweater out with both hands, arm's length, as if considering a purchase at a department store. "This is—I cherish this. Thank you," she says. "I donated Jamie's clothes to charity. I wanted to think of some part of her going out in the world, doing some good for someone."

"I'm sorry. I didn't mean to remind you...."

"Oh, honey, you didn't remind me. I was thinking about Jamie when I opened the door. When I poured my coffee. When I brushed my hair. I'm always thinking about her. Don't you worry about reminding me. I'm glad you did."

She shakes her head, puts the sweater in her lap.

"Sometimes that's a hard thing," she says. "I see it on people's faces. They're thinking of Jamie. But they don't want to say it. I know they're worried it would upset me. They don't say anything."

She sighs. "But look here?" She jangles her bracelet, a silver feather dangling from a chain around her wrist. "This was Jamie's. It was there, on her wrist through it all. They found it when they found her. I wear it now, because it was with her. Because I *want* to be reminded, see?"

She reaches out for me, like I'm supposed to take her hand. So, awkward as it is, I take it. Her palm is soft and the back is spotted with brown dots. For a second, the silver feather skims against my wrist, and I'm startled by its unexpected warmth.

"I'm glad you remember her," she says, the tears spilling over now, trickling down her cheek. "That's a gift."

She drops my hand to wipe her face with her fingers. "I must look a mess," she says with a quiet laugh. "You think I'd be all cried out by now."

"Well, I guess I should let you get ready for church," I say, backing toward the door.

"Hold on a second, honey." She stands, retrieves a

brochure from the drawer of a little table near the window. "Take this. And I want—" She reaches out like she means to touch my hair, but then her hand drops. "I want you to know I'm happy Charlie has found you. He's a special boy. This has been hard on all of us. I'm glad he has someone to help him through." She smiles again, her eyes glistening wet. "I think Jamie would be happy, too."

I remember the times Charlie has said we can't speak for Jamie. Somehow I doubt he'd argue with Jamie's mom, though.

"Thanks," I say, and it's maybe the oddest thing I've ever thanked anyone for. I look down at the brochure in my hand.

EVERY GIRL MATTERS
Advocating, Educating, Empowering
Below, there's a picture of three teen girls holding hands. "What's this?" I ask.
"It has some tips on how to stay safe," she says.
I flip open the brochure:

- Let people know where you're going and how long you expect to be out.
- Always carry pepper gel spray, your cell phone, and a whistle.
- When out, stay aware of your surroundings. Don't let your cell phone distract you.
- If someone harasses you, be vocal. Try to gain the attention of people around you.

- Alert the police when you see someone
  in trouble.
- If someone you know makes you uncomfortable, avoid that person and let your
  friends and family know.

The list goes on for two pages. All the things I should do to keep the monsters away.

"It's a group I volunteer with," she says. "We advocate for victims' families, educate young people about personal safety, share missing-persons alerts on social media, that sort of thing."

"Wow," I say, forgetting myself for a second—talking like I'd talk to anybody, not a mom, definitely not Jamie's mom. "That seems hard. Having to deal with everyone else's stuff, on top of, you know, what happened."

"It saved me," she says simply. "I can't tell you what a difference it makes—knowing I might be able to help some-one going through the same heartache, maybe even stop it from happening."

"You must hate me—"

"No. What? Why would you say that?"

"Because—because…" I can't say it, but we both know what I mean: *Because I'm alive and your daughter is dead.*

"Oh, honey, I don't hate you." And this time, she does touch my hair, gentle and familiar.

Mercy Garden

"I'm not doing it," I say.

"But it's *tradition*," Lindsey says.

"A *stupid* tradition!"

"Yeah, well, that's kind of what makes it a *tradition*," she says. "Is it *smart* that we pile a table with food and sit around eating until we puke? Or that we hide eggs in our yards once a year? Or encourage kids to sit on some old bearded guy's lap and tell him what they secretly desire? Traditions *are* stupid! That's how they work!"

"But willingly jumping into ice-cold water? That's just wrong." I pull my blue stocking cap farther down, past my ears, and shiver dramatically.

We're in Lindsey's Toyota, cruising down the highway in the dark on our way to Mercy Garden. By its name, it sounds like an old folks' home or maybe somewhere you're supposed to sprinkle your grandmother's ashes, but really it's just a regular park out in the woods next to Blue Haven Lake, about fifteen minutes outside of town.

It's also the site of the infamous December Dunk, held annually the first Sunday of December. The so-called tradition, which has been going on since sometime in the last century, involves open tailgates, music, a bonfire, and, contrary to all logic, swimsuits. The evening culminates at midnight, when everyone is beyond making good decisions, and all the seniors jump into the icy water.

I've been on the sidelines for the past two years, cheering on the idiots. But this year, Lindsey insists we *are* the idiots. "You're only a senior once. Assuming you graduate, which of course you will," she says. "So that's it. You're holding my hand and we're doing it."

There's no arguing with her when she gets like this, so I keep quiet and pray some miracle saves me before the stroke of midnight.

As we ride, I tell her about my visit to Jamie's mom that morning. I'm still trying to get my mind around how someone can be simultaneously so sad and so serene. And how that same someone can then go out and try to change the world.

"She was like a superhero, Linds," I say. "The Grieving Flower! The Amethyst Wind! The Protector!"

"Seriously?"

"Yep," I say. "Kicking butt and taking names!"

"You should be like her when you grow up," she says.

"What?"

She flashes me a look out of the corner of her eye as she

drives, like it's obvious. "Well," she says, "maybe *you* should be a superhero. Maybe *you* should change the world."

"Okaaay. And how exactly am I supposed to do that?"

"You're awesome," she says. "You'll figure it out."

"That's helpful," I answer. *Not.*

When we get to the Garden, Lindsey parks at the end of the tailgate line. She pulls out a cooler and a bag of chips from her back seat and sets them out on her trunk. "There's soda here, but if you want..." she says, wagging a six-pack of canned beer. "We might need some liquid courage."

"Yeah, sure," I say. I snap one free and carefully pry open the lid, holding it away from my body so the foam that bubbles out doesn't soak my coat. I think of the can as more of a prop than an actual drink. I'll carry it around, maybe nurse it a little, and the other 99 percent of my graduating class won't bother me.

Lindsey must have the same idea. She takes one, tucks it unopened in her coat pocket, and hides the remaining beers under her passenger seat.

Someone has strung fairy lights above the boat dock and set up some floodlights on stands. A guy from my psych class is deejaying, pumping low-key reggae into the chilled night air. To one side, a small bonfire flashes in the man-made sandy area near the water, and a few people are playing grab-ass in a clump near its fringe.

I spot Robert Leuger with a cluster of football dudes throwing crap into the fire. He stands behind a petite redhead from the cheerleading squad, his hands on her hips in that *I know her in the Biblical sense* way.

"Hey," I say to Lindsey, "you okay with that?" I nudge my head in Robert's direction. "I'm good with leaving."

"Nah," she says. "It's...whatever. I'm fine with it."

"Fine with what?" It's Charlie's voice, out of nowhere, right behind us.

I turn and, sure enough, there's Charlie's face to match.

"Hey, stranger," I say.

And suddenly the moth in my stomach starts doing kamikaze dives because I'm not sure how we left things yesterday, and I don't know exactly how I want to pick them back up again. I still haven't answered my own question: Can I be with Charlie as things stand?

"Fine with...getting that deejay to play something we can dance to," Lindsey says, heading off toward the dock. "I'll catch you later."

Charlie gazes out over the water. The reflection of the crescent moon squints up at us from the lake's rippled surface.

"So, what's the verdict?" he asks.

"What verdict?" For a second, I'm thinking Kyle, the case, *was there some new verdict?*

But then he clarifies, "You and me."

"Oh," I say. "I didn't know—I mean, I'm that transparent?"

"Maybe." He scuffs his foot into the gravel of the driveway. "Maybe I know how to see you."

"You know how to see me," I echo, taking it in.

He looks up then, eyes bright. "I'm wild about you. If it makes any difference."

His face is beautiful, but it's his eyes that do me in. There's a reason the poets call them windows to the soul. His window opens on a field at night, surrounded by woods. Leaves in the wind, a fox's cry. The encircling trees, both safeguard and temptation.

I say, breathless and eye-drunk, "You too."

"But—?" he asks. I let the word linger because I don't want to say what comes next.

I think about what Jamie's mom said, how glad she was that I could be there for Charlie. About what Charlie himself said, how I'm the one who just keeps digging.

I'm not sure either one of them is right.

"Me being with you now, it's kind of like asking the recovering alcoholic to work the bar," I say. "I'm not sure I have what it takes. Are you going to be okay with me? Am I going to be okay with you? I just—I don't know. It's not going to be easy."

He runs his hands through his hair, like he's trying to tug out words.

"It doesn't have to be so hard," he says. The phrase sounds familiar, and it's a second before I realize he's repeating the same thing to me I said to him weeks ago at the riverside. He leans in, just as I did then, and kisses me. A kiss that is an ask as much as it is an answer. "These last weeks, it's been difficult, *I've* been difficult, yeah, and you've been patient as hell. But I'm trying. That's all I want, is that you try. We don't have to agree about everything. We're not going to. We're not the same person."

He gives me a wry smile, then adds, "Thank God. I'm not really my type."

"You said you were right, though."

"I think I am."

"But I can't deal with that anger, Charlie. Even if it's deserved," I say. "I'm not going to hate him anymore. I have to let go of it. I have to."

"But you don't have to let go of *me*," he says, catching my hand, like I'm going to bolt any second. "And I—maybe I can, you know, in time, I don't know."

"You literally just said nothing."

"I could—I don't know. Jesus! You're a good influence on me, okay?"

"Really?" And I can feel the smile invade my cheeks. I never knew I'd been waiting for someone to say those words to me. But apparently, I have been. Boys will lie about love, but this—how could he even *know* to lie about this? I repeat his words, slowly, incredulous. "I am. A good influence. On you."

"Did you *see* me earlier this year?"

I think of the Ghost of Charlie Past, gray-faced, hoodie up, eyes down.

"You woke me up," he says. "You were so annoying. Like a tag poking the back of my neck. Just a little frustration at first, but it won't go away. And then you just keep thinking about it, but it's weird because the more the tag is *there*, the more you realize you kind of like how it feels. You think it's kind of a cute tag. And then a *really* cute tag. Smart and funny and deep. And then you realize you're awake. The sun is a beautiful thing. And the tag—it's even *more* beautiful. You don't know what you'd do without it. You fucking *love* this tag." He throws his hands up in frustration. "This is maybe the worst metaphor ever."

My super-identity—Tag-Girl. *Annoying People for Justice!*

"Let me try again." He holds my gaze like it's a bowl of water he doesn't want to spill. "I'm only here—I'm *here* because of you. I was pretty out there after that verdict. That was...hard. It was messed up. But I'm here now in the land of the living, getting ready to jump into a lake in forty-degree weather, because I'm still awake, and apparently that's what you do when you're awake. You undertake ill-advised and reckless acts."

I'd laugh, but I don't know where my face went.

"I'm here," he says again, "because of you."

Everything in me tells me this isn't bull. This is real. That Charlie is not just my boyfriend, but my friend. That, however frustrating I might be, I matter to him. Just like he matters to me. And isn't that worth fighting for, too?

Plus, God, he looks super hot when he's saying it.

"Okay," I say.

"Okay?"

"Yes, definitely." I nod.

The music shifts to a techno club mix. A group of girls on the dock start bouncing around in what approximates dance.

"Lindsey got her way." He holds out his hand. "Dance with me?"

"That's a yes, too."

Jump

So we do.

We dance on the dock like we're at the edge of the world, and we don't care if we fall off. We bop and twirl, flash our hands. One song bleeds into another, and we keep dancing. Others churn around us—thrashing grinding crunking. All the seniors are here—Jared, Randy, Nick Richert, the Allisons, Amanda Wells, Monica and Andie, Shavelle Rylan, Clarissa Coleson, Paige Sanchez.

Taylor even showed up with Kai—"for moral support only—*not a senior*"—she insisted, when Lindsey tried to convince her to do the jump.

By the time the midnight call comes, we're part of one big mass of dance, my coat's off, and I'm sweating in the cool night air.

Lindsey sashays up, holding a wad of beach towels, with Jared Hilley right behind. "IT'S TIME!" she yells over the music, but she needn't have bothered because the deejay announces on the mic, "Yo, the moment's here, people.

Time to show some skin! Get ready for the…DECEMBER DUNK!"

And everyone's yelling and hooting as the seniors start stripping down to swimsuits or undies. Thanks to Lindsey's insistence, I'm ready with a black one-piece under my clothes. She, meanwhile, is in a frosted-pink bikini. Charlie and Jared, no surprise, are not in actual swimsuits, but boxers. Charlie's gray knit, Jared's red flannel.

"Holy crap it's cold!" All the sweat I've worked up is making me colder now, as the air chills the perspiration on my skin. "Are we seriously doing this?"

"Believe it," Lindsey says, grinning. "Let's go!"

"Hold up," Charlie says, checking his phone. "Mark's here. Somewhere." He scans the crowd, sends a text. "He better get down here."

We pile our clothes and line up at the edge of the dock to jump with the other idiots. To be fair, some of the slightly less idiotic among us are down on the sand, so they just have to run in the water, dip their toes, and run out. Lindsey insists they're wimps.

"Bunch of pussies!" Jared yells at them, rubbing his arms to keep warm.

"Excuse me," Lindsey says, "but I happen to think that particular bit of anatomy is pretty fabulous. If you really want to insult those guys, maybe you should try something else."

"Yes ma'am." Jared tips a pretend hat to her, then yells toward the beach, "Bunch of dicks!"

I peer down at the water, which seems an abyss, even though I know it's not very deep here. My toes hang over the dock's edge. I'm cold, but there's freedom in this sort of cold. There's a *what the hell* to it that makes me want to spit in the face of cold and fear and everything else standing between me and the life I want.

Mark sprints down from the parking lot, panting, in green floral swim trunks and a navy swim shirt. "Am I too late?"

"Come on," Charlie says, and Mark falls in line beside him.

Lindsey grabs my left hand. With the right, I grab Charlie's.

I glance over to Mark, who has found his breath and is staring down the water like some badass in a Western.

I squeeze Lindsey's hand. "I'm your huckleberry," I say.

She laughs. "Oh, yes, you are."

Jared, on her other side, holds out his hand to her, and she surprises all of us, Jared included, by taking it.

"ARE YOU PEOPLE READY TO GET WET?" the deejay screams into the mic. The crowd cheers.

I feel my heart pounding, *I am alive and I am stupid* "TEN…NINE…" *and I am free* "EIGHT" *and I love* "SEVEN" *my friends and* "SIX" *my family and love* "FIVE" *dancing, even if I can't dance, and running* "FOUR" *and I'm annoying and it's good* "THREE" *that I'm annoying because* "TWO" *we are alive* "ONE!"

We jump, a high arc, holding hands, and splash down

into the ice-cold water. And Holy Hell! My heart is exploding at the same moment it squeezes the entire lake and the starlit sky and the park and everyone in it into a tiny grip of blinding light. I flail my way to the surface and gasp for air.

In a second, I will pull myself out of the water. I will rub off with a towel and hug Lindsey and Charlie and maybe Jared or Mark. I will wrangle into my clothes and spend the night warming up under quilts in someone's basement or garage, listening to music and talking and who knows what. But for now, this—this moment in the cold lake, intensely alive, in love with my life—is enough.

Acknowledgments

This was not a book I sought to write.

I was hard at work on an entirely different manuscript when this one overtook me. I had read in the paper about a lost girl—found days later, dead. The brutality of her murder, the senseless destruction of her life, left me outraged and grieving. Worst of all, I had seen equally horrific events play out in newsprint a dozen times before with different names and details, and I was gutted by the certainty I would read of such horrors again.

That story broke something in me. So I did what I do when I'm broken. I cried, consumed junk food, then picked up a notebook and pen.

How is a young woman supposed to find her way in a world where so many men quite literally want to kill her? And in many cases, not even to kill her specifically, but to kill any girl who happens to occupy the space she is in? Such a threat, both intensely personal and oddly generic, seems impossible to navigate.

I genuinely love the girls in this book, fictional though they are. I love Charlie and Jared, too, and Jamie's mom. I love these characters' resiliency and courage and ability to find some good to aim their lives toward. But those qualities in my fictional characters are a mere trick of the light, the dimmest afterimage, when compared to the astounding grace of the real women and men who are able to live lives of goodness (and in some cases even forgiveness) in the aftermath of violence against their loved ones. I do not believe I have such grace within me, and I hope I never have cause to find out.

It also feels necessary to mention how deeply I respect the efforts of groups like Help Save The Next Girl, which works in my own community to prevent violence against young women.

There are many people to thank for their contributions to this book's existence.

Emily Mitchell, my dream agent, has stuck with me patiently throughout the process. She has given me space to take risks, and she continues to support my outlandish ideas long after others might have given up on them. In short, she is exactly the person I need in my creative life, and I sincerely feel my luck in having her on my side.

I am equally fortunate in my editor, Nikki Garcia, whose driving force and keen insights have been invaluable. The fact that she saw something worthy in my manuscript at the exact moment that I had utterly given up on it was, quite frankly, life-changing for me. Her guidance has made this a much better book than what landed on her desk many months ago, and I thank her for her willingness to shepherd it through its various drafts.

I also wish to acknowledge the excellent work of the Little, Brown and Company copyediting, marketing, and design teams—specifically, Michelle Campbell, Elisabeth Ferrari, Stefanie Hoffman, Sasha Illingworth, Annie McDonnell, Victoria Stapleton, Angela Taldone, and Valerie Wong.

Thanks to Madelyn Rosenberg for writing Jared's song. (For the record, Jared's tongue-stud is for her.) Thanks also to Cece Bell, from whom I blatantly stole "Vessel of Sweet Relief." Madelyn and Cece's encouragement and good advice have been guiding lights in my life.

There are many who took time to read my work in its various forms and offer excellent feedback and encouragement. They include Cece Bell, Catherine Cone, Tom Cook, Nicole Foley, Patrick Knicely, Thomas Locicero, Chrissy Mortlock, Cindy Perdue, Madelyn Rosenberg, Amelia Ross, Angie Smibert, Kristi Stultz, Cyndy Unwin, and Julie Walsh. Thanks also for the contributions of Karen Adams and Lois Roach, who aided my research.

I am supremely grateful for the support of my family. They have all been excessively patient when I let everything else in our lives go to seed while focusing intently on some stage in the writing or revision process. My daughter was especially helpful, in that she read drafts, offered valuable suggestions, and helped care for her siblings (and me) when needed. Her own creativity has been an inspiration to me. I also wish to thank my mother- and father-in-law, who are astoundingly generous in their support of both my family and my personal endeavors.

Most of all, though, I want to thank my husband, who has been my champion in every sense of that word. He has been there each step of the way with whatever I needed, be it space, time, a sympathetic ear, moral support, lunch, chocolate, etc. He has put up with me holing up for days to work on this book, he has read every page and offered smart advice and encouragement, and he has continued to believe in me, even when I wasn't so sure.

Finally, I want to send a hug and a shout-out to anyone who has gotten this far in the book. It seems unlikely that after three-hundred-some pages, you're going to be reading acknowledgments, but if you are—wow! Thanks!

Mary Crockett

has worked as a toilet-seat hand model, factory grunt, staggeringly bad waitress, incompetent secretary, the person who irons name tags on industrial uniforms, history museum director, and, currently, teacher of creative writing at Roanoke College. She has her Master of Fine Arts degree from the University of Virginia, where she was a Henry Hoyns Fellow, and she has authored several award-winning books of poetry. Her website is marycrockett.com.